After receiving his grade twelve diploma and marking his eighteenth birthday, René Oshawee cannot fight the temptation seventeen-year-old high school junior Billy Redsky blatantly offers now that what they share has become taboo.

When their secret romance is blown into the open, Billy's foster parents send René to Toronto to complete the last of his schooling under the supervision of a family friend, leaving Billy behind at their Ojibway community.

Now Billy and René must make the biggest decision of their lives—fight for the true love they know they'll never find with anyone else or go their separate ways.

Knight Moves
Copyright © 2021 Maggie Blackbird
ISBN: 978-1-4874-3243-0
Cover art by Martine Jardin

Published by eXtasy Books Inc or
Devine Destinies, an imprint of eXtasy Books Inc

Look for us online at:
www.eXtasybooks.com or www.devinedestinies.com

KNIGHT MOVES
WHEN WE WERE YOUNG 3

BY

MAGGIE BLACKBIRD

DEDICATION

For Ava and Genevieve. I hope you grow up to love reading as much as your Auntie Koko does.

Thank you to my husband and the Mals for your never-ending love and support.

Thank you to my editor, Emmy, my proofer, Bri, my cover artist, Martine, and Jay, EIC.

CHAPTER ONE: I'M READY

January 8, 1998
Thunder Mountain First Nation, Thunder Bay, ON

The possibilities of turning seventeen today were endless. Possibilities such as . . . finally doing what had hounded Billy's crotch for the past six months.

Sex.

Not sex with any ol' dork, either.

Sex with René.

René Randall Oshawee.

Billy snatched his backpack off the dresser. He closed the door to his walk-in closet. Before leaving his bedroom, he cast another long look at the mural he'd finished of Pumpkin, the great *makwa* of Thunder Mountain.

His painting had captured the bear's magnificent color of burnt cinnamon and light tangerine. Since he'd used an autumn theme to paint, the wall burst with bold shades of red, purple, and orange. Pumpkin's mighty paw scuffed a couple of cones fallen from the pine trees.

Billy raised his thumb.

Thanks to the Oshawee family, life was a bowl of ketchup chips instead of stale popcorn. This was the second birthday he'd celebrate in style, not like his first fifteen Mom had destroyed. The moccasin telegraph was saying the pathetic lush was currently in rehab. As if she'd permanently cork the bottle and close her nostrils to blow.

Enough thinking about his useless biological mother and

1

brother. Today was a day for Billy to celebrate with his *real* family. He shuffled down the stairs.

The maid stood at the kitchen island, readying breakfast. She used to clean two days a week, but Mrs. O had hired Lucy on full-time after her husband had left her alone to feed three mouths in grades five, six, and seven.

"Happy birthday," Lucy called out. Her black hair was tied back in a braid. A full apron covered her big boobs. "Your pancakes are ready."

"You're tops, baby." Billy scooped his plate off the island.

A hint of wryness invaded Lucy's giggle. "I should be. I was your supervisor for almost a year."

Before landing in foster care, Billy had done a lot of break and entry he'd admitted to. As part of his punishment, he'd helped a family friend with the cleaning business she owned. Working off the money his foster dad had laid out to purchase new items for the people Billy had robbed was a better deal, considering he could've been charged with the offenses, and his career as a cop would have gone tits up before he'd finished high school.

"The best supervisor a guy could ask for." Billy set his plate on the table in the breakfast nook. He reached for the maple syrup.

"I cooked them exactly how you enjoy them. A bit crisp and extra blueberries." Lucy readied another plate. "Mrs. Oshawee said she'd call tonight. I think she feels bad not being here for your big day."

"It's cool." Billy cut into the stack. "All I care about is getting my license. Those two are always jetting off on biz trips."

"Is René taking you out tonight?"

"Yeppers. It's Thursday. No shift at the video store for him. We're doing dinner." Billy shoveled a helping of pancakes into his mouth.

Dates with René were the cherry on top of this new life

Billy was loving. Hell, he'd take a simple drive up the mountain and be finer than a baby sucking on a soother. All that mattered was spending time with the guy he loved.

More than loved.

Totally horny for.

Major wood for.

A total boner for.

This waiting until grade twelve to hit the sheets René had insisted on blew chunks. Billy had started his second semester of grade eleven after the Christmas break. He was more than ready to do the horizontal nasty. Just because René had been in grade twelve when he got to sink the pink didn't mean Billy had to wait. Shit, all he heard in the boys' locker room was the latest *home run* some dude had scored.

"I guess it's a good thing I asked." Lucy strolled over, hand on her generous hip.

"Err . . . asked?"

"You're supposed to tell me if you won't be home for supper, according to the rules laid out by Mr. and Mrs. Oshawee," she reminded him.

Oops. Billy's mouth molded into a sheepish grin. "Sorry. I know for sure René would've told you."

"I know so." A hint of teasing was in her tone. She meandered back to the island.

Maybe informing Lucy of his every little move was one of those supposed *responsibility tests* the Oshawees loved laying out for Billy. Since René's elder brother was also on a business trip, there was nobody to check in on them. Not that a *babysitter* was necessary after René had turned eighteen at the end of December.

They had the house to themselves. Billy smacked his lips together. Free from The General, Colonel, and Sergeant until Sunday night. The Oshawees were staying on in Toronto for the hockey game. Daniel's business meetings in Winnipeg ended late this afternoon, but he planned on taking his girl-friend to something Billy couldn't remember.

For sure this was the weekend he'd get laid — that was if he could con the guy he loved into taking the bait.

René gasped. He leaned on the tiled wall wet from the spray of the hot water. His breathing remained quick and short. The shower washed away the result of jacking off. He ran his tongue along his lower lip. This was definitely getting old, but he was sticking to his guns. Especially now that he'd turned eighteen two weeks ago.

The legality of seeing Billy kept poking the back of René's head. Although two grades separated them, technically, they were only a year apart, as Billy reminded anyone who bothered listening.

René reached for the shampoo. Since last June, he was a high school graduate but had stayed another year to earn his Ontario Academic Credit, something every person who chose to pursue their post-secondary schooling did. He was hardly enrolled at Lakeside University. That wouldn't happen until September.

So attending high school had to count for something while seeing a guy under the age of eighteen. Every year a couple of students pursuing their OAC dated a junior or senior.

He lathered up his hair. With the exception of Matt Gerhard, the rest of the rocker clique had moved on to the local college or trade institution.

Ian and Moxy had gone a step further. They'd split in his van for Toronto to attend The Franklin College of Music, the very place René had applied to before changing his mind at the eleventh hour to become a lawyer.

Ian and Moxy had returned for the Christmas holidays. René had jammed with them in the rehearsal space in the basement. They'd gone on and on, excitement in their eyes, about how much they were loving the music college.

That was another problem. Last May, René had been gung-ho about pursuing a career to help troubled youth like Billy. Now? René stood under the spray and washed the shampoo from his hair. Maybe this was why he was majoring in music for his undergraduate degree? Part of him couldn't shake his biggest dream—writing songs and drumming for a living.

Why had he assumed on his eighteenth birthday answers to his most urgent questions would magically appear? If anything, he was more confused now than when he'd been a minor.

Was he pursuing this new career for Billy's sake? Or did this stem from guilt because René had popped from the womb holding a silver spoon, therefore, feeling obliged to help others who didn't share his privileged upbringing? Or the biggie—he plain out didn't want to leave Billy behind?

Emptiness would fill his life without the guy who'd changed René's way of thinking, no matter if music earned him a gold record.

He snatched the soap and gripped the slippery bar. Big deal Ian and Moxy were chasing his dream for him. Love was about sacrificing everything for the person a guy had given his heart to. For Billy, René would do anything.

Billy sat in the driver's side of René's truck. His license was classed a G2, which meant major restrictions. Oh well, driving was driving. According to the new rules, only one person was allowed in the vehicle if he didn't have a full Class G on board, which René was.

"It's still a license," Billy said, more to himself.

"Yeah, it got kind of confusing when the new law was implemented this summer after you got your learner's permit,"

René replied.

"I coulda had my full G last February if your dad didn't make me wait until today."

"It was part of your punishment for breaking into those houses. He said no driver's license until you turned seventeen."

"I know." Billy could accept this, even understand Mr. O's reasoning, but the punishment still sucked ass.

René laid his hand over Billy's resting on the stick shift. "In a year, you'll have a valid Class G."

"The government's getting too strict. Now they're nailing everyone for seat belts." Billy drew the strap away from his chest. The constricting material bounced back just as fast.

"I'm wearing mine." René patted his.

"You're only wearing yours 'cause you're shotgunning with a G2."

"Try no. If I'm caught unbuckled, I get two demerit points on my license. Not going there. Mom and Dad already pay enough to insure me."

"How's insurance gonna work for me?" Billy downshifted for the lights at James Street and Arthur. The city was lit because the sun went to bed early at around five. He'd keep driving. Their destination was Port Arthur.

"You'll go on as a secondary driver for Mom's car."

"I don't get to drive your dad's boss truck?" Billy stuck his hand in front of the vent blasting hot air. Tonight was a crisp minus twenty-five Celsius.

René guffawed. "Nope."

"That's one lethal machine. What's he got under the hood, anyway?"

"More than you can handle—why he won't let you drive it." Teasing snuck into René's rebuttal.

"Aww, suck it." Billy half joked and half grumbled. "He only lets you 'cause you're his son."

"Of course he does." René pointed at the street up ahead. "Turn here."

"Where're we going why you asked me to lay out some wicked threads?" Billy hit his blinker and moved into the right lane.

"The Steakhouse."

"Hey . . ." Billy held out his palm for five. "That's a fancy place. You're going Fifth Avenue, aren't you?"

"Why not? You're my guy." René's straight white teeth brightened under the light coming in from the streetlamps. He was damn yummy in his three-piece suit while obliging Billy his five.

He should ask Mrs. O if she could buy him a suit. He had turned seventeen today. Every upperclassman owned one. "What about my present? I don't see you packing anything."

"You'll get your present. Later . . ." There was a hint of mystery in René's silky voice that always skimmed Billy's skin.

"Later?" Billy lifted his fingers off the stick shift and set them on René's firm thigh hidden beneath dress pants. "Is it on you?"

"The present?"

"Yeah."

"Why would you think it's on me?" René stared straight ahead.

If Billy had to draw the guy a picture, he was all for whipping out his sketchpad. While keeping one eye on the street, he walked his fingers until he reached the nest of warmth between René's gorgeous, long legs. "I figured your present's in here."

René softly chuckled. "You got a one-track mind. Then again, every guy in grade eleven is the same." He seized Billy's wrist.

"What's that s'posed to mean?" If anything, wasn't a dude

supposed to get turned on when someone made a play for the goods?

"Horny city." René's chuckle became a rare snicker.

"Oh? You had sex on the brain in grade eleven?"

"I was no different from my classmates." Dry ice was moister than René's tone. "You hit sixteen and a switch gets flicked. Every homie I knew was wanking to skin mags."

"You included?"

"Uh-huh."

"Me and my old buds used to watch a lot of humping. Hoyt was always renting the stuff." Billy couldn't help his grin. "Hey, question. How'd you get your dick mags? It's not like you could borrow Daniel's since pussy does nothing for you."

"Doesn't matter."

Billy snuck a quick peek. In the dark interior, he couldn't spy if René was blushing. "You lifted them?"

"No. I never stole anything in my life."

There was only one other way René could have gotten gay porn magazines. "Keith sent them to you, didn't he?"

Instead of continuing to stare straight ahead, René looked out the passenger window.

"Seriously? He's eight years older than you. I never heard of—"

"I never stopped bugging him about it. Okay?" Irritation and a hint of embarrassment crept into René's admittance. "I kept on until he caved—"

"Where did he mail them to? Your parents for sure would've—"

"He didn't mail them. He brought them when he came home for Christmas. The year I turned sixteen." René shook back his bangs.

"So you got 'em when you were still fifteen?" Billy snorted.

"Hey, I can't help that I was born at the end of the year. I was in grade eleven. Every guy in their junior year has porn

8

on stash," René replied with a hint of defensiveness.

"I don't have any. It's at my old crib. Not that I owned any. It was Hoyt's."

"I'm eighteen now. If you want me to get you some—"

"Pass. I had all the X-rated shit I could take 'cause of Hoyt. I want—" René's finger came over Billy's lips. A soft finger. A sexy long finger Billy enjoyed kissing. He glided his mouth over the slightly chafed pad.

"I know what you want." René's soft-spoken voice was a whisper. "You don't think I feel the same way?"

"Then why're we waiting?" Billy downshifted for the red light up ahead. "It's not like you made a promise to anyone other than yourself."

"Maybe that's what's important to me. Keeping my own promise." René had returned to staring straight ahead.

"Okay. Cool. I respect your promise."

René's stare slithered in Billy's direction.

"What?"

"I'm used to you always pushing." René's perfectly arched brows crinkled. "This is a first."

Billy shrugged. "Then tell me why the promise. Remember, you can't keep everything up here anymore." He tapped his head. "We're a couple. That means we gotta act like a couple. I'd say it's why I'm not firing a million questions at you anymore and giving you a good push. Well, maybe I am in some ways. I'm pushing about sex. Hah."

"Yeah . . ." René must have clucked his tongue, because a popping sound came from his mouth. "You're right. I've been working hard at sharing. I'm not doing too shabby, hey?"

"Yep. I'd say so." Billy waggled his brows. "Well?"

"Remember, I'm new at this talking stuff." René reached for a pen clipped to the driver's visor. "You had a pretty rough life up until we got together. It's only been a year and a half since you've been in foster care. You deserve . . ."

From the corner of Billy's eye, he caught René bouncing the pen on his knee.

"You deserve the ultimate respect." René's words were lighter than snow.

And light enough for goosebumps to jump up from beneath Billy's skin. He shivered. "Making us wait until I hit grade twelve is showing me respect? How so?"

René grasped Billy's fingers. "Because you deserve respect. Nobody showed you any up until you went into emergency care with Uncle Ned and Aunt Ellen." He squeezed Billy's hand. "Don't think this is easy for me. It isn't."

"Then if it isn't . . ." Billy squeezed back.

"If I give you the *Keith said* spiel, you're gonna get ticked." René used the thumb of his right hand to click the end of the pen, even though he was a southpaw.

A sliver of annoyance gathered at the back of Billy's neck. Not Keith Harlow again. Enduring his visit during the Christmas break had been trying enough, because René had gone for coffee with Mr. Toothpaste Smile. Twenty-six or not, and one year left to acquire his master's in art history, Keith didn't have any right butting his nose into their relationship.

"Has he figured out what's going on with us?"

"Of course, but y'know I won't confirm anything to him. I said the guy I'm seeing isn't out. He won't push. I mean, he's gay, too. He's very respectful of people who're in the closet."

"So what advice did he dole out about seeing *the kid* this time?"

"You're hardly a kid." René let out a low whistle of approval. "Them's are some serious guns." He clasped one of Billy's biceps. "Shit, you got bigger guns than I do."

A warm heap of flattery tickled Billy's insides. "Wanna find out who's got the other bigger one?"

René cracked a half smile. "I told you, I'd rather wait—"

"I don't wanna. Okay, now I'm going into *pushy* mode."

Billy snatched René's hand again. "I want you." His words were pleading, even begging.

"Oh man . . ." René's head fell against the headrest. "Do you know how hard you're making—"

"Yeah, that's it. I want you hard. Major hard." All this talk about boners stroked Billy's crotch.

"I meant how hard you're making this for me." There was a hiss to René's voice.

"Well?" Using his thumb, Billy caressed René's palm.

"If it's gonna happen, let's let it happen naturally. Okay? That's all I'm asking."

"And right now isn't natural?" Billy almost sputtered.

"Let's have dinner, first. Afterward . . ."

CHAPTER TWO: LET'S PLAY TWO

The waitress wove her way through the crowded restaurant. She held a slice of birthday cake. Under the dim lighting, people dined at the many tables covered in white cloths and the chairs outfitted in red felt coverings.

René curled his fingers together and set his elbows on his place setting. The flickering candle in the yellow holder caught the glow of Billy's smooth skin. He was seventeen but passing for nineteen because the hostess, at the beginning of their meal, had asked if they'd wanted anything from the bar.

With his hair cropped over his ears and light spikes to his bangs gelled slightly to the side, there was a true maturity to Billy now. The sprinkling of whiskers above his mouth offered a masculine depth to his boyish looks.

"Here you go. Happy birthday," the waitress announced.

"Thanks." Billy flashed her his cheeky grin. "Great meal. The best prime rib I've ever had."

"I'll be sure to tell the chef. Now, are you sure you don't want anything from the bar for an after-dinner drink? You turned nineteen today."

"It's okay," René replied. "Some coffee would be nice, though."

"Right away." The waitress left.

"C'mon, we could've had some beers." By the twinkle in Billy's dark eyes, he was jesting.

"You're driving. Neither of us is old enough. With the luck you generate, the bartender would've told her to card us, anyway. Coffee'll suffice." An itch to reach across and take

12

Billy's hand crawled along René's palm. God, this sucked having to hide what they felt for each other.

In the past, he hadn't minded. Why playing *closet* this evening irritated him, René wasn't sure. "Your present." He reached insides the breast pocket of his suit and withdrew the small, wrapped package.

"You did have it on you." Billy moved his chair in closer, since they sat on opposite sides of the table instead of adjacent from each other. Another way to hide their secret. "Let's see."

René placed the package down.

Still grinning, Billy scooped up the gift. He peeled away the blue paper the clerk at the jewelry store had used for wrapping.

The intensity of René's beating heart was his foot triggering his kick drum in the basement.

Next, Billy cracked open the white box. His lips formed into an O. He gaped at the black velvet case.

A hint of sweat rose at the nape of René's neck.

Using his thumb, Billy tipped back the lid, then slapped his hand over his mouth. "What the . . ." His fingers held the sterling silver chain. The locket in the shape of an army dog tag dangled in the air. "What is . . ."

"See for yourself." Gushes of delight sprinted through René's veins.

"Seriously? You got me this shape 'cause of — "

"You did say we were good little soldiers in Oshawee Army, didn't you?" René couldn't help the supple laugh gliding from his throat.

The waitress strode over carrying their coffees. Bad timing. Heat of annoyance gathered on René's face.

"Oh . . . a present." The waitress giggled.

"Um . . . yeah . . ." Billy palmed the gift.

Once she'd left, he clicked open the locket. His reddish-brown skin morphed to the shade of pink excitement. "It's . . .

it's us. This was taken at Christmas. Downstairs. In the rehearsal room. Moxy took it."

"Yeah. I asked her to give me a copy when she got the film developed." Pride filled René, pure satisfaction over Billy loving and understanding what the gift meant.

"Is that why you rested your chin on my shoulder? I see the metal horns you flashed are missing. It's only our faces." Billy kept inspecting the locket.

"C'mon, she would've wondered why I leaned in the way I did." Again, the urge to stroke Billy's hand and caress his fingers impaled René like a sword.

"I'm putting it on right now." Billy unfastened the clasp. Even with a collar, he managed to secure the chain around his neck. Regret flickered in his gaze, as if he loathed tucking the locket beneath his navy-blue shirt.

"Remember, it stays hidden." The same regret hovering around their table coated René's tongue with its bitter essence.

"I understand." Billy rubbed his chest where the locket lay. "They'd wanna check out whose picture is inside. I . . ." His eyes finished what he couldn't say in the restaurant. *I love you.*

"Me, too," René whispered. He lifted his coffee. If only the world was different and they could behave like a true couple.

He glanced around at the straight couples holding hands, gazing lovingly at one another, sitting adjacent with their knees brushing. Longing tugged at his heart.

Billy rode shotgun. During the drive home, he'd unfastened a few buttons to his shirt so he could keep touching the locket. So much thought had gone into the gift, from the picture René had tricked Moxy into snapping to picking out the perfect design symbolizing a cherished secret only they understood.

The truck rolled into the garage.

René switched off the engine. A wool dress coat swathed his upper body Billy would give anything to peel off. The guy sure didn't resemble a high school student in his three-piece black suit, red tie, and starched white shirt. No wonder the waitress kept offering them drinks from the bar. René had tucked his bangs behind his ears. The ends of his almost-black hair flipped up on his shoulders that weren't broad but a sexy square shape instead of rounded.

"I had a really great time." René pocketed his keys. He leaned over, stretching his arm across the back of Billy's seat.

Having the distance closed between them was being sucked into a wet dream full of hot steam. Billy kept toying with the locket. His underwear had suddenly grown a tad too sticky and prickly.

René's lips brushed Billy's mouth. The familiar scent of crisp, clean cologne wafted under Billy's nostrils. The most luxurious palms to ever caress him claimed his face. René's tongue searched out Billy's. Gladly, he swapped some spit. He matched René's lush strokes of sensual twirls and delicious licks. The taste was potent, a combination of the mint René had sucked on after the dinner with a smidgen of tobacco.

They'd made out too many times to count, starting with their first kiss up on the mountain two falls ago, but whenever René laid one on Billy, he was transported back at the lookout point, both standing by the railing and the reserve below them.

Maybe he'd never stop being the fifteen-year-old punk who'd been ready to burst from his running shoes, overcome by the most popular guy in school, his very dream dude, smothering his lips with a silky kiss.

The wet heat of René's tongue slipped from Billy's mouth. "We should get inside." His palm remained on Billy's face.

Still searching for air, Billy managed a nod. He'd never con

René into getting sideways, not when the man—yeppers, not boy—he loved had this much self-control.

Billy worked his jelly legs from the truck. He followed René's confident strides from the garage to the back steps.

René fished his keys from his coat. He reached the top of the deck. His dress boots left prints in the dusting of snow on the shoveled stairs.

"I got some nasty wood," Billy muttered. "Man, you always do this to me."

"Seriously?" René stood beneath the outdoor light. He hiked a brow and unlocked the door.

"Yeah." The groan was lodged in Billy's throat. "Not surprised you don't have one."

"That's because I take care of biz in the shower."

Billy edged into the mudroom. He removed his parka and hung the heavy jacket on the hook. Fuck hiding his boner.

René's gaze flicked over Billy. He settled the focus of his delicious chocolate-brown eyes on Billy's crotch, and his casual stare intensified. "Guess you weren't needling me." He let out a low whistle.

"It's yours if you want it, but you don't want it," Billy muttered. He set his boots on the rack. "I'm gonna change."

"Into something more comfortable?" There wasn't teasing in René's question. His voice was pure sandpaper, tormenting every goosebump Billy possessed.

The silver locket resting on his skin reminded Billy he owned René's heart. "I get it. I do."

"Get what?"

"Why it ended in your truck." Billy withdrew the gift from beneath his shirt and rubbed the warm metal. "I'm not gonna rag on you about always following what your parents say. I respect it. Seriously. This is your first time watching the house without Daniel hanging around. I know you wanna ace their test."

"Test?" René's eyes crinkled.

"Yeah. They're always testing us."

"It's not a matter of acing a test. It's about making an adult decision."

"Hey, you've only been an adult for two weeks. Cut yourself a break." Billy turned to go change his clothes. Just as he spun on his heel, René's fingers wrapped his wrist.

He glanced over his shoulder at the same look that had almost drowned him in the truck.

"Y'know, maybe the way you're acting is what's the turn-on." René's voice was the same sandpaper scratching along Billy's skin.

"What d'you mean?" Any sass Billy had left in him died under the potent stare.

"Again, you're not giving me your usual spiel or twenty questions. You haven't for a long time . . ." In two steps, René closed the distance between them.

"I . . ." The words crumpled in Billy's throat. "I . . ." He coughed. "Maybe I'm learning how to respect your point of view. I get it. I do. Does it mean I'm down with it? Fuck no. But I can accept it.

"When I woke up this morning, I was going to . . ." Using his finger, Billy drew a line down René's chest buried beneath the vest and shirt. " . . . try figure out a way to con you into bed."

Shameful heat claimed Billy's cheeks, especially at the amusement flickering in René's gaze. "Something tells me nobody can . . . con you into bed — unless you're willing to be conned."

"You make me sound like I'm made of steel. Hey, even Superman had his Kryptonite." The slight rasp to René's voice continued to scrape Billy's goosepimples in the most seductive way.

"It doesn't matter. Take Olivia. She blackmailed you. You

only agreed to her proposition to save my ass. Nothing more."

"True. And . . . proposition?" René's eyes twinkled.

"What?"

"You don't use as much slang as you used to. I mean, you're still a slang monster, and will probably always be." René reached out and ran his finger along Billy's cheekbone.

"Maybe 'cause the advanced classes have us writing essays and reports." Billy folded his arms. "Hey, I was a good little soldier and took your advice. I'm learning lots on the debate team. It's a great class."

"I know you are." René's lips tugged at the corners. "They teach you different techniques. Are you using one of them now?"

"Nope." Maybe Billy should.

"I see the horns sprouting out of your head." Although René lightly chuckled, a smoldering campfire danced in his irises, flames ready to stretch out and burn Billy. "What're you cooking up?"

"Nothing. Honestly." Attempting to seduce René had been a dumb idea. Where was Billy's pride? Probably on the floor where his tongue sat from this constant stroking on his cheekbone. If he had any dignity, he'd wait for René to give in to his feelings.

Aww, screw his pride. "You wanna fuck or not?"

"You know it's what I want more than anything." René's confession was pure heat to Billy's crotch.

"But your promise . . ." Billy gripped René's finger still gliding along his cheekbone.

"It hasn't been easy, that's for sure." There was something in René's expression Billy couldn't read.

Whatever lurked there was enough to massage Billy beneath his pants. He laced their fingers together and steered René to the basement stairs.

Billy took the steps one by one, moving carefully so he

didn't trip. There was nothing to worry about, though, because René kept a tight grip

Something waited for them down there. Something Billy could almost smell, because he was drawing in the deep scent of excitement. The same unfathomable expression simmered in René's dark-brown eyes.

Anticipation boomed in Billy's chest. He ached to lick his dry lips, but he had no saliva. His spittle had drained away on maybe the eighth step.

His socked feet brushed the cool ceramic tile on the floor. Not only was excitement ripening the atmosphere, fear was present. His own fear. He'd asked for this. He'd begged for this. Now that he clutched what he'd constantly hounded René for, a red alert siren wailed in Billy's brain. Maybe the continuous impenetrability in René's eyes was responsible. Perhaps this was how he'd feasted upon Olivia when he'd taken her to bed.

Billy's knees became rubber, ready to give out under him. "Were you s-s-cared?" he sputtered through clacking teeth.

"Scared?" Even René's voice was undistinguishable. He spoke in his soft tenor, but there wasn't a trace of emotion.

"When you first did it?"

René finally peeled his peepers from Billy, but still held his hands. At least this brief moment of respite offered Billy a chance to gulp a helping of air. As for his rubber knees, they were hopeless.

Too soon, René glanced back with the same ambiguous gaze. He released one of their hands and unknotted the red tie.

Heart a roaring fire, Billy gaped.

René cast aside his tie. He worked on the buttons to his vest. One by one, with the flick of his thumb and index finger, he unfastened them. Sure, Billy had witnessed René removing his rocker apparel after the day was done and then slipping into his sweatpants, white t-shirt, and boring socks, but he sure hadn't observed the guy shedding his clothes in such a determined yet suggestive fashion before.

"Are . . . are you gonna answer me?" Billy's knees jittered.

"My first time doesn't count." René let go of Billy's other hand. He slipped out of his jacket and vest. Then he draped the garments over the chair at the fancy phone desk by the staircase.

"It-it doesn't?"

"No." Very slowly, René shook his head. He worked on the buttons to his dress shirt.

If Billy's heart kept going from a raging fire to pounding thunder, the crazy thing might stop beating.

"What about you?" René's question was gentle yet seductive.

"Wh-what about me?" The cold never ceased, even with fine linen covering Billy's arms.

"Am I the only one who's gonna strip?"

"Uh . . ." First a too-dry mouth, and now Billy's tongue was thicker than Pumpkin's rump.

"If you're not ready, say so. I don't want you to do anything—"

The anxiety coursing through Billy's veins died. "I am. I'm more than ready." The words dribbling from his mouth had more courage than what trickled inside him.

"You sure?" René removed his cuff links. His voice remained smoother than satin.

"Aren't you nervous?" Billy spit out through his still-clacking teeth.

"Of course I am. You don't think I thought about this moment in the shower all the time?"

If René kept speaking in his cotton-caressing tone, Billy might melt all over the floor.

René finished with the cuffs. Those were also set on the

small table. He curled his finger in a gentle *come here.*

Rubbing his biceps, Billy managed the one step to seal the tiny gap separating them.

René laid his palm on Billy's face. This time his gaze was readable. Tender. "I love you," he quietly said. "I love you so much. It hasn't been easy for me, although you think otherwise."

"It's been about me, hasn't it?" The cracks in Billy's voice was reminiscent of puberty.

"Yeah, it has. I don't want to hurt you again. When you dumped me after I . . ." René kept stroking Billy's face. "Being dumped wasn't the kicker. It was why you dumped me. I never wanna let you down again. Ever. I won't let myself be the person responsible for your pain. Your family and buddies fed you enough of that crap."

"Oh man . . ." Billy croaked out. "I got more than your heart, don't I?"

"Yeah, you do." René's mouth came down on Billy's.

He was enveloped in a kiss gentler than the brilliant white clouds he'd painted the other day that had floated by on the azure sky. René's lips were plusher than the puffy pillows Billy rested his head on every night. He locked his arms around René's shoulders.

His first time wouldn't be the disaster he'd heard about from a couple of guys in the boys' locker room, one confessing he'd had no idea where to put *it.* When love was in play, each took care of the other. And René was cherishing Billy, even though the guy admitted he was also nervous.

With his mouth still being dusted with delicate kisses, Billy glided along the ceramic floor and past the pool table. His socked feet hit the carpet just as René's tongue slipped between Billy's lips. The licks weren't deep or probing. They were as gentle as the kisses lavished on him moments ago.

This was dreamier than a dream. Sweeter and softer than

cotton candy. The guys in the locker room were wrong to do the deed without love involved. Holding someone's heart was a guarantee of tender care during a time of apprehension and fear.

René was going to make this the best experience of Billy's life. He knew it. Felt it deep in his bones. He lavished René's tongue with bold strokes. The saliva Billy needed after his mouth had gone dry was replenished by René's offering.

The backs of his knees bumped the sectional in the TV viewing area. He was guided onto the smooth fabric, straight onto his back with René following Billy downward.

Chapter Three: Hands Are Tied

In the past, René had constantly practiced self-discipline, drilled into him by his parents, his uncles, his aunts, his elder brother . . . everyone. So taking his sweet time with Billy should be a simple piece of birthday cake. Try *no*.

His fingers had morphed into eagle talons, ready to tear off Billy's clothes and devour his naked flesh. In the shower, René had jerked off to different scenarios of claiming Billy, but fucking was not on the agenda. Not tonight. Billy deserved to be eased into sex. So keeping the kisses slow and gentle was imperative.

Although Billy had wheedled and nagged to get between the sheets, from his sweating, hiccups, and stiffer-than-a-board tongue, it was clear terror had claimed him. The kind of scared everyone faced during their first time. Neither did Billy have the benefit of tipping back a few beers and snorting a couple of lines of coke, like René had.

Billy's boner pressing on René's own hard dick said the guy he loved wanted this bad, though. The ache in René's underwear became unbearable. So much for beating off this morning to maintain some level of control, because having his tongue deep between Billy's lips sure wasn't helping.

Only high school boys shucked the foreplay and went greedily for the goods. As a graduate and OAC student, René wasn't about to do that. He was a man, and must take Billy like a man would, which meant lots of touches and caresses until Billy begged for an undressing.

Finally, and much to René's aching relief, Billy's tongue got in on the action. The time had come for René to remove his damned shirt that stuck to his back. He slipped his hand between their rising and falling chests. Before he could touch the button, Billy laid claim to René's wrist. He broke their kiss.

Billy blinked a few times. Fear still lurked in his dilated pupils, but also excitement. "I . . . let me . . . let me."

To have each button unfastened, no matter how clumsily by Billy, was what René had longed for. When the tips of Billy's shaking fingers brushed René's bare chest, he couldn't help the hiss leaving his throat. He fisted his knuckles into the sofa for leverage since he lay over Billy. There was a tug and another to René' shirt. The hem slid from the waist of his pants. Billy squeezed his eyes shut.

René leaned in and feathered his lips along Billy's hot cheek that was ripe with fever. Sweat pimpled his unruly hairline.

"It's okay," he murmured. "We can stop any time you want." He nuzzled Billy's just-as-hot ear.

"N-no." Billy's voice crackled. "Not a chance."

"Oh man . . ." Another groan left René's throat. He managed to wiggle off the rest of his shirt. The linen material fell to the carpet.

Billy reached up and draped his arms around René, forcing him back on his chest.

The ache in René's underwear had vanished and was now rushes of pleasure stroking him. His skin was smothered by the softness of Billy's shirt. Being almost the same height, their crotches were pressed tight. The hard excitement beneath Billy's pants tugged at René. He yearned to slip his hand inside and grip Billy's boner. But the guy he loved was still a bit nervous, given the heavy breaths coming from his nostrils. So René kept rubbing his groin along Billy's.

Their hips moved in the same rocking rhythm, producing luxurious sensations jerking off in the shower had never created before.

Billy inched his hand between their chests. From the twisting of his fingers, he was trying to undo his shirt buttons.

René slipped his tongue from Billy's mouth.

Panic filled Billy's eyes. "What're you —?"

"Easy . . ." René pecked his lips. "Just giving you a hand."

Their mouths continued to feast on one another's tongues. The saliva René tasted was pure heaven. He used his other hand to prop himself slightly. Now he was able to reach a very stiff Billy and unfasten his shirt.

"You okay?" he murmured. His fingers rested on the first button. He kissed Billy's neck that was pure silk to his lips.

Billy managed an even stiffer nod.

"Any time you wanna stop, just say so." René undid the third button since the first two were already open.

"Quit saying that. I'm no blue-baller." Defensiveness smattered Billy's reply.

"Didn't say you were and wouldn't think you are if you do ask me to stop." René drew Billy's earlobe between his teeth and suckled.

"There's no stopping . . . not a chance." A slight rasp of determinedness drenched Billy's voice.

"And what if I stop us?" As if René could hit the brakes at this point of no return. He unfastened another button.

"I'll call *you* a blue-baller." Heavy pants came from Billy's mouth. He relocked his arms around René's shoulders and held tight.

Being clung to, although wonderful, was making it difficult for René to get the rest of the shirt open. He had to use his sense of touch while continuing to ply Billy's neck with silky kisses, supple enough to hopefully relax him.

"You don't . . . don't know . . . how long I-I-I w-waited for this."

"Me, too." René groaned. The last of the buttons were

undone. He tugged, and the hem slipped from Billy's pants.

"I can't believe it's happening." Billy clung even tighter. "You're mine. Really mine now. All mine."

"I'll always be yours." René melted his mouth on Billy's.

"Wait." Billy broke the kiss. He set his hand on René's cheekbone. "It can't happen down here. It's gotta happen upstairs. In your room."

"We can do that." The last thing René wanted was to get up, but if being upstairs made Billy happy, they'd make the hike to his room. "C'mon." He used his palms to push himself off the sectional.

Billy followed. He tossed his opened shirt beside René's lying on the carpet.

"Let's go." René tangled their fingers. Walking backward, he led them to the staircase. He received the same starry-eyed look as when they'd first made their way downstairs.

René gently tugged. They reached the top. He guided them into the mudroom.

Billy released their fingers. He locked his arms around René' shoulders. In turn, René hugged Billy's waist. They were crotch to crotch.

René clamped his teeth together. He moved his hips, rocking in sync with Billy's light grinding.

"Oh shit. That feels good . . ." Billy smothered René with a deep kiss.

Billy's desperate searching tongue, gnashing hips, and shoving feet sent René against the wall.

The eager response coming from Billy, his fear now having dissipated, allowed René to finally give in to his own urges. He slid his hands lower until his palms gripped Billy's plush ass. This was the first time he'd ever gotten to feel him up. Sure, he'd copped a grab here and there during their make-out sessions on the sectional, but nothing like this.

While still caressing the finest butt he'd ever stroked, René glided his fingers to Billy's crotch, ready to slip his hand between their melted-together groins and cup the spot he'd always wanted to touch.

A gust of wind blew into the mudroom. Then the back door slammed shut.

René's heart almost burst through his rib cage and flew out from his chest. Before he could blink, and with fear digging into his backside, he pushed Billy with all the strength he possessed.

Billy stumbled backward. For a split second he teetered, on the verge of falling over, but he threw out his arms to steady himself. He spun on his heel.

The worst person who could've caught them stood clutching a suitcase and his mouth fully open.

Danny!

"What the . . . What the . . ." Big brother's shocked stare whipped from René to Billy, then back again. "What the hell's going on?"

Heart still going full tilt, the words René hoped to speak wouldn't jive in his brain to formulate a coherent explanation or tumble from his burning throat.

"You . . ." Danny used his free hand to point at Billy. "Upstairs now." His once-rounded eyes narrowed at René. "You. To Dad's study. Now."

There wasn't a shirt for René to smooth. The most he could do was clasp his fingers. "I—"

"No. I don't want to hear it. Upstairs." When reproaching Billy, Danny used Dad's commanding voice. "I'm storing my belongings in the spare room. I'll be right back." He huffed down the basement steps. His bootheels banged with each clomp.

"Oh fuck . . ." Billy's fearful stare latched on to René. "What're we gonna do? What're we gonna do?"

Gone was the young man who'd engaged René in risqué

foreplay. In his place was the trembling boy who was a mere junior in his second semester of high school.

René was about ready to cuff himself across the face. How could he have been so stupid? Mom and Dad trusted him. He was an adult now. His dick had led him to the worst place possible.

Danny poured a glass of scotch. Instead of meeting in Dad's study, they were downstairs at the wet bar. René sat on one of the leather stools. He'd slid on his shirt earlier. His head remained hanging. There was nothing he could say or do to explain his actions.

What had felt so right at the time had really been terribly wrong.

Danny rested his hand on the bar. He was Dad, from his jet-black, thick, short hair to his stocky build. "Is this why Billy wanted to become friends? Because he had a crush on you?"

René stiffened. "Don't be bringing him into this. I'm the adult." He tapped his chest. "I didn't use common sense—"

"No, you didn't," Danny barked. He planted his other hand on the counter while leaning in. His dark eyes burned a hole into René. "Mom and Dad were going to speak to him when they got home on Sunday night. Now this—"

"Speak to him? About what?"

"His mother." Danny shook his head. He snatched his glass and drained the last of the scotch in the tumbler. "She's finishing rehab next week. She wants to reestablish a relation-ship with him."

Disgust spread its bitter taste across René's tongue. "Reestablish a relationship? There was never a relationship to begin with."

"Don't shoot the messenger. I'm simply telling you what's going on." Danny refilled his glass. "Let's not get off topic, either. What you were about to do if I didn't show up — "

"Danny — "

"No." Danny slammed down the glass. The scotch shook in the tumbler. "How long has this been going on? And don't lie to me. He started it, didn't he?"

"What do you mean *he* started it?" An inch of defensiveness climbed up René's back. "Why're you coming down hard on him?"

"Because everything's adding up. I always thought it was a bit odd the way I'd catch him looking at you. I swore I was imagining the, well, err . . . love in his eyes." Danny smacked his lips together. "You know better. He's your foster brother. He's two grades behind you. He has too much to adjust to as it is. Why didn't you tell him no?"

"Because I was in my first semester of grade twelve." René folded his arms.

"First . . . Did this begin before he started living at Uncle Ned and Aunt Ellen's?" The look on Danny's face was Dad seated in his leather chair in the study.

"No. When he started living with them, we were friends first."

"It never occurred to you to tell Mom and Dad the truth? They took you out for dinner to let you know they were fostering Billy. Why didn't you open your mouth then?" Danny's lecturing became harsher.

"I wasn't about to tell them I was gay. At the time, I couldn't even admit it to myself," René fired back, but his tone lacked Danny's critical bite.

"I know what you're like. Your common sense always prevails. Billy pushed until he got his way, didn't he? Don't think I didn't notice how he wheedles and cons until he acquires what he's after."

"He doesn't wheedle and con." René sputtered. "He's intrepid."

"Intrepid?" Danny flicked his hand. "That's a nice way of twisting what he really is — manipulative."

"Why're you so quick to come down hard on him?"

"Because he's streetwise. That's why. Don't get me wrong. I like Billy. He's done well for himself."

If René didn't say something, Danny would paint a gruesome picture to Mom and Dad about Billy and lay all the blame on him. "Y'know, I didn't have to offer him a lift that day."

"What're you talking about?" Danny's thick eyebrows bunched.

Dammit, René loathed opening his mouth, but he had no choice. "Billy asked me once why I offered him a lift at the beginning of my senior year. I told him I'd offer anyone a ride who'd missed the school bus." Heat gathered on his face. "It's true. I would, but I also offered him a ride because . . ."

He glanced to the sectional where he'd been on top of Billy earlier. "He kept coming into the store."

"What store?"

"The video store. He'd stay around for an hour or two. Every day. I . . . I'm not stupid." René couldn't admit that Keith had made him wise in the ways of men's interest in one another, because Danny had no clue about his best friend's sexual orientation.

"I . . . err . . . I sort of put two and two together. I thought . . . I thought he might be interested in me." If René's face burned any hotter, he'd become one of the wildfires that raged through the forests surrounding the reserve and city.

"A guy with the worst rep was giving you vibes and you thought to—" Danny's summarization was incredulous.

"No," René quickly said. "I only wanted to feel him out. Even then, I changed my mind." He snatched a straw from the tall glass since he didn't have a pen to twirl. "I couldn't figure out what I wanted. I knew he dug me. I felt it. But I wasn't ready to . . . ready to admit what I didn't want to admit. As a matter of fact, I was really tough on him at the beginning. It drove him nuts."

"So he put the vibe out and you went for it." Danny rubbed his face the same way Dad would.

"Uh . . . yeah. Can you let it pass?" René set his elbows on the bar and folded his hands. "If Mom and Dad find out, they'll stick Billy somewhere else. He's not ready to—"

"Why didn't you think of this before I found you two in the mudroom?" Danny pointed upward.

"You don't think I did?" René gasped. "I thought about it all the time. I swore to myself I wouldn't touch him until he hit grade twelve—"

"But you didn't." Pure accusation dripped from Danny's mouth. "You're an adult. He's a minor. You're done high school. He isn't. He's your foster brother, for cripe's sake."

"I didn't expect him to be my foster brother." René sat his hand on his chest. "Mom and Dad blew me away when they told me they were taking him in. By then it was too late. We were already seeing each other."

"Welp, they're not gonna like what I have to say. Dad's gonna—"

"Please don't tell them. Please," René begged. "I promise you I'll end it tonight. Right now. Just don't tell Mom and Dad."

"Yes, you'll end it. You're going straight upstairs afterward and tell him to date people in high school. That Carla girl is always lurking around. Tell him to ask her on a date."

A flicker of jealousy crawled through René's blood. Still, hadn't he admitted in the past they'd make a cute couple when he was previously trying to cut Billy loose? "Will you keep this to yourself?"

Danny's thick shoulders drooped. "Renny, y'know I'd do anything for you, but this is serious business. Mom and Dad are his foster parents. If David finds out, we're cooked."

Great, he would bring up their cousin's name, who was Billy's caseworker. René rubbed his temples. "Even after I promised you I'd end it, you're still going to tell them?"

"I wouldn't be an adult if I didn't. Welcome to eighteen, little brother. Nobody said doing the right thing is easy. Do you think this is easy for me?" Danny pointed at himself.

"Can you at least sleep on it? Please?" God, René had done so much begging, he might as well get on his knees.

Danny ran his hand over his face as if lathering up with a bar of soap. "We'll talk some more tomorrow. I need to unpack."

"What're you doing here, anyway?" René squinted. He motioned at the luggage.

"A long story I'm not ready to talk about. Let's say Paula doesn't want me at the condo tonight." Danny rounded the bar. He picked up his suitcase and made his way toward the hall that led to the spare bedroom. Before departing, he pivoted. "Remember, you end it tonight."

Chapter Four: Pieces of the Night

Billy couldn't stop pacing his room. They were cooked. Burnt toast. For sure Daniel was going straight to The General and Colonel. He was probably on the phone right now.

Footsteps padded down the hall. They weren't the familiar clomp of Daniel's formidable gait but René's smooth saunter. Billy dashed to his door and threw it open to René on the other side. There might as well have been a thundercloud above his head with pouring rain.

"He's gonna tell your parents, isn't he?" Billy managed to squeak out through the ball forming in his throat.

This couldn't be happening. They were in love. Madly, deeply in love. They hadn't fought after René had pulled the unthinkable last year. They'd been getting along perfectly. Naturally, what they'd shared had almost led to sex. That was what happened when two people were crazy about each other.

Regret and hopelessness loomed in René's eyes. He reached out and drew Billy into his arms, smothering him with his familiar crisp, clean scent. Being blanketed in such a tender embrace was enough to expand the lump in Billy's throat. He couldn't stop the tears from welling up.

"Wh-why?" Releasing those words when he could barely speak was like trying to suck a boulder through a straw.

"You know why," René whispered. He stroked Billy's back and used his broad chin to nuzzle him.

"Wh-what'd he say?" But Billy had his answer already. He clutched René tighter.

"What I keep telling you. I'm eighteen. I'm a high school graduate. You're fostering at my place. You don't need to take advanced grade twelve algebra to figure this calculation." Pure misery was in René's limp reply.

Then if he didn't want to see them come to an end, why not fight for them? Billy squirmed until he was free of René's clinch. He set his palms on René's biceps and bore down on his despondent gaze. "You're eighteen. You can make your own—"

"No." René shook his head. He trailed his finger down Billy's cheek. "You know why we had to keep *us* a secret."

Billy buried himself back in René's arms. "Can't you talk to him? Can't you tell him to keep it quiet?"

"I can try talk to him, but I know already what he's going to say, Billy."

First thing that morning, Billy marched downstairs to Daniel in the breakfast nook. He was sipping coffee, munching on toast, and glancing over the newspaper. A brown bathrobe wrapped his sturdy body.

"Good morning." The greeting didn't match the storm clouds gathering in Daniel's eyes. "Renny still sleeping?" He motioned at the available chairs.

At least Billy was receiving an invitation to sit, or was Daniel going to pull a lecture from the pocket of his robe? "Yeah."

Lucky René had a spare for first period, so he never left for school until second class.

"Do me a favor and wake him before you leave." Daniel turned back to his newspaper.

That was it? Billy's fate would be decided without even consulting him. "About last night—"

Daniel held up his hand while staring at the paper. "We can talk when you get home. Now fix yourself some breakfast. I imagine Stu will be here pretty quick."

Stuart picked everyone up for school, but Billy's best bud could darn well toot his horn until Sunday, because he was talking to Daniel first. "About last night . . ."

"Get yourself some breakfast. I already said Stu's going to be here to get you soon." Finality was in Daniel's order.

Okay, Billy would try the polite approach, so he used his most respectful tone. "Don't I get a say in this matter? Don't I get a chance to explain myself?"

"There's nothing to explain. Renny more than explained enough for the two of you last night." Daniel turned another page of his newspaper.

"I think you're being unfair. I'm seventeen—"

Daniel set down his paper. He focused his steel gaze on Billy. "Then if you're seventeen, act like it. Your priority's getting ready for school, not engaging in a discussion that could make you late for first class. Any adult would know the time to talk is after you get home."

Spine stiffer than a board after receiving more than a spanking, Billy tromped to the walk-in pantry. This was incredulous. The damned family was still determined to treat him like a ten-year-old, even when he was being as placid as he could muster, considering the circumstances.

Fuck this shit. He snatched the box of *Graham* wafers off the shelf and trounced back into the kitchen. "I love him."

Daniel's gaze shifted from the newspaper to Billy.

"I love your brother."

"Nobody, when they're seventeen years old, knows what love is." Daniel's voice was dryer than unbuttered toast.

"Your parents didn't then? Mr. and Mrs. O got married when she was eighteen and he was nineteen."

"That was the trend in their day. It's not the nineteen seventies anymore. Everyone on the rez married young back then. We're closing in on the twenty-first century."

"I don't see what the difference is. Seventeen is seventeen."

Billy strode over to the cupboard, still clutching the box of cereal.

"No, it's not. When I was seventeen, I wasn't thinking about getting married."

"Neither am I." Billy gathered up the milk, spoon, and bowl. He returned to the breakfast table. "But it doesn't mean you can't fall in love."

"No, it doesn't." Daniel actually nodded. "Still, you—" He folded up his newspaper. "I'd better finish dressing."

Billy's mouth fell open. The Sergeant never shut down in the middle of a conversation, much less backed down. Daniel was going to tell the Oshawees. For sure René would listen and do the unthinkable—tear Billy's heart from his chest.

When René strode downstairs, Danny was showered and dressed. He stood at the kitchen island with a cup of coffee.

"Did you tell Billy about his mom?" René beelined for the buffet where the coffee pot was kept. He poured himself a mug full.

"I'm not his foster parent." The same serious tone from last night was in Danny's voice.

Fair enough. René grabbed his coffee and sat at the eating bar at the island. Although he'd tossed and turned in bed for a solution, none had come. The fact was, they were busted. Like every adult on planet Earth, he must face up to his deception and take full responsibility. No amount of begging would change Danny's mind, because big brother was viewing this from the perspective of a reliable person in their mid-twenties who'd earned his post-secondary degree and worked full-time.

"I won't ask you again to keep it to yourself. I understand now. I do." René squeezed the handle of the mug. "All I ask is they let Billy remain here. If he's moved, I'm not sure how he'll react. If you want . . ." He swallowed. "I'll move."

"Move?" Danny cocked a brow. "Where would you move to exactly? Living from home is expensive. Why do you think university students stay in residence or triple or quintuple up to a house? You're not even in university. You're in high school."

"I'm officially done high school," René calmly replied. "There are other high schools . . . like . . . Toronto."

"Toronto?" Danny sputtered. "Renny, there's more to living away from home than making the monthly rent payment. You don't even know how to wash your own clothes or make a bed."

"Everyone's gotta start somewhere. Mom can show me how." Tension appeared on René's forehead.

"There's no way they're allowing you to move to Toronto to finish your OAC. This convo is finished. I'm speaking to them Sunday morning before they check out. I don't want to tell them any sooner because I refuse to ruin their weekend." Danny rinsed his mug in the small sink built into the island.

"Fine. Tell them. I'll talk to Dad when he gets back." René also rinsed his mug. "I'm outta here. My class is starting soon."

Danny was as hard-assed as Dad.

Billy sat in the computer lab. Matt Gerhard was present, working on another student's computer that had gone bonkers, something the teacher couldn't fix, so whenever shit hit the fan, the high school's Bill Gates was dragged from one of his OAC classes and hauled in to fix the problem.

Matt, of course, was one of the rockers. He was also dating a senior, and she was seventeen. If Matt got to see an underage chick, then there shouldn't be an all-out SWAT team drawing their weapons on René for daring to see a guy in grade eleven.

The bell rang. Billy stood and snatched his books. Matt remained at the station, continuing to work on the broken computer.

Billy plopped in the other chair. This was the ten-minute break. They had a moment to talk. "How's it going with you and Erin?"

"Pretty good." Matt's voice was as monotonous as his blank stare.

"So . . . uh . . ." Dammit, this wasn't any of Billy's business. He sure as shit didn't want the scoop on Matt's love life, but he had to start somewhere. "Are you two gonna keep dating when you're done school at the end of the year?"

Matt stopped staring at the computer screen. His blank blue eyes became one of seeing a two-headed man. "What?" He squinted.

Oh great, Billy had come off as a total dork. "Just wondering. Y'know? How it all works if people date others who still have to finish school."

"Why don't you ask Renny? You live with him." Matt turned back to the wonky computer screen, still firing off weird numbers that didn't belong.

"He's not dating anyone."

A hint of a smirk snuck up on the corners of Matt's slim mouth. "Yeah. Too bad he's married to his drums."

He is not. He's seeing me, and his parents are going to try break us up. "Well?"

"She's cool and all." Matt shrugged. His fingers kept gliding over the keyboard. The numbers peppering the screen were diminishing. He was closing in on fixing the problem that had stumped the teacher for a good half an hour.

"And . . ." No wonder why the guy Billy loved had picked Matt to cozy up to over Mike. Even though the Gerhard twins were facsimiles, Mike was Sheldon and Vince's speed — a true rocker with a nose piercing and two tattoos. As for Matt, even though his long hair matched his brother's, the dude was a bookworm and computer geek.

"My priority's this." Matt pointed at the screen. "Moxy and Ian are in T-O. I'm planning on applying to the U of T. They offer a better computer program. They told me if I get accepted, I can crash at their crib."

Billy sank so low, he almost slid from the chair. Great. Matt was choosing his schooling over love. There was no point in continuing their conversation.

René shoved away his textbook and binder. Closing time was drawing in at the video store. He still had to prepare the float and lock up. In the morning, Billy would do the main cleaning. Hopefully, he'd managed to enjoy his night at the movies with his buddies.

Headlights flashed in the main window. Stuart had gotten his own wheels — his mom's old minivan after she'd bought a new one. The sliding door opened. Billy hopped out. With a toot, the red vehicle drove off.

Billy pushed on the door. The bell above tinkled. His new curfew was twelve-thirty on weekends and ten-thirty on weeknights. He no longer had to choose which two nights he'd use for socializing during the school week because he'd shown the proper maturity and responsibility to be granted his new set of rules, something René was familiar with since Mom and Dad had applied the same system when he'd been a junior.

The usual light in Billy's dark eyes wasn't present. "Hey . . ." He set his hands on the counter.

They hadn't had time to speak today. Fridays were crammed with tests and new lessons. "I was just about to close off the till and start the z reading."

"I'll help." Billy's voice was as dead as his blank stare. He rounded the counter. "What's Daniel doing at the house anyway?"

René hit a few buttons on the keyboard. "Paula's pissed at him about something. I think it's why they came back early from the 'Peg. He's bunking in the spare room and that's that."

"I think he's fakin' it. He came home early to check up on us," Billy muttered.

The till drawer banged open. The printer cartridge spewed out the reading. "I doubt it. If Danny wanted to stay at the house, he would've."

"What about us then?" Billy grabbed a handful of quarters.

This was going to be the worst conversation René had ever had. "Y'know what's gonna happen. What I'm trying to do is make sure you stay at the house."

As for Mrs. Redsky, Billy would flip when he heard Mom and Dad drop the bomb about the drunken lush. Maybe René ought to tell Billy. Then the lecture coming from his parents might not be as shocking.

The night was a crisp midnight blue. Besides the glow of the moon, the high beams from the truck Billy drove cast light on the skeleton underbrush that crept right up to the road. The last time he'd witnessed René smoking inside the interior was before he'd confessed his love. They were also heading to the same place where they'd truly become a couple, but the path was a snowmobile trail now. If they drove the truck down where René had used to dirt bike, they'd get stuck, four-wheel drive or not.

"Why're we going here? We'll freeze." Billy stopped at the start of the trail.

"I just felt like coming here." René threw open the passenger door and vacated the vehicle.

Billy turned off the engine and followed René, who'd already started down the trail, hands shoved into his coat pockets and normally straight shoulders rounded.

"Wait," Billy called out.

René removed his gloved hand from his pocket and held out his fingers. Billy jogged forward. He stopped beside René and took his hand.

The spruce trees were lit by the silver glow from the moon. The snow shone up an iridescent blue. As they walked, their boot heels crushed the packed trail.

There wasn't a breeze present, only the chill of winter surrounding them. Although they were enshrouded in cold, their linked hands generated a fuzzy warmth that was a crackling fire, toasting Billy from his toes to his toque-covered head. Not very often could they stroll together hand in hand. Each time they walked like a true couple, a *this is so right* feeling softer than the pima cotton sheets of his bed smothered his skin.

"This is weird, huh?" Billy said, glancing around. "January's always windy."

"Yeah, it is." René dug inside his pocket and withdrew his cigarettes. He easily manipulated a smoke from the packet, flicked his platinum lighter, and set the tip in the flame while swinging their hands back and forth in a singsong sort of way.

Perhaps the peaceful night was a good omen.

"What'd Daniel say?"

"You already know what he said." René took a drag. He squeezed their gloved fingers.

Billy swallowed. "He's gonna tell your parents?"

"He's calling them Sunday morning before they fly out to give them the heads-up."

Something fisted Billy's heart. He stopped. The *crunch, crunch* of their boot heels squashing the snow ceased. Before he could will them away, tears surfaced in his eyes. A vicious lump emerged in his throat.

The Oshawees were going to take René from him.

"Y'knew if we got caught this was gonna happen." René's words were gentle on Billy's ears.

"B-but . . ." Finally, after fifteen years of pure shit, Billy had captured what he'd always wanted, now only to have love torn from his grasp. "Wh-why? We're not doing anything wrong."

René used his hand holding the cigarette to lift Billy's chin upward. "I'm sorry. It's their house. Their rules. You're their foster son."

"I'm not their son. I never thought of myself as their son," Billy choked out through the expanding lump in his throat. "They're people who're looking out for me until I turn eighteen. All I got is one more fucking year to go. One measly year."

"I know. I know." Passion Billy had never heard before shot from between René's lips. Such agony. Such pain. He dropped the cigarette and yanked Billy into his arms. "Do you think I want this to happen? Do you think if I could find a way to stop it, I would? I can't. I can't. And I'm sorry I let you down."

He laid his head against Billy's and stroked the toque. Wetness came from somewhere, ready to freeze on Billy's skin. René's tears. He was crying.

Billy clutched him in a bear grip. The tears in his own eyes seeped from his shut-tight lids and rolled down his cheeks.

The General held the cards, and they could only wait to see what the top dog would deal them.

CHAPTER FIVE: NOT ONLY NUMB

The General had slammed down his iron fist, informing the household to be home when he walked through the back door. René had switched shifts. He'd left for work that morning and arrived home around five. He'd gone straight to his room.

Billy lay on his bed, arms and legs crossed . . . waiting.

Daniel had retrieved Mr. and Mrs. O from the airport over an hour ago. The clock on Billy's nightstand read seven. He'd heard the duo come up the stairs and make their way to the royal chamber on the other side of the second floor. Then they'd left the master suite about fifteen minutes ago and had gone downstairs.

René's phone rang. Then his bedroom door opened and closed. He'd probably been summoned to sit in the chair that faced the front of The General's desk in the formidable study across from the formal living room at the front of the house.

Billy bolted off his bed and dashed into the hallway just as René strode to the staircase. "Wait."

Stopping, René slowly pivoted. He'd changed into his comfy outfit of sweatpants, a t-shirt, and white socks. The same pain smothering Billy's chest loomed in René's eyes.

"Th-they can order us to stop seeing each other, but . . . but nothing can make me stop loving you." The words from Billy's mouth were filled with the same agony tearing him in two.

"I know . . ." René spoke so quietly, Billy had to strain to hear.

"And . . ." Billy inched forward. His feet dusted the carpet in the hallway.

"Nothing can stop what I feel for you." René fisted his hands. Pain burned in his pupils. "I gotta . . . I gotta . . ."

"Renny!" Mr. O bellowed.

Oh boy, this was bad if The General hadn't bothered to try calling René's separate phone line again.

"I gotta get downstairs." René turned. He vanished from the hallway. His socked feet brushing the stairs carried to where Billy stood.

Billy dashed back into his bedroom.

René stopped at the small drink fridge in the butler's pantry to retrieve a cream soda for his parched throat before facing off with his parents. He dragged his feet into the main hall. The balcony above him showed no sign of Billy looking down.

Somehow, he had to convince his parents to approve his plan. Already, he'd instant messaged Ian and Moxy. He'd done so after he'd gotten home from work, explaining he was considering finishing his OAC in Toronto, and could he possibly stay at their place. They'd said yes, naturally. The time had come to get on his knees and beg.

Being an adult sucked. If this was owning up to his age of majority, he'd take his high school years any day of the week. Then, he could act out, demand they had no right telling him and Billy what to do, pull a fit, get as emotional as he wanted. But he'd never done so when he'd been a minor and he wouldn't now, because his biggest priority was ensuring Billy's time in foster care was meaningful, giving him life skills he'd require to become a successful adult.

There wasn't any sign of Danny, who must be downstairs in the basement. René couldn't get angry at his elder brother for ratting on them. Only teenaged kids became hostile if anyone dared to expose their wrongdoings.

But was falling in love wrong?

He stopped in front of the study where the double doors were open. Mom sat in the chair opposite the desk. Dad was in his usual leather high-back.

"Hey . . ." René meandered into the room. On shaky legs, he took the chair beside Mom.

Mom fiddled with her fingers while Dad's hound dog face said he could use a drink.

René's heart pinched. He'd let them down. Dammit, why did *that* look always overload him with guilt? Probably because they had complete faith in him, and he'd broken their trust. Now he'd put them in a horrible predicament.

"I'm sorry," he softly began. The tab of his cream soda glistened under the silver lighting in the study from the chandelier overhead. The desk lamp was off. He opened the can. "I'm really sorry. If you'd let me explain—"

"How long has this been going on?" Dad's voice was somber.

"Danny didn't tell you?" René glanced up. His shoulders stiffened.

"It wasn't his place. He simply informed us what he witnessed in the mudroom." The weariness in Dad's tone matched an old man of eighty and ready for the grave.

"I see." René set the can between his legs. Fountain pens were neatly placed in the glass holder in front of him. His fingers pleaded with him to snatch one to twirl.

"I asked you a question." Dad's voice sharpened.

René shifted. He crossed his ankles. Uncrossed them. Then recrossed them. "I . . . uh . . . we started out as friends first."

"Friends?" Dad quirked a brow.

René nodded. "I didn't know about him and he didn't know about me."

"How did the two of you find out about each other?"

"When . . . I don't know. It's hard to explain. I picked up vibes from him, and he picked up vibes from me."

"Did this start in the house?" Dad tapped his finger on the blotter.

René shook his head. A smidgen of sweat trickled down his back. "No. It . . . uh . . . when he . . . when he was living at Uncle Ned's."

"I see. Now, accounting for the agony you endured informing us about your sexual orientation, and accounting for your secret desire to live how society deems a normal life, I'm assuming Billy pursued the relationship."

René winced. His family were too smart, too perceptive. Considering he'd done his best to hide his true self, whatever that might be, his parents and brother seemed to know him better than he knew himself. "Yes . . . but . . . I gave him a reason to."

"Reason?"

Why did Dad have to sound so serious? He had Darth Vader down pat. "I . . . I told Danny this already. I didn't have to give Billy a ride to school that morning, but I did."

"Ride to school?"

"It was the fall, the beginning of my senior year. He was late. He missed the bus. So I stopped and offered him a ride." The embarrassment shimmering through René seeped into his confession.

"Was there a motive?" At least there wasn't a hint of accusation in Dad's question.

"Maybe . . ." René picked at his sweatpants. "I . . . he kept coming into the video store. He'd stay there, like, forever. Keith . . . he was a big help, y'know. It made me wise to the vibe. Signals. I knew Billy wanted something from me, but I wasn't sure what."

"I think you're far more insightful than what you're acknowledging."

Great. Busted. "Fine. I had a good hunch he dug me. I felt it in my gut. The thing is, as much as I wanted something to happen, I didn't want anything to happen either — if that makes sense. I kept . . . he called me a tap once. He accused me of not knowing whether I wanted to run hot or cold water."

Mom and Dad simply stared.

René cleared his throat. This meant he was supposed to keep talking. "He . . . he helped me." He flicked back his bangs. "He helped me lots. If not for him, I'd still be . . . still be denying who I really am. Even when I discouraged him, he never gave up. He, uh, also likes girls."

Dad pursed his lips. "Yes . . . I see. He was dating Julie Handorgan briefly. Carla Morrisseau has also been around."

"I tried to tell him to live a normal life, but he said his *normal* is with me."

"I understand how you two helped one another." Compassion filled Dad's lecturing tone. "I really do. But you also hinder one another."

"Hinder?" René squinted.

"You sat with me and your mother last March, declaring passionately how much music means to you. I know the courage it took for you to ask us to support your request to attend the Franklin College of Music. You and Chunk planned on going to Toronto together. Now? You wish to become a lawyer."

René rubbed his thumb on the pop can.

"As for Billy, since we confirmed he enjoys the company of girls, he isn't allowing himself to examine that side of himself. He desires to become a First Nations constable, whereas when we first spoke to him, his dream was to become an artist. How did the two of you arrive at your decisions? Did your relationship influence your goals for the future?"

Well, yes, but René wasn't changing career courses all for

Billy, or was he? Hadn't he questioned himself already?

"You don't need to speak." Dad raised his hand. "Your silence tells me everything."

"Wait a second." René straightened. "You're assuming—"

Again, Dad raised his hand. "Let me finish, please."

"Sure." René lifted the can and tipped back a sip.

"I know you couldn't tell us about your relationship when we informed you we planned on fostering Billy. At the time, you couldn't admit to yourself who you truly are. But when you told us the truth, why did you fail to inform us about you and Billy then?"

René gripped the pop. He hung his head. In a small voice he murmured, "Because we knew you'd disapprove."

"If you knew this, you also knew what you were engaging in was wrong. Correct?"

Keeping his head bowed, René nodded.

"You're aware your mother and I are responsible for Billy. If Family Services learns what's occurring under my roof, they'll take him from our care."

René swallowed. He wiggled his toes. They pushed up and against his socks.

"Billy's future is what's important here, isn't it?"

René nodded.

"Then what happened in the mudroom cannot ever happen again. Is this understood?"

"Yes," René whispered. "I fully understand." He glanced back up. "Does this mean he'll stay here?"

"I don't know." Dad sighed. "How can I keep him here when I'm aware how you two feel about each other? This will hinder him from living a life he's supposed to explore because he's too devoted to you."

"No. No." René almost leapt forward. He set his hand on the desk. "I . . . I . . . I talked to Ian."

"Ian Fletcher?"

"Yes. I talked to him. I told him I'm gonna finish my OAC in Toronto. He said I can crash at his place—"

"Renny. Renny." For the bazillionth time, Dad's hand came up. "That is an emotional decision based on a reaction. Not a logical one, is it not?"

"Yes."

"Decisions must be based on logic. They must be thoroughly explored. Even though you're eighteen, I cannot permit you to up and move to Toronto based on an emotional reaction. Adulthood means investigating your options. Understood?"

"Yes."

"Until I speak to Billy, no decisions will be made. You don't see me reaching for the phone to contact David, do you? Your mother and I are going to discuss this matter further tonight. Sleeping on it is imperative. You don't think we discussed this on the plane trip home? It was important we agree on which direction to take when we finally sat down with you."

Pleading filled Dad's eyes. "Renny, please understand, I know this is your first . . . romance. I was young once. I'm aware the heart has great influence on teenagers. Although you're an adult, turning eighteen is more than a number. Do you think you made an adult decision when Daniel discovered you two?"

That was an easy answer. "No." René licked his lips. "I didn't want it to happen. I asked Billy to wait. I'm not saying it's Billy's fault, either. I—"

"As I said, I was young once. I know how a young man's hormones work. Believe me . . ." Dad rubbed his brow. "The fact is, you and Billy cannot stay under the same roof any longer. How we're going to resolve this problem is what we must tackle next."

At least Mom and Dad weren't hollering in René's face, calling him an immature clown who couldn't keep his dick under control. "I just want to say this — letting Billy stay here is important to me. Very important. If he's placed somewhere else, I'm worried . . ." He drew in a breath. "I know his mother's getting out of rehab soon and she wants to reconnect. I don't want to see him regress. He's come so far."

"Did Daniel tell you?"

René nodded.

"We're contemplating and exploring options regarding Billy's situation. We don't wish to see him fail any more than you do." Dad flopped back. "Dismissed."

René stood. All he could do was wait.

Dread gripped Billy by the shoulders. He inched into the study where The General sat behind the desk.

Mr. O glanced up. "Please, sit. I thought you'd be more comfortable if you only had to speak to one of us."

Thank fuck he wasn't hollering or accusing Billy of seducing his son. He made sure to sit straight in the chair. Then again, the soft tap on his door from René five minutes ago had been a quiet sign, telling Billy not to fear.

"I'm sorry—"

Mr. O raised his hand. "An apology isn't necessary."

Billy's heart was the revving of the throttle of the dirt bike. Maybe The General was going to let this pass. Maybe he'd allow them to see each other, as long as they didn't do the nasty in the house. "Oh?"

"Renny explained to me the two of you began . . . dating, before Mrs. Oshawee and I started fostering you. Naturally, you'd want to keep seeing each other."

"Yeah. I—"

"Unfortunately, because we're fostering you, and you're living under our roof, we can't permit you to see each other anymore." Regret lurked in Mr. O's words.

Billy's rising chest deflated. What he'd feared all along was a reality. The Oshawees wouldn't give their blessing.

"Billy, please look at me."

Forcing his head upward and away from the plush carpet, Billy focused his gaze.

"Understand, Renny is an adult and graduated, whereas you are a minor and in your junior year. You two are living under the same roof. This wasn't an easy decision for us." Mr. O pressed his thin lips together.

"Does this mean —?"

Again, Mr. O raised his hand. "Please let me finish." He folded his fingers together and rested them on the desk blotter. "I know how an older person can influence a younger person. Although you and Renny helped each other greatly, your . . . ah, relationship, also stymied your growth."

Huh? What did Mr. O mean?

"Do you recall when you first moved in and I requested you take the bus instead of riding with Renny to school every morning?"

Billy nodded.

"There was a good reason — for you to develop new friendships and your own social circle within your grade group. You did. Yet he still holds great influence over you. Although you can't see this, I can. Your dream to become a police officer is noble, however, Creator gave you a talent in art, did He not?"

"Y-yes." Where was this leading?

"Last March, Renny begged us to let him attend the Franklin College of Music in Toronto. Then he changed his mind and informed us he wished to pursue a law degree. I know what music means to my son." Mr. O rubbed his brow. "What I'm trying to say is you have two more years to think your future through. Renny has five months, maybe even less, because he has to apply to the university he wants to attend . . ."

He sat back and steepled his fingers. "Mrs. Oshawee and I are going to talk some more. We'll have your answer as soon as possible. Once we give you our answer, there is something else we must discuss."

"Uh . . . something else?"

"Yes. But we won't get into that now. I don't want to overwhelm you. Unless you have further questions, you're dismissed."

Billy had questions, but those answers wouldn't come until the Oshawees gave him the new rules. "It's okay. I understand."

He wouldn't whine or wheedle to get his way. René was right. If they wanted to be treated as adults, they had to act like adults by accepting the consequences for their actions.

He left the study, but he couldn't stop his head from hanging.

CHAPTER SIX: END OF THE WORLD

M om had informed René a half hour ago to shower earlier than usual so they could talk. Billy wasn't present. Wednesday mornings he cleaned the video store, and Stuart always picked him up there for school.

Dread coasted along René's spine. The parents had made their decision. During the past two days, awkward silence had permeated the house. Thank God for his job so he didn't have to be home for dinner to suffer more unease in the dining room. What pained him, though, was Billy's absence in René's room whenever he returned from work around quarter after ten, and seeing Billy's closed door with light coming from beneath.

He grabbed his textbooks and binders off the desk and gently shut the door to his room.

As he made his way downstairs and into the foyer, his chest kept tightening. Dad's study was empty. Well, they wouldn't be meeting in there. The parents weren't in the formal living room, either. He'd find them in the kitchen.

Mom stood at the island, buttering toast. Dad sat in the breakfast nook, sipping coffee and glancing over the newspaper. Lucy, who always made the morning meal, wasn't present.

With a deep breath, René set his books on the table and beelined to the buffet to get himself a cup of joe. If Lucy wasn't around, this reaffirmed the parents had made their decision. If he had to lace up his boxing gloves and fight for the boy he loved to remain here, he would.

René filled his mug and sat at his usual spot just as Mom approached, carrying two plates of food. She set one in front of Dad and the other in front of René. His weary stomach wasn't in the mood for scrambled eggs and toast, but out of respect, because Mom worked hard at her job and shouldn't have to cook, he'd eat what was in front of him.

When he bit into a helping of scrambled eggs, the taste buds on his tongue revolted.

Mom set down her own plate and sat. "More coffee, anyone?"

"I'm good." Dad shoveled food into his mouth.

At least one of them could eat.

While René forced down his breakfast to silence, his stomach continued to protest. Naturally, they'd wait on speaking to him until after the meal was done.

Once he ate the last of his eggs, he shoved away his empty plate. Mom had brought the carafe to the table. He poured himself another cup of coffee to wash away the bitter taste in his mouth.

"How's Chunk doing?" Dad took his coffee black. He picked up his refilled mug and sipped.

Why were they asking about René's main man? They knew Chunk was working this year at his parents' restaurant to bank more money before he entered trade school in the fall to become a chef. "S'okay. I haven't talked to him in a few days. We've both been busy."

"Has he decided which college he's applying to?" Dad had also set aside his plate.

"Not yet." René palmed the mug.

"We've reached a decision. It took us a couple of days because we had some researching to do." Dad cleared his throat. "This wasn't easy."

The pattering of René's heart slowed.

Dad again cleared his throat. "I . . . I hoped you'd remain

here and attend university at Lakeside as your brother had done. We spoke to Keith. He lives east of the university in Church and Wellesley."

The pattering of René's heart increased.

"He informed us the area where he lives is rich in . . . a certain culture. A place you'll find comfortable to be yourself." Dad's pitch lowered. He didn't look up but stared at his coffee mug. "I believe this is for the best. As Keith said, perhaps what occurred is a blessing in disguise. You can be your true self there if you are comfortable enough to be . . . err . . . out.

"Keith's roommate is the owner of the house. A lawyer. He's a partner at a practice downtown. His name is Brooks Avery. He has a basement apartment he rents to university students. We are in luck. The renter is withdrawing from school. Something about a family emergency and he must return home. I spoke to Mr. Avery and asked him to hold the apartment for you — and Chunk, if he decides to move with you."

René's mouth fell open. For real he'd reside in Toronto's *gayborhood*? He'd heard great stories from Keith about Church and Wellesley. Gay-friendly bars. Gay-friendly restaurants. The possibility of actually coming out . . . He came close to slapping his hand over his mouth.

"There's a school on Jarvis Street where you can finish your OAC." A tinge of sadness hovered in Dad's words. "It's within walking distance, so you don't have to worry about parking. Parking is extremely expensive in downtown Toronto."

Mist settled in Mom's eyes.

"Speaking of parking," Dad continued on, "it's best you leave your truck here until the summer. Once school is complete, you can fly home to retrieve it. Under the circumstances, we don't have the luxury of making the drive east. You'll fly. You'll need to retrieve your truck, because Mr.

Avery is more than open to the possibility of providing you with a job for the summer. He's aware you wish to become a lawyer."

A surge of shock clambered up René's spine.

Dad picked up his mug and sipped. His face contorted slightly, as if he'd drunk dishwater. "Perhaps . . . perhaps I've been selfish. After speaking to Keith, I fully understand now why he moved to Toronto."

He shifted his gaze from the coffee mug he still held in the air. "You're my youngest. It's not easy for a parent to lose the last in the nest, so to speak. But it's all for the best. Keith can help you in a way I can't.

"As for your drums, I checked into shipping them ground. What I'll need you to do is take your kit apart and prepare it for travel. I know how much drumming means to you, and you'll need something familiar once you're settled.

"Believe me, after attending the Indian Residential School, I know how lonely being away from home can be. But you won't be fully alone. As I said, if Chunk wishes to go with you, he's more than welcome to. You also have friends there. Your mother and I are always on business in Toronto. The same for your brother. And you'll be under Keith's tutelage.

"Keith's more than aware how I feel about this matter." Dad's eyes narrowed. "I'm trusting him with my youngest son. He assured me he'll take good care of you. The city can be an unsavory place at times. People take advantage of one another in certain ways. I told Keith I don't want anyone near you unless they have his full approval.

"We're flying out this weekend. I already spoke to your Uncle Vernon. Billy will have your shifts at the video store."

Mom raised her head. "I'm contacting the school after you leave to arrange to have everything transferred to Jarvis Collegiate."

A roar filled René's ears. Billy was safe. But what if he

began dating girls? What if he started seeing Carla Morris-seau? Even worse, what if the two fell in love?

René glanced away. To save Billy, what if he lost him . . . forever?

Something was up. The tension in the house seemed to spread throughout like heavy fog. When Billy had first arrived home, the haze of doom had greeted him in the mudroom, hovered in the kitchen where Lucy was absent at the island, snaked upstairs with him to his bedroom, and then crept along behind him into the dining room where Mr. and Mrs. O waited.

"Did you cook?" Billy sat at his usual spot adjacent to Mr. O.

Mrs. O was across from Billy. It was their informal eating style when guests weren't present, since the big table could hold eight people. There was even a leaf in the closet to extend the seating to accommodate up to twelve.

"Yes." Mrs. O's reply lacked its usual pleasantness.

Once Mr. O dug into the pork chops, Billy followed. Eating wasn't easy. Not when his mouth wouldn't cooperate. His chewing was stiffer than the starched shirts Daniel dug wearing. The delicious taste of garlic and honey became vinegar and Tabasco sauce.

After forcing down dessert, Billy breathed a sigh when Mr. O poured a cup of coffee. Finally, they'd get this discussion underway.

"We spoke to René this morning." Mr. O was in full general mode. "We spent the day preparing to send him to Toronto."

Why, oh why did they make Billy eat first, because his pork chops were about to barf their way from his shaking stomach. "Uh . . . wh-what?"

Mr. O set down his mug. "I know this is hard for you —"

Billy tossed aside his chair and bolted upstairs to his

bedroom. He slammed the door. The pork chops kept grumbling, but he wasn't about to puke. Still, the shock roared in his ears and blasted down his spine. His breaths came too fast, and he was forced to pace the room because anxiety was threatening to burst through his skin.

A knock came at the door.

"No." He whipped on his heel just as the door opened.

Mrs. O entered. Sorrow filled her gaze. "I'm sorry.".

"Wh-why? Wh-why?" he sputtered. At least he hadn't spat out what banged in his brain. *Get the fuck away from me. I hate you. I hate you all. How could you do this to me? How could you take away the one person who matters to me on this earth?*

"You can say it," she reassured him in a quiet voice. With small steps, she moved across the rug. Her arms came around him, halting Billy from his pacing.

He hugged her, something he hadn't done before. But she was here, offering a comforting shoulder that he laid his head on. He buried his face into her fresh-smelling hair. Tears sprang from his eyes. Fuck it, he didn't care he was ready to bawl like a baby.

He cried.

Billy sat in his desk chair. He hugged himself. The crumpled tissue he'd used to blow his nose and dry his eyes remained in his palm.

Mrs. O sat on the edge of the coffee table. She placed her hand on his bobbing knee. Five minutes ago, she'd gone downstairs to get them some tea to drink.

"I-I n-never cr-cried this way before . . ." Billy gulped. "N-not even when René . . . hurt me and I dumped him. N-not even when he dumped me."

"I'm sorry. So sorry." Her hushed words were fingers stroking his hair. "We don't want René to leave either, but it's for the best."

"H-how?" Dammit, Billy had promised himself he'd

behave as an adult, not a bawling little shit. Talk about em-
barrassing having a major meltdown in front of the
Oshawees.

"We had a long talk with Keith . . ." Mrs. O sighed. "Please
try and understand the predicament Mr. Oshawee and I are
in because of what happened. We don't want to uproot René
from his schooling. That is the last thing we want to do. But
we can't have the two of you living under the same roof anymore. Family Services trusts us to honor our agreement when
we applied to foster you."

"What if — ?"

"René was insistent you live here. I agree. I want you to
keep living here until you're done school. From there, we can
discuss where you'll further your education," Mrs. O continued on, as if unaware she'd cut him off.

"René wants me to live here . . ." Billy said slowly. "This is
his idea, isn't it?" A ball of red-hot hate formed in his chest.

"He suggested it. He suggested it because he told us you
come first before his own feelings." Mrs. O smoothed the
thighs of her pants.

The red-hot ball of hate died. Billy clutched his stomach.

"He also informed us you sincerely enjoy the company of
girls," she added quietly.

Not that bullshit again. Billy threw out his hands. "I told
him already, I don't care about girls. All I care about is him.
Why does he keep insisting I date girls? I thought we were
over this 'cause he stopped bringing it up last . . ." *After he told
me he loved me.* "But I guess we aren't, hey?"

"Billy . . ." She reached out and stopped him before he
stood. "I know how hard your life's been. I know you believe
René is all you have. But there are other people who care
about you. Starting with Mr. Oshawee and me."

He bit down on his tongue to keep his anger in check. This
wasn't Mrs. O's fault. He was at fault. Now he had to own the

destruction his category-five bullshit had caused. If he hadn't kept bothering René for his dick, they wouldn't be in this mess. He was the very reason why they were having this conversation, and why René was leaving.

Billy buried his face in his palms.

"Try and see this from René's perspective. Keith told us the neighborhood he resides in is rich in the . . . well, René will fit. I guess they have parades in the summer. The residents respect gay people. Maybe this is what he needs to come out. I know you don't have a problem with who you are, but René does. He can accept who he is now, however, he still has to embrace everything that Creator made him."

"Creator?" Billy blinked. "Mr. O said something similar downstairs in the study. I never heard you two mention Creator before."

"Just because we don't mention *Kitchi Manitou* doesn't mean we don't believe."

"You don't go to the annual powwow. Chief Oshawee goes, but he's only there for the opening ceremony, then I don't see him again."

"Everyone worships in their own way," she murmured.

"Then why doesn't René believe?"

"Maybe one day he will. Maybe being apart is what you both need? As Mr. Oshawee said, you two help each other, but you also hinder each other." She reached out and set her palm on his cheek. "I heard a different CD coming from your room last week. It was much mellower than what you borrow from René, and I know the music doesn't belong to him."

Heat crawled along Billy's face. He'd been blasting *Congratulations I'm Sorry* by the Gin Blossoms. Carla had loaned him hers, insisting the band wasn't *chick music* and to give the group an honest try. He'd agreed, and after spinning the CD a few times, he'd unearthed that he loved power pop.

"I get it. I do."

She again brushed his face. "I know there are a lot of changes for you. In a way, I wish this didn't have to happen. I really do. The last thing I desire is to take away your best friend." She led them back into a sitting position. "There's also something else I need to speak to you about."

There was more doom about to enter his life? Shit, he could barely process René leaving. "Can it wait?" he begged.

"You know, I think it can. I'll talk to David first thing in the morning."

"Mr. Oshawee?" David Oshawee was Billy's caseworker. "What about him?"

"As I said, it can wait. We can talk when we get back from Toronto. The house is going to be extremely busy. We have to get René packed and ready because we're flying out Sunday morning."

"Sunday . . ." Billy gulped. "So soon?" The lump returned to his throat. "I'm gonna go see René." He stood.

"By all means. Go ahead. Keep in mind you'll be starting at the Video Store on Monday at six."

"I am?" Billy stopped short since he was on his way to the walk-in closet.

"The job will do you good. It'll keep you busy. Vernon has agreed to let you take over René's shifts . . . as long as the hours don't interfere with your schoolwork. You're seventeen now. I believe you can manage your own schedule."

"Yeah . . . I can." Billy opened the closet door and yanked out his parka.

His world had gone from sky blue to rainfall gray.

Chapter Seven: Lost Horizons

The locket was always slightly cool on Billy's chest, but he refused to remove the precious gift, no matter if the cold wind of January cut into any patch of skin that wasn't covered. Every day after he showered, he refastened his birthday present around his neck and tucked the dog tag beneath whatever shirt he'd selected.

Anger and grief had a stranglehold on him. Anger because René had gone and decided without even consulting him. Grief because René had sacrificed his own home, his own bedroom . . . all for Billy.

He pushed on the door to the video store and entered to toasty warmth. The bell overhead tinkled. One customer was looking through the drama section and another stood at the comedy rack.

René stopped stocking the videos he was putting away.

Billy glanced around. This was happening too fast. On Monday, he'd be standing behind the counter, a spot where René should be—where he should always be. A wave of dizziness swamped Billy. He steadied his wobbly gait.

"Hey." René set aside the videos.

The two customers never glanced up but kept staring at the box covers they held.

Doing his best not to storm across the store, Billy forced his feet to walk softly. He removed his gloves and set them on the counter.

"Your parents more than dropped a bomb on me." He held up his chin.

Flecks of pink dotted René's smooth cheekbones. "I'm sorry." He stole a peek at the two customers then focused his sorrow-filled gaze on Billy. "There was no other alternative."

"No other alternative?" Billy sputtered. He did his best to keep his voice down. "You offered to move to Toronto. What about us now?"

"I had no choice. If I didn't, they would've had to tell David, and he would've sent you somewhere else." Pleading surfaced in René's eyes. "Try and understand. I wasn't going to let them send you to the city. Especially not with your mom wanting to play her role now."

"Uh . . . what?" A hammer seemed to appear out of nowhere and bonked Billy on the head. He clutched the counter to keep from keeling over. "Play what role? She-she wants me to move back home?"

"I thought they told you over dinner. They told me they were going to tell you over dinner," René blurted out, as if he was stumbling over his tongue.

"Th-they didn't tell me anything. I . . . I left the table. I went up to my room. Your mom came up. We talked. But she never said anything about . . ." If Billy's life got any worse, he'd be stuck in a permanent nightmare with the Hook hollering *he knew what they did last summer.*

"No." René's reply was quicker than the shaking of his head. "No. David wouldn't allow that. She can only visit you. Nothing more."

"V-visit? She wants to visit?"

René nodded.

"You knew all along and you didn't tell me?" The red-hot anger resurfaced.

"I didn't know how to tell you." René again glanced at the customers. He angled his head slightly down, adding, "It was bad enough we got caught. Danny told me when he was confronting me about . . . us."

One of the customers approached them, holding a movie box.

Billy made his way around the counter to wait until the time came to ring off the till.

Guilt clamped its ugly paws around René's throat while he showed Billy how to complete the z reading. Again, he'd sucker-punched the guy he loved, but what else could he do? There wasn't any other solution.

"I don't want this any more than you do." René rolled the last of the coins. Grief continued to dangle from his heart like the icicles hanging from the eaves trough of the building.

"What're we gonna do? You're leaving on Sunday." With a shaky hand, Billy offered over the rolled dimes. "That's it? We're done?"

René stuffed the coins into the bag he used for the float and till reading. "You don't think this is just as hard for me?" He pulled the strings closed on the bag.

"Then why volunteer to leave?"

"We've been over this already. You know the answer." René began showing Billy the lock-up procedure, which he already knew, having watched René do this a dozen times, but stalling was what cowards did.

Once they had the door properly secured, they got into the truck.

René started the engine. "You'll be driving this until the summer."

"Th-the summer? Y-you mean you're coming back then?"

Wincing, René shifted the stick into reverse. "Only to get my wheels. Keith's getting me a job working at his room-mate's law firm."

"Where're you staying? With Moxy and Ian?" Billy stared out the passenger window. His chin rested on his knuckles.

"No. I'm renting the basement apartment at Keith's room-mate's house." René turned onto City Road.

Billy whipped his head in René's direction. "What the fuck . . ."

"Please, chill. I love you, not Keith. And I can guarantee you, nothing will ever happen between me and him."

"You promise?" A tear seeped from Billy's eye.

"You have my word." René crossed his heart. He glanced from Billy and back at the road. "I told you . . . I . . ." No, he couldn't let the lump beginning to form in his throat force him to cry. He had to be strong for them. "I love you."

"I can't believe they're breaking us up." Billy sniffled. He swiped at his eyes. "I can't believe it. Yeah, I get it. They don't want us fucking in the house. But if we promise them we won't—"

"Try *almost fucking in the house* is why we're having this convo," René reminded him. "We can't un-ring the bell."

"Un-ring the—what?"

"It's an analogy used in law. When a judge asks a jury to ignore inadmissible evidence, it's a questionable request because the jury has already heard it. Even if they try to ignore what they heard, they can't." René pulled up at Uncle Vernon's. He reached inside the console and handed Billy the bag.

While Billy left to give Uncle Vernon the float, René tapped his fingers on the steering wheel. The ache wouldn't subside. Normally, he'd be excited about leaving for school, but walking away from Billy was gruesome fingers reaching into his chest and wrenching out his heart.

Billy had been suspicious about Keith. The same suspicion René couldn't shake scratched again at the back of his head—Billy dating Carla, Billy falling in love with Carla, Billy doing the deed with Carla.

The truck door opened.

René jerked.

Billy slid inside.

"We haven't had a real chance to talk. Let's go for coffee tomorrow night. I don't have to work. Friday's my last evening."

"Yeah, your uncle already told me," Billy said quietly. He was staring out the passenger window again. "Coffee's cool."

Getting to use René's truck for five months should have Billy reaching for the clouds, but what good was a truck when the price he must pay was his heart? He meandered downstairs to the dining room. Lucy had left an hour ago. Whatever she'd made, the delicious scent wafted under his nose.

He inched into the dining room. Mr. and Mrs. O sat at the table. The same tension he'd experienced the other day was present. René was right. They'd rung the bell. From the stiff shoulders of The General and fussing about of Mrs. O, they were the jury who couldn't ignore the evidence they'd heard.

Billy pulled out the chair at his usual spot. René always sat beside him if he was home.

"Where's Renny?" Mr. O's question lacked warmth.

"Downstairs. He's taking apart his drum kit," Mrs. O replied. "I told him already we're getting ready to eat. Give him a moment."

Because René always obeyed his parents, naturally he'd be trucking up the stairs to munch on his roast beef like a good soldier in Oshawee Army. Billy squeezed and un-squeezed his fingers to stop any further negative thoughts from developing. The adult way was to take responsibility.

"I know about my mom." Billy reached for his glass of water.

Mr. and Mrs. O both whipped their gazes on him.

"René told me last night." Billy set down the water.

"I see . . ." Mr. O grasped the platter. "It wasn't Renny's responsibility to tell you."

"It's okay." Billy shrugged.

Footsteps barreled through the kitchen. René appeared. "Sorry. I was working on padding the cases. They're nylon and I don't want anything bumping around in the moving van." He scooted in beside Billy.

"We're going out for coffee after," he added, glancing at his mom and dad.

Doubt was splattered all over Mr. and Mrs. O's exchanged looks.

"Of course." Mr. O plucked two big pieces of meat from the serving tray and passed the dish on to his wife. "Remember what we talked about—"

"Dad, I think we need time to say goodbye," René muttered. "Please, cut us a break. We didn't run off to Winnipeg or anything after you laid down the law. We're accepting and respecting your decision."

Mr. O flushed.

A hint of shock slapped Billy upside the head. He'd never witnessed René throwing shade at his parents before, although impudence hadn't filled his words, but simple reality. Still, this more than proved René was as pissed and upset about the Oshawees' decision. Maybe nothing would happen between Keith and René, then.

With a hand heavier than cement, Billy dumped four teaspoons of sugar and added three containers of cream to his coffee. They were at the Olive Table, a restaurant on Arthur Street The General and Colonel dug dining at for informal gatherings. Gold's Coffee, their normal hangout, was out of the question, or everyone from the high school would want to join them to chat.

René sat across from Billy, also fixing his coffee with the

same cement-hand style, which was weird for a dexterous drummer.

"I'll tell you what I'm scared of if you tell me what you're scared of." Billy lifted his coffee and sipped. The contents in the mug shook.

"What do you mean by scared?" René also raised his mug and sipped.

"I'm scared you'll go and fall for Keith again and forget about me." Beneath the table, Billy's knee bumped on its own.

"You don't gotta worry about that." Reassurance dusted René's words.

"Wh-what about you?" Billy glanced around. At eight o'clock, only a few people were in the restaurant with the cheery lemon painted walls, white chairs with lemon padded seats, and a golden buttercup floor.

"What else." René removed his cigarettes and lit one. He laid his platinum lighter on the packet.

"Well . . ." Billy leaned forward. He set his hand on his bobbing knee.

"I . . . I don't wanna say it 'cause I . . ." Pain surfaced in René's irises. "You deserve to be happy. You deserve to live a great high school life. I want you to enjoy every minute of it. Lookit you, you get as many high-fives in the halls as I do. Before, nobody glanced your way. I know how you hated being referred to as Loser Billy Redsky and how bad you wanted to fit in."

"Say it. Please. I need you to say it." Billy couldn't help the begging in his voice.

René folded his lip over the other. He glanced toward the front of the restaurant and then back to Billy. "The same thing. I don't want you to forget about me."

"How could I?" Billy sputtered. "I'll never forget you. Ever. I'm gonna count the days until you come back to get your truck—"

"Don't. Please. Don't count." More pleading smothered René's intense gaze. "I want you to . . . Y'see, this is why I didn't want to tell you about my fears. I . . ." His pitch lowered. "I love you. I want you to . . . I want you to do everything I wanted to do in school. For me. Please. Can you do this?"

Billy had never heard such passion coming from René before. Or witnessed such passion in his eyes. Not even when they'd gotten close to undressing. If they weren't in a restaurant, ten bucks René would've taken his hand, laid his lips over the back, and pressed his mouth against Billy's skin.

"Why're you asking this of me?" A little tear of a wound seemed to open in Billy's heart.

"Because it means a lot to me. I want you . . ." René tapped the ember of his cigarette against the bottom of the ashtray. "I want you to . . . I just want you to have the life I always wanted to have."

Why was René so insistent about this? He hadn't shut up about Billy living a dumb normal life after they'd first gotten together. He shouldn't be surprised the guy he loved was still rambling on about the same ol' bullshit. Fine, if this shut René up for good, although Billy had no intention of honoring the request, he'd spit out the words. "Sure. I get it. I'll enjoy high school. Do prom. Do parties. Dances. Everything you're asking of me."

René blinked. The cigarette he held fell into the ashtray. "Oh . . . I thought, uh . . . cool. Thanks." There was something unreadable in his expression. He fumbled to grab his fallen smoke. "Prom's cool. You should go to junior prom."

"I will," Billy lied.

Again, René's expression was unreadable. He peeked at Billy's hand on the table. "I . . . I . . . I wished I coulda taken you to prom. But . . . I guess it's something that will never happen, even if Mom and Dad hadn't caught us."

"Yeah, 'cause you're not out."

"Neither are you," René quickly said.

"That's 'cause you won't let me come out to anyone." Billy padded the reminder with a hint of harshness.

"Y'know, I don't get it. I really don't. Why doesn't it bother you? Is it 'cause you can go both ways? It always baffled me how you're so casual about it." René's mouth was close to falling open in astonishment.

"I told you already. If being bi means having you, why should I give a shit? All I ever wanted is you." Billy folded his arms. Why couldn't René feel the same way—not give a hoot and be happy they'd unearthed they shared the same sexual orientation?

"I'm glad you wanted me, 'cause you made me want you, too." René's free hand sneaked across the table. He lightly brushed his fingers against Billy's before withdrawing his hand to clutch the coffee mug.

Shock fluttered in Billy's belly. That was the first time René had ever touched him in public. The guy he loved was begging to free himself from the closet but couldn't yet. Maybe Toronto might help him, as Mr. O had insisted.

In a way, Billy wished he had to work on Saturday night, because The General and Colonel were throwing René a going away party, which was another slap to Billy's face. Now he'd have to force himself to smile and play happy at the house for Daniel, Chunk, Vince, Sheldon, Eddie, the Gerhard twins, Ned and Ellen Atatise, and whoever else had been invited.

They were closing off the till. Billy had taken care of everything from renting out videos to restocking the shelves for the Friday night shift under René's supervision.

Sunday was coming too fast. To make Billy's life more miserable, he had to meet with David Oshawee on Monday about

Mom, who'd gotten out of rehab today.

From what Billy had heard, Hoyt was in the city, crashing at some chick's pad. Whether Mom had given the moron the boot or not, Billy wasn't sure. Considering she was requesting visitation rights, David had probably told her Hoyt couldn't be in the picture.

"I don't get it." Billy shut off the lights. Only the exit light at the back of the store gave off a hint of illumination.

"Get what?" René tossed Billy the float bag.

"Why Mom wants to reconnect. Weird."

"Maybe she's had enough of drinking."

"Yeah right." Scoffing, Billy huffed to the exit to double-check that the back door was properly closed. "I lived with her for fifteen years. She loves booze more than her own liver. Something's up why she went to rehab. Why she's trying to quit drinking? Fuck, she might've even kicked out Hoyt."

"She did?"

"I dunno for sure. He's been crashing at some chick's pad in the city." Billy strode to the front of the store to lock up the main door.

René followed.

A shiver spooked Billy's spine. He didn't have to turn around to know René's gaze was stroking him from top to bottom. His breath was close to Billy's ear, moistening his lobe with steamy heat. He swallowed. René's lips were on the back of his neck, pressing ever so softly on the nape.

Billy dropped the key. A loud clank came from the floor. "What're you doing?"

"Wishing I could change my mind and fuck off with you to Winnipeg," René murmured.

A surge of elation pumped through Billy's veins. "Let's do it. Let's fuck off to the 'Peg. We can find jobs." Hope beat hard against his ribs.

"We can't," René whispered. "You're underage. And I

promised—Dammit."

He spun Billy around. Their chests bumped. René's mouth came down on Billy's and smothered him with a desperate yet sultry kiss full of pathos. Billy clung to him and kissed René back with all the passion he could muster.

Chapter Eight: Wave Bye Bye

The party had sucked. Sure, René had enjoyed saying goodbye to his family and buddies, especially since Chunk wouldn't be joining him in Toronto until the middle or end of February, but he'd spent the evening wearing a pasted-on smile instead of having a blast.

René shut his toiletry case. Everything else had already been packed. The room he'd slept in from the age of four when the house had been built was empty enough to create an echo.

His bookshelf was bare. His desk was bare. His closet was bare. Now he'd taken everything from his bathroom, except for the towels. His stereo, drum kit, and other larger belongings had been shipped off on Friday.

At the end of August, excitement had blazed in Moxy's and Ian's eyes at their going-away party Sheldon had naturally skipped. They'd sincerely been ecstatic about kissing off Thunder Bay to a place where they stood a chance at securing a record deal.

René clenched his fingers and squeezed his eyes shut. Becoming an adult wasn't special. Turning the big one-eight simply reiterated the responsibility he must undertake that his parents, brother, and Keith loved lecturing him about.

His high school years were finished. He'd complete his OAC at the school in Toronto and then—what? Begin his BA.

He wrapped his arms around himself. A smidgen of a lump surfaced in his throat. His eyes pinched.

The bedroom door opened.

Tugging in a big breath, René craned his neck to Billy slowly entering the room.

"I already told your mom and dad I'll drive you guys to the airport, but I'm not going in."

"I know." René swallowed. He couldn't blame Billy. He sure wouldn't stand silent while watching the guy he loved walking away, and not being able to share a goodbye kiss, either. "I'm sorry. I really am."

Billy inched in closer.

René grasped him by the waist. They were face to face. "I love you. I love you. I've said this a million times. If I could figure out a way to stay, I would, but I can't."

Shivering, Billy laid his head on René's shoulder. "I know. I know." He rubbed his face on René's shirt. "Maybe . . . maybe we can still change their minds? Mom's sober. And if Hoyt's crashing at some chick's pad — "

A massive steel ball seemed to fall out of nowhere and land on René. "Absolutely not." He hugged Billy firmer. "No way. I'm not letting you move back to your house. Mom and Dad won't go for it either. David, he'd shit twice and die if you even brought up the suggestion."

"It's our only chance." Billy's voice cracked. He gripped René strong enough around the neck to almost choke him.

"Please . . . please," René begged. "You can't go back there. This is the only way. Can't you understand I'm doing this for you because I love you? Because I love you so damn much, I'm willing to move to keep you safe? Here, everyone cares about you. If you move back to your place, I'd never sleep. I'd always worry about you. And it's too dangerous. Your mom's seeing a biker. Your brother's an affiliate of a biker gang."

Billy kept his head on René's shoulder and nodded. "I can't stand to say goodbye. I can't."

The sobs heaving from Billy were enough to crush René's heart. He moved Billy's head so they were eye level. Tears streamed down Billy's cheeks. René laid his lips over Billy's sobbing mouth and kissed him.

Just in case he weakened and grabbed René's hand, Billy kept his fingers clasped together while riding in the back of the crew cab of Mr. O's truck. Since he was on the right side of the vehicle to the Kaministiquia River, his visual was the train tracks, hydro polls, and bush. The businesses and bike path were to the left on City Road.

The suitcases had been stored in the box that had a covered lining to keep away the snow or rain. Snow, in their case. But the sky was a clear azure to match the chill in the air. The heater was turning the interior into a desert. He should've worn a jacket instead of his parka.

The railroad tracks disappeared behind the mounds of snow and skeleton trees. They were getting closer to the T intersection. Billy rubbed his arms to stop from trembling.

Once they reached the gas bar and video store, instead of going left or straight, Mr. O guided them onto James Street. They were officially heading for the airport.

This drive was too short. Why couldn't the airport be in Port Arthur?

Too quickly, they were on the swing bridge, crossing the river separating the reserve from the city.

Billy had never chewed on his nails before, but biting down on something kept his throat in check or he'd make a fool of himself and start bawling.

They were now passing beneath the tunnel of the railroad tracks. Normally, they went straight up to Arthur Street when going to the city, but Mr. O steered them onto Gore Street, which led them to the most hated place in Billy's life right now.

There were houses to look at and the occasional business.

He snuck a peek at René, who also glumly stared out the window with his arms folded.

Soon, the houses on René's side of the street vanished. In their place was more railroad tracks.

They were on Neebing Avenue now. It didn't take long to reach another railroad crossing. If only there was a big-ass long train. In seconds, they were merging onto the highway. Billy couldn't stop trembling.

When the sign appeared, stating Thunder Bay Airport was just up ahead, he stiffened and sat straighter.

The truck made a left from the highway. A plane lifted off from behind the two-story airport and climbed high in the sky. Mr. O drove them down Princess Street. They went under the direction sign, indicating they'd reached the airport. He never steered them to the parking area but kept following the road until they came to the terminal.

From the reserve and to the airport, they'd taken all of ten minutes.

Mr. and Mrs. O vacated the vehicle. A hint of wind swept inside, but the heat on Billy's skin kept him from shivering. A buzzing sounded, followed by a *ding ding.*

Already, he knew the drill—take the truck home, park the vehicle in the garage, and leave the keys in the master bedroom on the chest of drawers.

René continued to stare straight ahead.

With his tongue too big for his mouth, Billy stumbled through "I'll... well, I'll... I guess we'll talk sometime soon..." Fuck, what was he supposed to say? "I mean, I guess this is..." *This can't be goodbye.* "Take it easy—"

René reached across the seat. Billy jumped slightly. Gooseflesh poked up on his skin. René's palms melted on Billy's cheeks, and his mouth was claimed by the silkiest lips he'd ever caressed. A surge of shock blasted through Billy's veins. The kiss was gentle, barely a whisper but enough to capture him in a moment of time that stood still.

The silky mouth that he gently explored vanished, leaving him puckering the air. He cracked his lids open to René's tormented gaze. Billy was engulfed in an embrace constricting enough to break his ribs. René's cheek feathered Billy's. Cozy. A true fire on a cold night. He was about ready to melt all over René's chest.

"I love you." Moist steam peppered René's crackling whisper. "You take care of yourself. Okay? If you need me, call. Promise?"

"I . . . I . . . I will." Billy kept his cheek on René's. His thundering heart galloped madly to catch up to his shaky breaths.

"Remember what we talked about? You're gonna own the school and make the best of this, right?" They still remained locked in their embrace.

Billy's stiff neck could use a good oiling because he couldn't get his head to nod.

"Renny!" The General's deep baritone pretty much smacked the truck's interior.

"I gotta go." René untangled his arms from Billy's death grip. His deep stare cut through the chill on Billy's skin and wrapped him with warm comfort. "I'll be waving when we take off. Okay?" He slid from the truck.

Even though the back door gently closed, René's familiar crisp, clean scent lingered in the cab. Billy scrambled to his side of the vehicle and pressed his face to the window.

René was helping Mr. Oshawee with the mounds of luggage. Mrs. O came out of the airport, pushing a baggage cart. René loaded the first suitcase onto the contraption. Once the last piece of luggage was plopped on the cart, he wheeled off for the entrance doors, never looking back.

Shaking, Billy wormed his way from the back seat and into the front. Under any other circumstance, he'd be excited about driving Mr. O's boss vehicle. Not today.

He wriggled his fingers into his shirt and withdrew the locket. People passed in front of the windshield. Some were laughing, others talking. He snapped open the dog tag to a picture of friendship and love, their eyes full of delight, big smiles, cheeks brushing, and René's slightly broad chin on Billy's shoulder.

The lump in Billy's throat was a boulder threatening to careen down a steep hill. Somehow, René had predicted their future by giving Billy the most precious gift possible that summed up what they'd shared for over a year and a half. Maybe René had known the time they'd borrowed was coming to an end.

From the airport and back to the reserve, Billy couldn't stop the tears sliding from his eyes. He kept glancing at the clock. The Oshawees' flight left in an hour. Once he pulled into the garage and parked the truck, he made his way toward the house. His knees were about to give out as he ascended the deck stairs and headed into the mudroom. He wobbled his way upstairs and left the keys on the chest of drawers in the royal chamber.

His feet wouldn't stop moving. Anxiety's snarling claws were ready to cut through his skin. He had to get outside and do something. Anything. He bolted down the stairs, snatched a drink from the mini fridge in the butler pantry, and ran for the deck.

So far, he'd killed a half an hour. In another half hour, René would be flying away until June.

Even though January's cold chill nipped at Billy's exposed skin, he remained outside for the thirty minutes in the minus twenty-five temperature. His teeth rattled. He hugged himself to keep warm.

The plane appeared. The roar of the engine filled the air. All he could see was the tail, because René was flying east over Lake Superior. Through tear-filled eyes, Billy gazed up at the bright sky. He lifted his hand and waved.

You said you'd be waving. Wave back. Wave back.

He never stopping staring at the plane until the sleek white vessel disappeared from his line of vision.

René was gone.

Billy bowed his head.

At the video store, Billy sat behind the counter. While customers browsed through the movie selections, he cracked open his books. He swilled back a taste of root beer to ease the ache in his throat from crying most of the afternoon.

Thank fuck a worker had called in sick and Vernon had phoned Billy to fill in. Here, he could try his best to keep his mind busy.

A few friends from school had stopped by to congratulate him on his new job and getting to use René's boss wheels while he was in Toronto. Even people from the reserve who'd rented a movie had congratulated him on his new position.

Big deal. Vernon's Videos now sucked without René's presence in the store. God, trying to swallow the perennial lump clogging his neck was growing more difficult. If Billy didn't get his shit together, he'd break down and cry in front of everyone.

The bell overhead tinkled.

He glanced up to Carla entering. Only a hoodie protected her from the weather. She spanked her mittens together and removed them but held on to her car key, since she'd probably driven her mom's wheels over.

"Hi." She sashayed up to the counter, where she placed her hands. Concern filled her oval-shaped eyes that flattered her round face and plush, wild berry painted lips. Her long, black hair was braided into one tail. "I wanted to see how you're doing."

"I'm cool," Billy lied.

"C'mon. It's me." She reached over the counter and poked

him in the chest. "We're friends. Friends share stuff. I know how close you two are. I expect you're bummed about him leaving. He was the older brother you always wanted."

Older brother? Billy stiffened and forced a smile. "Thanks."

"Don't thank me. We're friends. Friends don't have to thank each other." Her stare hardened. "Now, are you gonna tell me how you're really doing?"

As if Billy could bawl on her shoulder like a little kid. Guys didn't do that kind of stuff over a buddy. For sure Chunk, Sheldon, and the other homies from the former rocker clique weren't crying in their bowl of potato chips over René leaving. Sure, Sheldon had probably broken down after Moxy had dumped him and left, but he was allowed to because he'd lost his girlfriend whom he'd dated for a good four years.

Wait a second. Moxy had always carried a torch for René. What if they wound up together? Probably not. René was gay, and he'd promised not to go anywhere near Keith Harlow.

"You're thinking and not talking." Carla poked him again.

Funny, Billy used to say the same thing to René.

Just then a customer strode up to them.

"I'll let you work." Carla slid on her mittens. "But you can't hide how you're feeling from me. Got it? You can pick me up for school."

Pick her up? He didn't want anyone near him while he lugged around his heavy heart that weighed sixteen tons. "Sure."

"Later." She swiveled and left.

Billy readied the customer's video. Maybe he should talk to Carla. Out of the chicks who hung around him, she was his best girl friend.

Billy guided the truck into the driveway after leaving the float and bank receipts at Vernon's place. René's scent still lingered in the interior. Fresh. Crisp. Clean. Daniel was already here to spend the night. His vehicle was parked in front of Mr. O's stall.

Fuck, so much for finally having a minute to give in to the loneliness that had clung to Billy's heart all evening. As he hauled himself into the house, the ghost of pain followed him, refusing to be blown away by the harsh wind.

"That you?" Daniel called out.

"Yeah." Billy hung his parka. "I'm tired. I'm gonna turn in."

"Understandable. Have a good sleep. Don't forget that you gotta meet with David after school before you go to work."

"I won't forget." Groaning, Billy placed his boots in their proper spot and meandered into the kitchen.

Having to see David Oshawee about Mom was another strike against this week. Billy dragged himself upstairs to his bedroom. Sure, he should attempt optimism by telling himself René, who refused to leave the closet, had boldly kissed and embraced him in the back of Mr. O's truck while The General had been watching, but the goodbye had only reaffirmed they were kaput.

He glanced around his room. Finally, he gave in to the tears hiding behind his eyes and the lump lurking in his throat. He sank to the carpet. The ghost of heartache claimed him in its clutches. There was no way he could go on without René. Not a chance. He put his face in his palms and wept.

Nobody understood. Nobody cared. All they gave a fuck about was telling him what was good for him—and they'd taken away the only good thing about his life.

How the hell was he supposed to sleep tonight, knowing René wasn't across the hall?

Billy snapped his head up. That was what he'd do—he'd move into René's room. At least in his bedroom, Billy could absorb the remaining energy left behind. Ned had said a person's energy always lingered for a few days.

He stood and marched for the walk-in closet. For over forty-five minutes he worked like a madman, storing his toiletries in René's bathroom, stuffing his socks and underwear into the drawers of René's walk-in closet. Hanging his clothes on the hangers René had used. Placing his books in René's empty bookshelves. Where René had set his laptop on the desk, Billy set his sketchpad and charcoal pencils.

A glow seemed to fill him.

Yawning, he hauled himself to the king-size bed and tucked himself beneath René's covers. The smell of the guy he loved loitered under his nose. He clutched the pillow René had used and laid his head on the other two, where a couple of strands of hairs from René's thick mane lingered.

CHAPTER NINE: NEW MISERABLE EXPE-RIENCE

Billy drove down Missionary Road to Carla's crib. He wasn't feeling on the brink of heartache after getting to wake in René's bed, reach for his clothes in René's closet, and shower in René's bathroom. In a weird way, this experience was similar to René taking an extended trip. He could pretend René had never gone far away. But the locket beneath Billy's shirt kept reminding him René had left and was starting his first day of classes today.

Carla's parents owned a bi-level. Her dad was the economic development officer, and her mom managed the bingo hall. She also had two younger sisters, one in grade eight and the other in grade six.

He pulled into the driveway. The front door opened. Krystal, the one in grade eight, appeared. She was the striking image of Carla in elementary school.

Krystal dashed up to the truck, hugging her books. Her puffs of breath floated on the air.

Billy lowered his window.

"Oh my gosh, are you giving Carla a ride?" She giggled.

He almost smirked. Had he looked the same way in grade eight whenever he saw René about the reserve, a lovesick fool dying for attention? "Yeah. She asked me to get her last night."

"Renny's wheels are super-bitchin'. I bet he's having a boss time in Toronto, hey?"

Any cheer Billy had managed to find to inflate his broken bones died right then. "Yeah. He's probably having a blast . . ." *Without me.*

"I betcha he'll be as popular there as he was here." Krystal kept giggling. The dark-purple toque stopped the wind from blowing her glossy black hair about.

"He probably will. Wherever René goes, people dig him." What wasn't to like about René? Or love about him? Billy wrapped his fingers tight around the steering wheel.

"It's cold." Krystal stomped her feet, shivering.

Someone was hinting for a ride, even though the school was only two roads over. "Get in." Billy motioned at the interior. "Let me flip the console up."

"Oh my god. You're, like, totally awesome. Thank you!" Giggling even more, Krystal darted around the truck.

The front door opened. Carla appeared. She frowned and stomped over to the vehicle. "What're you doing?"

Krystal had the door ajar. "Billy's giving me a ride 'cause it's cold out."

"Uh-uh. You conned him into giving you a ride. Get inside. You're supposed to wait for Tonya." Carla pointed at the house. "I had to walk to school every day. You can, too."

"You're such a bitch." Krystal wrinkled her pretty nose.

Billy slapped his hand over his mouth before he laughed.

"Call me a bitch again, I'll shove your face into the snowbank. Get inside and wait for Tonya." Carla hip-bumped Krystal away, then hopped in and closed the door to her sister's sneering face. "Let's go. She can walk."

"Oookay." Billy wasn't about to get between the sisters. This was their fight. He guided them out of the driveway while Krystal continued to glare. Then she whipped on her heel and stormed up the stairs. "It is pretty cold."

"Big deal. I had to walk in the cold." Carla sniffed. She shook back her black locks. Pink muffs covered her ears. "I hate the wind. It always ruins my hair."

"You'd better get used to it. Winter Maker loves blowing his breath on us during January." Missionary Road led straight to City Road.

"Yeah, I remember Mr. Atatise telling us that in Ojibway Culture class in grade eight." Carla turned her head. "How're you doing today?"

A pool of loneliness expanded in Billy's heart. Maybe he should tell her the truth? No, he couldn't. René was in the closet. To exclaim he was consumed by a pit of grief would out the guy he loved.

The scent of her perfume was deep in the interior, expunging René's crisp, clean fragrance that was a big part of him — a beautiful bouquet that had caught Billy's nose from the first time he'd sat in this truck. He had to stop the urge from telling Carla to quit changing the smell. He had no right saying such shit to her, not after their friendship had survived the mutual attraction between them he'd kiboshed.

"How's Xander?" he asked.

Having tried out for the cheerleading team at the beginning of the school year and then joining the squad, Carla had gone out with the captain of the hockey team a few times. At the games, in between periods, she'd skate around on the ice in her tiny skirt with the other cheerleaders.

"I dunno." She shoved a stick of gum into her mouth. "I haven't seen him since Saturday."

"Yeah? Go out somewhere?"

"The movies."

Normally, juniors and seniors caught a flick on Sunday, but if they were on a date, they went the night before and sat in the balcony, because the freshmen and sophomores had laid claim to Saturday evening at the theater. Shit, Billy would never experience the balcony now.

"More than dating?" He guided them down City Road.

Carla guffawed. "No. We're friends. Like you and me are."

Billy nodded. From what he'd overheard in the locker room, guys wanted to be more than Carla's friend, especially Xander. "True."

"What're you doing this weekend?"

"Working." Billy motioned at the video store since they were at the T. He steered them onto James Street.

"Do you have Renny's shifts?"

"Yeah. All of them. Monday, Wednesday, and Friday from six to ten. Saturdays and Sundays from two till ten."

"How about we get something to eat after you're done work on Friday? It'll do you good to go out and not mope." There wasn't a hint of flirtation in her suggestion, only worry.

Maybe he should go out and nab some food. She was an ear he desperately needed right now, especially since he had to meet about Mom after school.

Mom was setting up the basement apartment today, so last night René had stayed in the guest room upstairs at Keith's and Brooks' place. Roommates? Highly doubtful. They'd retired to the same bedroom around eleven, after sitting in the living area and informing him about the neighborhood.

As Dad had previously mentioned, the school wasn't far from the one-way street where René now lived that was full of Victorian houses, brand-new condos, and brick apartment buildings. Some homes even had driveways, which was rather strange for downtown cribs. On his trek, he'd met joggers and dog walkers.

He could've taken Church and then veered off on Wellesley, but he'd wanted to check out the hood, so he'd gone straight down Gloucester and then hit Jarvis. The walk hadn't taken long. Only ten minutes to reach the school.

The three-story brick building was in front of him. All he

had to do was ascend the endless pile of cement stairs that led to the main entrance.

Dad had been right about not bringing the truck. From the looks of things, there wasn't a school parking lot. Even when René retrieved his wheels this summer, he'd walk everywhere.

Because he loathed backpacks, he'd gotten a leather briefcase off of Dad. To make carrying his books easier, he'd attached a shoulder strap diagonally across his chest. Since he was early, he'd locate the office first to complete his registration.

During the walk to school, Billy had clouded his thoughts. Where he was going. What he was doing. At least they shared the same time zone.

René pulled on the handle and entered. The building was old, but the interior had undergone some updates. Well, he was only here for five months. Making friends wasn't required. He already had some here. Plus, he'd promised to visit Ian, Jennifer, and Moxy once Mom and Dad flew back to Thunder Bay.

He strode down the hall. Whispers came from behind him and stares in front of him. Girls smiled.

"Oh my God, he's fucking hot," a female said.

No big surprise he'd have to put on the same false façade from back home. He stopped. Wait. Nobody knew him here. Last night, Keith and Brooks had talked about the importance of starting over in a place that welcomed people of the rainbow flag, as Brooks had eloquently summarized Church and Wellesley.

Keith was out here. Brooks was out.

René fisted and unfisted his hand. Could he leave the closet? What if word traveled back home? Hang on, nobody knew about Keith in Thunder Bay, but he hadn't come out in Toronto until his second year living here. That was a long time to be gone. If Danny didn't even know the truth about Keith, nobody from their former group of friends would, either.

René glanced around. Which way was the office?

"You look a little bit lost." A guy with long black dreadlocks came to a halt. His thick, rose-colored lips spread into a broad grin. "Need the four-eleven on something?"

"Yeah." René pasted on his famous flashy smile. "Where's the office? I'm finishing my last semester of OAC. I need to complete my registration."

"Figured you were new." The dude held out his hand. "Trent Johnson. Call me Fab, though. Everyone else does."

"Good meeting you." René shook. "René Oshawee, but—" He bit down on the inside of his cheek to stop the brazen sassy comeback of *call me Renny 'cause everyone else does.* This was his chance at a new life, a new beginning, even if he was carrying six loads of miserable inside his chest for Billy.

"But what?" Trent's grin was bigger than Chunk's, and he seemed to possess the same gregarious personality of René's main man. Whereas Chunk was packing a good eighty extra pounds, Trent was gym-trim with a nice set of muscles filling out his smooth, almost-black skin.

"Nothing. How's about the office?" René motioned at the hallway.

"Right this way, my man. Right-o this way." Trent patted René's back. "You're starting a week late. The new semester began last week."

"Yeah. I'm applying to the U of T in the spring. Since I'm going to be here in the fall if I'm accepted, I thought I'd get an early start on the city. My parents finally gave me the okay." As René walked, a few girls cast him admiring glances.

"Oh? They here, too?" Trent steered them to door with the lettering *office* written on the glass.

"Yeah. We flew in last night."

"Flew in?" Trent opened the door. "You're not Mohawk?"

"Mohawk? No. Ojibway." René entered the reception area.

"Ah, I get it now. I thought you were from around here. We got a lot of reserves down this way."

"Lots up north, too. I'm from Thunder Mountain."

"Where's that about?"

"Northwestern Ontario. A stone's throw from Thunder Bay."

Trent let out a low whistle. "Thunder Bay? You are far from your hood, homeboy."

"Yeah, sure am." René set his hand on the counter.

The secretary rose from behind her desk. "Can I help you?"

"I'll let you finish getting registered. We'll probably be in the same classes. I stayed for the extra year, too." Trent stuffed his large hands into the pockets of his cargo pants sitting low on his hips. "How's about lunch? You don't wanna be eating alone."

"Lunch sounds cool." The miserable clouds seeming to hang over René's head parted a smidgen to let in some sunlight.

"I'll introduce you to my buds. Later." Trent made a clicking sound and fired his index finger with his thump up at René.

René fired back the same shot. Maybe he could poke his head from the closet. Still, if he did, and word got back to T. Bay, he'd have to permanently stay here like Keith. Staying here meant releasing the last bit of hope from his fingers that held tight to somehow being with Billy again.

"Your mother has completed her rehabilitation program." David Oshawee sat behind the desk in his office. The blinds were open. Sunlight streamed inside the window behind him.

Billy rubbed his thumb along the strap of his backpack he'd

set on the floor before having a seat in front of the desk. When school had let out fifteen minutes ago, he'd bolted straight for the Family Services building on the rez after the ringing of the bell. He had to keep his mind on the meeting, and not let his thoughts wander to how René's first day of school had gone in Toronto.

If only they could call. Impossible. For sure the Oshawees would spot the long-distance charges on the telephone bill. If only they could instant message. Impossible. Billy didn't have a computer. There was email he could access on his computer in the lab at school, though.

"Are you comfortable meeting her?" Mr. Oshawee continued on in his same monotone voice that was as interesting as oil paint drying.

"It doesn't really matter." Billy's world had already gone up in flames. Reconnecting with Mom was the last meteor crashing into a fiery earth dead of human life.

"I informed her of your school and work schedule. She asked if I could set up a supervised visit on Thursday at three-thirty." Mr. Oshawee twirled his pen.

The pulse point in Billy's throat fluttered. Of course Mr. Oshawee shared the same trait as René. They were cousins. Physically, though, the family services worker was a true Oshawee. Dark skin. Bold features. Stocky build. "Uh . . . sure. Sounds cool."

"How do you feel about this? You haven't talked to her since you've been in care."

What was there to feel? Billy had written off Mom before he'd been tossed into the foster system.

"Are you comfortable meeting her by yourself in the visitation room?"

Billy shrugged. She'd say what she had to say and then he'd split. "It's cool."

"Okay." Mr. Oshawee wrote in the file. "But if you need

anyone, we're here for you."

Yeah, they all said that, even Mr. and Mrs. O. So much for being there for him. If they truly were, they wouldn't have tossed René on a plane and taken him one thousand and four hundred clicks from Billy.

"Everything's ready." Mom sat her hands on her hips. "Linen. Furniture. The delivery men also dropped off your belongings. Tomorrow, I'll start on the groceries, dishes, and small appliances."

René removed the strap from across his chest and set his briefcase on the floor. The small living room had a couch and chair. His TV and VCR from home were on a new entertainment stand, along with his stereo.

"Your drums are in the spare bedroom. I wasn't sure where you'd want them, so I told the delivery men to leave them in there," she added while folding a dish towel at the small eat-in kitchen where two chairs and a table were set up.

"There are two parking spots at the back of the house. Brooks uses one. He said you can use the other. The lease expired on yours. I guess the last renter didn't have a car and walked everywhere, so Brooks made a nice tidy sum on renting out parking. Make sure and thank him for his generosity."

"I will." Thank fuck, he didn't have to fight out on the street for a spot, as he'd feared. The vehicles he saw were bumper to bumper. He couldn't get over how tight parking was, unlike Thunder Bay where a person could pull their vehicle in anywhere, even if they had to pay.

"You won't have to worry about plugging in your truck. The temperature only gets as low as zero, maybe minus four at the very coldest. Your father did bring a cord. Brooks said there's an outlet."

René stifled his snicker because Mom and Dad were totally

old school and went by the imperial system instead of metric. "You mean minus twenty *Celsius*. That's pretty warm, considering it's the average for us."

"The average here, *in your* Celsius . . ." Her smile was mocking. " . . . is between zero and minus seven. Remember, if the city gets a snowfall like we do, it almost shuts down. They're not used to driving in our conditions."

"Almost shuts down?" René blinked.

"A lot of people don't own four-wheel drive. Small cars are easier to navigate and park. Where do Ian and Moxy live?"

"They're over in Mimico. They said it's cheaper there. They even have a driveway. I have the four-eleven in my book. I told him I'd call this weekend once I get settled." René removed his jacket, set it on the hook at the door, and sat at the kitchen table. "Did Billy meet with David yet?"

Mom frowned.

"What? I'm only asking." An inch of defensiveness wormed up René's backside.

"He'll be fine. Your father doesn't want you to concern yourself—"

"It's only natural for me. I—You know how I feel about him." René reached for the salt and pepper shakers.

"Yes, I do." Mom set the dish towel on the counter. She pulled out the other chair. "I wish you'd understand this wasn't easy for us."

Great, now he'd get to experience guilt. All his parents did was make him feel guilt if he disagreed with their decision, because they insisted their judgment was for his benefit whenever he received a lecture.

"Billy still has so much growing up to do. And you need to . . ." She wet her lips. "You need to find your own identity. Keith assured us you will here."

"Can we at least call each other?" Hope filled his words.

Mom sadly shook her head. "Let him be. Please. You know

92

we'll take good care of him."

"I know. I trust you." He stood. "I may as well start unpacking. I kept everything in my suitcases since there wasn't any point in taking anything out in the spare room upstairs."

"Did you make any friends?" Mom's question carried into the bedroom.

René's new sleeping quarters were a far cry from his previous one. The tiny box barely fit a double bed, nightstand, and dresser. His luggage was parked in front of the closet that wasn't even a walk-in. "Yeah. A few. This one dude Trent is pretty cool. He's in most of my classes. At least I'll have a study partner."

"That's good." Mom stood in the doorway.

"Yeah. We rapped quite a bit over lunch."

"It sounds like the two of you have quite a bit in common."

Maybe they did. René could admit he'd enjoyed Trent's company today.

Chapter Ten: Mixed Reality

Billy pulled up at the family services building on Loon Drive. The clock on the truck stereo read three-thirty. Mom had always been a late sort of person because of her drinking. Maybe she wasn't even here yet, or maybe she'd uncorked the bottle and was passed out somewhere.

He got out and lowered his head to avoid the icy strong wind and darted into the building. Once he told the receptionist why he was present, she pointed down the hall, informing him the visitation room was the second door on the right.

"Your mother's already here." The receptionist lit a cigarette.

Great. So much for getting to blow off the old lush. While he inched down the hallway, noise came from the other offices. Someone on the phone. Another demanding she wanted her *fucking kids back or else*. He snorted. The woman was probably a total drunk like Mom and deserved to have her children placed somewhere other than her party crib.

Heart colder than the wind outside, Billy pushed on the closed door and stomped into the visitation room done up with a small table and tiny chairs, a box of toys, adult chairs, and an adult table. There was even a couch, coffee table, and armchair.

Mom sat on the accompanying ottoman to the armchair. He'd seen her drunk around the rez a couple of times over the last year and a half. Her yellowish skin, dark circles beneath her eyes, and hair twisted in a ponytail confirmed sobriety wasn't agreeing with her, either. She was still the same miserable bitch. An oversized hoodie dropped past her skinny thighs that barely filled out her sweatpants.

Her trembling, bony hand held a cigarette. Her other bony hand clutched a shaking cup of coffee. "Billy . . ." A washboard road was smoother than her grittier-than-dirt voice.

He never bothered shucking his coat and sat on the edge of one of the plastic chairs.

Mom stood. There was a bump under her hoodie that didn't match her skeletal frame. Oh great, did her boyfriend, Caveman, knock her up? That was just what the Sons of Satan needed — an innocent baby to groom into a monster.

"You and your boyfriend expecting one?" he muttered, pointing at her stomach. "Weird. Since you were an epic fail with me and Hoyt."

Red flooded Mom's gaunt face, giving a smidgen of life to her walking corpse. "I'm not with Caveman anymore. He left me after I stopped drinking."

If that was supposed to generate sympathy from him, she was wrong. "Beer gut then?"

"Cirrhosis."

"Huh?"

"Cirrhosis of the liver. Doc said if I don't quit, I'll die."

He folded his arms. "I see. This quitting drinking thing is only about saving your ass. Not what a shitty excuse of a mom you are. Whatever."

"It's more than that." She shuffled across the space between them.

"I recommend you park your butt back on the ottoman. Don't you come any closer to me." He thrust his finger at her.

She stopped and sat on the couch.

"You're dying?" His voice was flatter than a pancake.

Mom puffed on the cigarette. "It's a disease of the liver. Scarring is irreversible, the doctor said. Coughing up lots of blood." She took a drag. "He said if I don't drink . . . there's a chance . . . maybe."

She was turning thirty-nine at the end of October but looked like she'd be celebrating eighty instead.

"Is there any kind of treatment?"

"They want to slow the scar tissue on my liver. They have me on meds for fluid build-up, toxins in the blood . . . that sort of stuff. The doctor said most important is attending recovery meetings." Mom puffed again. She glanced away. "We talked about a transplant. I'm not a good candidate. But we'll see . . ."

"They think if you get a transplant, you'll just go out drinking again."

Mom's lower lip trembled. She nodded. "I'm not high on the priority list."

"So you're dying? Is that what you're trying to tell me?" After not seeing her for over a year and a half, he should feel something, but everything was robotic—his voice, his movements, even his emotions, as if they stood on a stage and he was reciting lines.

"The doctor said some can live long lives. Some don't. All we can do is keep treating it."

" . . . and staying away from booze," Billy wryly added.

"Yes. No booze."

"Are you gonna boot Hoyt out then? His partying at the house is—"

"He's my son. I can't throw him out."

"He's turning twenty-two at the end of February. He's old enough to live on his own." This time a hint of emotion flickered in Billy's chest.

"He's all I have left after you . . ." She stubbed out the cigarette and reached for another. "Do you think I wanted them to take you away from me? Huh?" With shaky hands, she struggled to light the smoke she held.

"Yeah, you fought really hard for me, you stupid drunk." This was bullshit. He rose.

"Billy . . . please." Begging filled her words.

He refolded his arms. "Fine. I'm waiting." He tapped his foot. "I got a job to go to, unlike you. I don't go down to the band office on welfare day and demand my free ride." Not that he had to work, since his shift wasn't until tomorrow. But he'd say anything to get out of here.

"Do you think it was easy for me?" Mom gasped. She had finally lit the cigarette. "Your father left when you were only two."

"And you *left* when I was only four," he fired right back.

"Left?" She sputtered.

"Yeah. Left. Walked out the door to go get drunk and laid. You don't think I remember? I do. I . . ." He clenched his teeth. The heat on his skin intensified. "I cried for you to come back, but you didn't care. You kept leaving up until I packed my shit and moved in with the Atitises."

The resentment he'd stomped down somewhere deep inside him was rearing up his throat and firing from his mouth. The hate for this woman he'd also buried was rising like a monster from Lake Superior. And René wasn't here to take away the pain, because the fucking Oshawees had stolen from Billy the one person who always massaged away the hurt.

"Fuck this shit." He whipped on his heel and stormed from the room.

Mom's cries for him to come back followed Billy down the hall and out the main door.

When he stepped outside, his eyes burned from the toxic resentment still gnawing at him.

Daniel got out of his vehicle. He strolled over. "Hey," he called out.

Billy let out a big breath and meandered down the stairs. He was a popped balloon. Deflated and defeated. At least someone was here.

"I thought we'd grab a bite to eat at the Waffle Wigwam. My treat. I already told Lucy we wouldn't need dinner for tonight." Although concern lurked in Daniel's suggestion, his tone didn't match the gentle reassurance René had used to stroke Billy into submission.

"Sure." The wind whipped about him.

Daniel patted him on the back. "C'mon. Let's go."

"Did your parents tell you to check on me?" Billy trudged to his truck.

"Yeah, they did. But they didn't have to ask, because I would've anyway." Daniel got in his vehicle.

After leaving the Waffle Wigwam, Billy drove his truck straight to his former foster father's crib. Ned Atatise might not be René, but the comfort the man offered might help some.

Throughout supper, while Daniel had blabbed, Billy had been unable to shake the gloom and doom. He didn't know what his heart ached over more—not having René present, or not having René present to wrap his arms around Billy after his disastrous meeting with Mom.

The Atitises bunked in the older part of the reserve. Billy turned into the driveway of their eggshell-blue house with the white trim. Ned's old pickup was parked. Ellen's car wasn't around. Maybe she was in the city.

Billy got out into the icy chill and headed straight up the steps. Before he knocked, the back door opened.

"Hey, c'mon in." Ned's dark-chocolate eyes brightened. He offered his calming smile and motioned at the living area beyond the utility room. "I've been expecting ya."

"Really?" Billy shrugged off his parka and hung the heavy coat on one of the hooks. He removed his snow boots.

"Yep. Sure did. Renny left on Sunday. I got a pot of tea

going." Ned wandered into the small eat-in kitchen.

Billy followed. "You emerg fostering anyone?"

"Nope. And that's a good thing. Every day without a child in care makes me happier than the July sun." Ned stood at the counter. He fixed a mug of tea.

Billy pulled out a chair at the table. "So you knew I'd be bummed about René."

"You two were very close." Ned set down the mugs. He also pulled out a chair.

The way Ned had said *close* hinted at something more than buddies. "Uh . . ." Nobody was supposed to know about René except for the Oshawees, Keith, and Chunk. "Is something obvious to you?"

"You're forgetting I have more life experience." Ned's light chuckle was as smooth as René's. "But my sister also took me into her confidence." For once, emotion flecked his easygoing tone.

"You know then, don't you?" Billy squirmed.

Ned sipped his tea and peeked over the rim of his mug he had tilted at his mouth.

"Uh . . ."

"She said I'd be hearing from you." Ned set down the mug.

Billy couldn't help the scowl forming at the corners of his lips. "She wasn't supposed to —"

" . . . tell anyone?" Ned rubbed his chin. "You were gonna tell me, weren't you?"

A flicker of warmth dusted Billy's cheeks. "How'd you know?"

"Because you always come to me when something's troubling ya. I'll admit, I was piecing you and Renny together before she told me the truth. I had no proof, and it was Renny's place to tell his parents, not mine."

"You knew I was talking about René all along?" The heart to hearts Billy had shared with this man seemed to almost swallow him whole.

"I had a good hunch. If you hadn't spoken to me about being two-spirit, I wouldn't have guessed how close you two really were, but after you came clean, I figured the boy who was causing you so much heartache was Renny."

"Then you know the Oshawees busted us. Well, Daniel busted us. He told Mr. and Mrs. O." Billy toyed with the handle of his mug. "As for Mom, nothing new to say. Same ol' bullshit."

"Let's take care of one thing at a time, hmm?" Ned's suggestion was light.

"It's not fair." Billy glanced up. "I finally had what I wanted. Now it's gone. I got nothing."

"I wouldn't fully agree. You got a family who cares about you. Right?"

"I guess so."

"You're not living under your mother's roof. If your mother had caught you and René, what would she have done?"

"Nothing." Billy shrugged.

"Doesn't that tell you something? My sister and brother-in-law care enough about you to do something, because whether you agree or not, you two can't be seeing each other while you're living under the same roof when you're in care and underage. As I mentioned when we last talked, two years is a big gap. Renny's done high school. You're in your second semester of grade eleven."

"René said the same thing." Billy slumped in the chair.

"Of course Renny agrees. He's classed as an adult," Ned pointed out. "The thing is, nobody's doing this to hurt you. They're doing it for—"

" . . . my own good." Billy slumped even lower.

"The spirits are sleeping, but I think come the spring ya should seek your path," Ned gently said.

"Huh?" Billy dragged his wayward stare from his mug back to Ned.

"A vision quest. It can't be done right now. Winter is when the spirits sleep. But in the spring, we'll go in the bush together." Ned cupped his mug. "It'll do you some good to find your path."

"Find my path?" Billy sat up. "Vision quest?" He thought only old Indians from long ago went on those. "Really?"

"Are you still smudging in the mornings?"

Billy ducked his head. "Uh . . ."

"There's a reason you have to connect with Creator every morning. When you talk to Him, you are heard. He wants to hear from you."

"He doesn't answer my prayers anyway." Billy stifled his snort.

"He's not there to grant your wishes like a genie in the cartoons. He's there to offer you strength to meet what's in store for ya today. Think about if everything went your way. You wouldn't grow spiritually, would ya?"

That was true. "Yeah."

"A vision quest is there to offer direction. That's why in the old days when a boy reached puberty, he was sent out alone to seek his vision."

"Okay. We can try the vision quest." Billy traced the jagged scratch on the table.

"Ya don't try. It's something ya simply do."

Fine. Billy folded his arms.

"We're going to visit Ellen's family this summer. Ya wanna come along? It'll do you good to get away and watch the sun dance ceremony."

"What about my job?" Maybe leaving behind a René-less Thunder Bay was what the doctor had ordered.

"I'm sure something can be arranged. We take a three-week vacation, but if we bring you, we'll have you back here

in a week. The sun dance is also something you should consider."

"Uh . . . what?" Billy squinted. "I'm not Lakota."

"If you're invited to participate, you can."

"Even if I'm Ojibway?"

"Yeah. I've been sun dancing ever since I met Ellen." Ned
unbuttoned his blue shirt that contrasted with the bronzed
color of his skin and his almost-black hair.

Billy tilted his head. Curiosity flecked the back of his neck.
Then his breathing hitched at the scars Ned exposed on his
chest.

"My dancing scars. I got more on my back. They're my of-
ferings to those who I love and who I danced for." Ned refastened his shirt.

"Really?" Billy leaned into the table. "You're supposed to
dance for someone?"

Ned nodded. "Yep. A sun dance isn't about you. It's about
your prayers to Creator for someone ya love who needs the
strength of the Great Mystery."

Billy swallowed. Yes, he'd think good and hard about sun
dancing next year, after he watched the one this year. He'd
dance for René. For them.

"Are your parents taking you out for dinner tonight?" Keith
stood in the living room, touching the various stuff René still
had yet to put away.

"Yeah." René grabbed his wallet off the small kitchen table,
and his one and only key, which was weird. He fingered the
key chain that used to contain one for his truck, the video
store, the house, and Mom's office.

Billy had the truck key now. René dug in for a big breath
to calm the pinches in his chest.

"It'll take time." The softness from Keith's voice feathered the back of René's neck.

"We'll see." René lifted his jacket off the hook. His heavy coat hung in his closet because he had no need for Arctic wear now that he was far south.

"First love always hurts. Always." Keith leaned his butt against the back of the armchair. He folded his hands over the other. "You'll move on, though. You'll build a new life here. Soon, the reserve and Thunder Bay will become old friends. They'll feel like old friends when you go back to visit."

René withdrew a cigarette from the packet on the table. At least he could smoke down here and didn't have to stand outside. "Can't see it."

He lit the smoke and shut the platinum lighter he still used. Home was an ache in his heart, longing to be a thousand and four hundred clicks west. No, home was more than the reserve and his parents' house. Home was where Billy was.

"He was supposed to meet with his mom. I wonder how it went," René said more to himself, because the visit had probably been a disaster and he wasn't there to comfort Billy.

"He's seventeen. He'll deal," Keith assured him.

"Deal?" René snorted. "He—"

"René. René." Keith made a tsking sound. "Can't you see what you were doing to him?"

"Wh-what?" René gasped. "What do you mean?"

"He has to learn how to handle upsetting situations on his own. It's part of growing up." Keith continued to lean his butt on the armchair. "The assistance of friends or family is necessary, but you're still attempting to save him. Think about what you learned when you accepted Olivia's offer."

A smidgen of heat edged along René's cheekbones. "Yeah, I get it. A friend would have been there, not selling his body to keep his buddy from facing the music."

"Exactly." Keith nodded. "You must forget about home. Have faith. Your parents are there. Your uncle is there. Your brother is there. Billy also has good friends he can count on. I can assure you he won't retreat to his former behavior."

"It's not that. I know he won't. I just don't want him to feel . . . alone."

"Because you feel alone?"

The heat remained on René's cheeks. "Totally alone."

"This, too, shall pass." Keith strode up to him. He set his palm on René's shoulder. Their faces were inches apart. "You'll find — if you start living your life as a gay man here — the weight holding you down will lift. That's why you feel alone, why you always felt alone — even with Billy. As wonderful as your romance was, Billy can't fix what's broken in here." He laid his long index finger on René's chest and tapped. "Only you can."

Start living his life as a gay man. René shivered. "What's the first step?"

"First step?" Keith scrunched his slightly thick brow.

"To coming out."

Chapter Eleven: I Can Sleep

Daniel had retrieved the Oshawees at the airport. Billy had welcomed them home, shared dinner with them, and then bolted upstairs to René's bedroom to study.

A knock came at the door.

Ten bucks the visitor was Mrs. O. The General never entered Billy's domain. "Come in," he called out.

Sure enough, Mrs. O entered. She glanced around but never frowned her disapproval. However, there was disapproval coming. Her dissatisfaction was in her stiff walk to sit in René's former love seat. "You don't like your room anymore?"

"I like it." Billy kept his hand on the binder at the desk.

"I know your visit with your mother didn't go as anticipated —"

"It did. She behaved exactly how I expected her to."

Mrs. O glanced about, almost seeming to sigh, or maybe she was looking for the right words. "Yes, it's been difficult —"

"More than difficult. I love him. And he loves me." Billy shut his binder. Given her widening eyes, he should've kept his mouth shut, but he had a big trap and always spoke his mind. He might as well keep doing so.

"What about Carla? Daniel said you went for dinner with her after you finished work on Friday."

Boy, nothing got past the Oshawees. "We're friends. Nothing more. We had something to eat. Talked. I drove her home."

"She's aware of where she stands?" Mrs. O's gaze was searching.

"I told her already I'm not dating while I'm in high school. I told her I wasn't ready."

"I see." Mrs. O motioned at the closet. "Tomorrow, you begin moving your belongings back to your room. This is René's bedroom."

"He left." Dammit, Billy didn't mean to bite his reply in defiance, but he couldn't help himself.

Mrs. O lightly smiled. She stood, walked around the coffee table, and stopped in front of him. Patting his hand gently, she said, "I know it hurts. The last thing Mr. Oshawee and I wanted to do is upset you and René."

"He's . . . he's major bummed?" Billy almost flew from the chair.

"Of course he is. But as I told him, and as I'm telling you, you know why we made the decision we did. And nothing will change our minds." She leaned down and wrapped her arms around his shoulders.

Her lovely scent drifted under Billy's nose. He hugged her back, his first true hug for this woman. Yes, she meant well. She cared. But his heart was shattered into a million pieces only René could fix.

"Move back into your bedroom." Her soft command was in his ear.

"Rockfest?" René stuck the end of the pen into his mouth. "Really?"

"It's going down in July. Barrie's only an hour from here." Trent dug into his macaroni and cheese.

They were in the crowded cafeteria that was noisier than a Tool concert.

René closed his textbook and binder, since he'd been

attempting to study before Trent had joined him. He had a lot of catching up to do after missing the first week of the semester, although he'd attended his classes back home up until his move.

"Fab, my man," his buddy, Fernando, called out from the food counter line. "Gimme one sec."

One thumbs-up René gave the city was the different races in the school. He'd made friends with Indians, Pakistanis, Chinese, Hispanic . . . the list was endless. There was no white dominating red like in Thunder Bay, at least not that he'd encountered yet.

"What's with the colors, Fab?" another guy named Jagmeet teased. He playfully gave Trent a noogie. "You flying the rainbow flag twenty-four-seven? Pride ain't till June."

René's gaze zeroed in on Jagmeet's direction.

Abbas finally made his way from the line and set down his tray.

Peeking at Trent, René said under his breath, "What was the comment about the rainbow flag and pride?" He hadn't heard sarcasm or cruelty in Jagmeet's tone.

"Ah, they're razzing me about my threads." Trent pulled away the snug t-shirt in tie-dyed hues from his honed chest.

"Oh . . ." Maybe they had been making fun of gay people. René lowered his gaze to his untouched soup and sandwich.

"They figure since I'm gay I'm flying the flag." Trent snickered.

For a moment, René stopped breathing. His gaze zoomed upward on Trent. Gay? But nobody at school had mentioned his new buddy dug dudes.

"Ren-Man!"

Again, René's breath ceased. He whipped his stare in the direction of the voice. Kyle, who was in grade twelve, was part of their group.

"Hope you don't mind. The name just came naturally."

Kyle leaned in and squeezed René's shoulders.

"Lay off." Trent poked Kyle's side. "He's straight. He don't wanna see what's under your zipper, my man."

Kyle snickered and drew out a chair.

René fumbled for his bottle of water. Not only Trent, but Kyle, too? He should've known better. Toronto was a huge city. Students came from all walks of life. Of course nobody gave a shit two gay guys were at the table. Well . . . three, if René finally reached for his balls and left the closet.

His breath kept stalling, so he sipped water to soothe his dry throat and calm the anxiety fluttering his pulse points.

"Whoa, René, you look like you saw Kyle's underwear," Abbas teased.

"C'mon, my underwear are stylin', dude. Totally stylin'. Cleo LaSalle. Boxer briefs. Dust gray." Kyle waggled his light-brown brows. He unwrapped his sub and bit into the meaty sandwich.

"Okay, let's get this meeting back on track." Trent motioned at everyone.

"What meeting?" This came from Jagmeet.

"Rockfest. What else?" Trent tapped the table. "This is a major happening concert. Every Canadian band that is hip will be there. We'd be crazy not to go."

The rest of the lunch hour went over René's head. He was still trying to digest two gay guys were in his new circle of buddies. When the bell rang, he went through the motions of gathering up his books, emptying the garbage off his tray, and setting the tray next to the counter on a stack a mile high.

"Everything okay?" Alarm invaded Trent's question. "You not only look like you saw a ghost earlier, but I swear a zombie bit you good."

"I . . . uh . . ." René strode away from the counter. They were caught in the flow of students leaving, so he slowed his pace to a crawl.

Curiosity flickered in Trent's black eyes.

The rush of students passed them.

Still striding to the door, René stared straight ahead. "I . . ." He licked his lips and forced the words from his mouth. "I had no idea you were gay."

Trent stopped.

From René's peripheral vision, he caught the clench of Trent's strong jawline.

"That a prob for you?" Ice was warmer than Trent's question.

"No . . . not a prob at all. 'Cause . . .'cause . . .'cause . . . I'm . . . I'm g-gay, too. It's why . . . why I'm here." The pounding of René's heart was powerful enough to re-bust his healed ribs Billy's dumb cousins had dared to break.

"Dude." Trent set his big hand on René's shoulder. "We gotta do coffee after school. I gotta hear your story."

René sat on the cast-iron stool, opposite Trent at a hangout on Jarvis where classmates gathered after school. They were in the back, far from the usual crowd, who preferred to sit up front and window-watch at their tall tables.

"You're not out yet, are you." Trent's words were a statement.

René shook his head. He busied himself by adding cream and sugar to his mug. They should have gone to his place, because he could use a cigarette. One thing about Toronto, they really enforced the no-smoking law in bars and restaurants that came into effect, Trent had mentioned, over two years ago.

"You gonna tell me your story?" Trent lifted his mug. "We've been sitting here for over five minutes, watching you stare at your coffee."

René's reflection in the stainless-steel tabletop of his bright-red cheeks stared back. "I guess you can tell I'm not quite out yet."

"Not quite?" Trent quirked a brow. "Dude, you're so far in the closet, you're hiding behind the luggage and clothes. Does anyone know?"

"My parents. My best buddy. My brother. The guys I'm renting the apartment from."

"That's a great start. Your parents don't approve? Is that why they sent you here?" Trent frowned.

"They approve. I have their full support. I didn't want to come out back home 'cause . . . well, it's sure not Toronto. Where I'm from . . . it's sort of backward. It takes a good decade for everyone to catch up."

"I get it. Smaller, remote places are always like that."

"We went grunge long before grunge existed." René's chuckle was hollow. "Toques. Flannel. It's the normal everyday wear."

Music blasted from the antique jukebox next to the long counter with the red-covered stools. The place was something out of the nineteen fifties gone high tech.

"Are you glad to be here, then? It sounds pretty repressive where you're from."

"Here." René tapped the table. "No. Not really. But I had no choice."

"I see . . ." Trent drummed his fingers against his strong cheekbone. "You'd rather live where you can't be yourself?"

"It'd be different if . . ." René cupped and un-cupped his mug. "I got sent here because there's this guy . . ."

"Oh . . ." Trent drew in his cheeks and nodded. "I get it. So your folks didn't approve — "

"We were fostering him . . ." René wasn't about to let anyone get the wrong impression of his folks. As shitty as moving here was, they were his parents, and he'd always stand by their decisions whether he agreed or not.

"That could get pretty sticky." Trent nodded. "You two got

together when he moved in?"

"No. We were together before that." René finally sipped some of his coffee. The caffeine helped where he couldn't have nicotine. "He was emerg fostering at my uncle and aunt's until my cousin could find him somewhere permanent."

"Your cousin?" Trent squinted.

"He's the family services worker. I have lots of cousins who are older than me. Old enough to be my parents." René sheepishly grinned. "A big family. They work everywhere on the rez."

"Is he from a big family, too?"

"His are deadbeats. Think of the stereotypical native, and you got Billy's fam."

"That his name?"

"Yeah. He's two grades behind me. My folks weren't down with us. Me being eighteen now, and him in their care."

"Yeah, I get it. Sucks. How come they made you move?"

"I asked them to." René sat back. He continued to cup his mug and stare at the brown coffee. "Billy's had it tough his whole life. I wanted him to have a chance. Y'know? With my folks, he does. If they were to move him again, I was worried he might . . . well, he'd have a rough time. He was pretty badass when we met. Now he's doing super decent."

"Glad to hear that. Sounds like you're really into him." There was a hint of something in Trent's stare René couldn't put his finger on.

"I am. He's a great guy. Really artistic. Spiritual."

"Spiritual?"

"My uncle's been teaching him lots about our culture."

"Oh . . ." Trent scratched his chin. "I thought you were all into that."

"No." René lightly chuckled. "It's not my bag. Billy . . . he digs the stuff." The weight on his chest lifted after finally confessing the truth to someone who wasn't family.

"So . . . you and Billy . . . you two still an item?" Trent kept glancing at his coffee and then back to René.

"Considering my parents don't want us to have contact . . ." The awful word René had to choke out was the door he loathed having to slam shut on Billy's face where he stood on the other side. " . . . no."

"I'm sorry, man. I'm really sorry." Trent reached over. He laid his big palm over the back of René's hand.

René was smothered in warmth. There was even a slight comforting squeeze being offered. He peeked up from the shiny table surface to the concern reflecting in Trent's pupils.

"It's okay. You didn't know until now." Strange, but being touched by a guy in public should have sent René scampering for the closet. Not sitting quietly, letting the sympathy Trent offered wash over him like a fine cloth of soapy water massaging his bare skin.

"I get it, but it still sucks. I can tell what he means to you." Trent again squeezed René's hand with his luxurious embrace. "What's it like? I gotta admit I never felt that way about anyone before."

"You haven't?" René worked his hand out from beneath Trent's to grab his coffee. For sure he'd assumed Trent would have been in love. The guy was smoking hot. More than smoking hot. The dude could start fires.

"You sound surprised." The tenderness had faded, and amusement flickered in Trent's reply.

"Well . . ." René let out a low whistle under his breath. "You're sure not ugly."

Trent threw back his head and laughed. His baritone howl was as masculine as his pumped biceps and deep chest. "It don't matter how hot someone is. Even choice people have a tough time finding the right one."

"You're not seeing Kyle?"

"Why would you think I'm seeing Kyle?"

"Err . . ." Shit, René had stuck his foot in his mouth. This was a first. "I assumed 'cause you're both, well . . ."

"'Cause we're both gay?"

Heat flecked René's cheeks. He forced a nod.

"Look, just 'cause two people are gay doesn't mean they're gonna be into each other, right? You don't see straight people into every person who walks by."

Huge lesson learned. Yeah, René found Trent attractive, but as for Kyle, as cute as he was, he wasn't his type. If he had a type. Perhaps he did. "Excuse me for one second."

"Sure. 'Sup?"

"I need to remove my foot from my mouth. I never had to before. It feels a bit weird. I always wondered what my boot tasted like." René's chuckle was strained.

Again, Trent threw back his head and laughed. The guy put effort into everything, even a simple hardy-har-har.

"Mmm . . . boy. I bet he's missing you pretty bad, too." Trent lifted his coffee and sipped.

"I don't want him sitting around his room, bummed." René rubbed his brow. "He's bi, and I want him to—"

"Really?" Curiosity resurfaced in Trent's stare.

René nodded. "It was weird. Maybe even dumb. I kept urging him to date girls so he could live a normal life—"

"Dude . . ." Trent thrust his finger. "We. Are. Normal."

"Uh . . . huh?" René blinked.

"We're normal. You and me." Trent pointed back and forth. "One thing you're gonna learn fast living here—there is no such thing as normal. Normal is what you make your reality. If you think your reality's unnormal, it'll be unnormal. If you make your reality your normal, it'll be normal."

René had never thought to change his thinking that way. But reconsidering his sexual orientation as his new normal was something to contemplate. His budding friendship with

Trent was going to do him a world of good.

René was stretched out on his new double bed in his room. His laptop was plugged into the phone line. He scrolled through his email. Every time he did this, his heart clung to the hope Billy would bust the rule and send a letter, a note — something. But the inbox was filled with the usual messages René received.

He shouldn't do this, but he had to. Not knowing how Billy was kept rolling through René's mind like a treadmill. Before he could stop himself, he started typing.

Billy, it's me. Duh. Like you couldn't tell from the email addy. I just wanted to tell you my fingers are crossed the meeting with your mom was a big thumbs-up. I know it's tough trying to reestablish a new relationship with her, but it wouldn't hurt to try.

Remember, if you need me, I'm here. I get it. We're supposed to move on, and I'm trying to, but it's only been over a week.

How're you treating my best girl? Is she running okay? You taking good care of her for me? LOL. As if I need to ask. I know you're gonna baby her like I do.

It's not too shabby living by myself. Lonely? Yeah. But I got Keith upstairs to talk to. I'm also making new friends at school. Dad's coming up on another biz trip before the end of the month. Mom's coming with him. So you get the house to yourself again. Like that'll happen. LOL. Danny'll be there.

He paused before he typed in about meeting Trent, although he should mention who his buddies were, even that two were gay. Still, he couldn't bring his fingers to hit the letters on the keyboard.

You take care of yourself. You can do this. I know you can. June seems like forever when I'll be back to get my girl, but we'll see each other then. Remember what I asked of you? Please make sure and do it. Please. I love you, René.

He closed his eyes. Mentioning Rockfest wasn't a good idea, either, even though he probably wouldn't go because of his new job at Brooks' firm. He pressed send.

No doubt, once Billy sat at his computer in the lab, he'd find the message. So René shouldn't expect to receive anything until tomorrow.

Receiving an e-mail from Billy, and having a new friend who could help him come out, René shut off his laptop and easily went to sleep.

Chapter Twelve: Till I Heart It from You

After receiving René's email, Billy had spent the week walking on top of the gray clouds that had hovered over Thunder Bay, bringing in snow and some major wind. For sure they'd figure out a way to get through this bullshit. René never busted rules. Ever. To send a message meant he was suffering as much as Billy.

There was one problem, though. René had high hopes Billy would reconnect with Mom. So did Mrs. O. She'd told him he had to meet Mom again after school today. What was so imperative about visiting a pathetic lush who'd never cared? Bullshit.

He pulled up at the family services building and switched off the truck. The moccasin telegraph said Hoyt was still bunking at the house. If Mom was sincere, she'd give the loser the boot.

Billy slammed the door and huffed up the steps. He never bothered stopping at the receptionist's desk and went straight for the visitation room.

Mom sat in the same chair, smoking a cigarette. She brushed at her stained sweatpants. "I'm sorry . . . sorry we didn't get off to a good start."

"Sorry?" A surge of disbelief was an electrical shock to Billy's system. He was a computer ready to black screen. This woman never apologized or admitted to being wrong. "Uh . . . what?"

"I mean it. Making amends . . . this is more than what we call the ninth step for me." Her gravelly voice shook.

Oh, her recovery meetings bullshit again of being forced to do something. "Whatever." He plopped on the sofa.

"I'm not going to make excuses. The fact is, I'm an alcoholic, and being one, I ruined a lot of lives." She possessed the same unsteady hands from their previous visit.

"You didn't ruin mine." Billy slumped and folded his arms. "I was smart enough to get out."

Mom rocked slightly, something she always did whenever she was upset. Her bony jaw twitched. She puffed on the smoke. "How's school?"

"Fine." He shrugged.

The silence in the room should've pierced Billy's ears, but he picked at a few frays on the sofa arm. Some of the threads were wound into tight little balls. He rolled them along his fingers.

"I guess that's it? You don't wanna talk?" Mom puffed some more on the smoke.

"What's there to talk about?" The ice freezing Billy's heart slithered into his cold words.

"I dunno. About anything." Mom reached for her coffee in the paper cup.

He had nothing to say. Instead, he'd admire the pictures on the walls of cool native art. Maybe his would hang there one day.

Mom grumbled under her breath. Yep, she was readying to get all pissy, because that was what she did best. The stupid bitch didn't have a clue how to talk. She took a few more puffs on the cigarette. "You never ask about your father."

What was the point? Billy had never known the prick. Hoyt had mentioned in the past Dad was doing major time for armed robbery at a gas station in Medicine Hat.

"He left me with two kids to raise. It wasn't easy."

"Growing up with a drunk wasn't easy either." Heat appeared behind Billy's eyes.

Life flooded into Mom's sallow face. "I said I'm sorry. I know words are words. They don't mean nothing until it's proven. That's what I wanna do. Prove it."

He rolled his feet in a circle. "Yeah? How you gonna do that?"

"By telling you I love you and I miss you." Mom shook back her loose, thin hair that had once been thick and the rich color of bluish-black. "I don't expect you to say anything. But I miss you. I missed watching you grow up. I missed watching you become a young man. I missed a lot of things about you."

Something sharp dug into Billy's chest. The affection he'd yearned to receive from her had died each time she'd walked out the door in her skimpy outfit to find a bottle and a man.

He stood. "Seeya at the visit next week." He headed out the door, never looking back, his stomach twisting.

At the video store, where a couple of customers stood around picking out movies, the bell above the door tinkled.

Billy glanced up to Carla walking in.

"How'd it go?"

The concern in her dark eyes helped untangle some of the knots in Billy's gut. "Same ol' bullshit."

"Are the visits done then?"

"I dunno." He closed his binder and textbook. "I told her I'd see her next week."

"That's promising." Carla rested her elbows on the counter.

"The Oshawees said I have to see her. René does, too."

"You heard from him?"

"Yeah, he sent me an email."

"How's he doing?"

He seems to miss me, thank fuck. "Good. Making new buds."

"What about your mom? You told me she has a drinking disease."

"Cirrhosis of the liver. As for how she's doing, nothing new to report." He offered a smile because he owed props to Carla for stopping by to check on him. If only he could tell her the truth that was burning a hole in his pocket.

"You wanna go to the movies tomorrow night?" she asked.

"What's playing?"

"Deep Rising."

Billy snickered. He was lucky she loved horror as much as him and wasn't into those romantic comedies and chick flicks. "Sounds cool."

"Okay. Get me for the first showing."

"No prob. Seeya tomorrow."

She left the store with a light skip to her step. Always, he could count on Carla. Hitting a flick together was the perfect way to keep his mind busy.

René was only home for a quick change before Ian arrived. They were loading his drums into the van to begin jamming again. Ian was convinced they could score a record deal as a threesome, with Moxy and René both singing. That was major iffy. Neither had Sheldon's range, and Sheldon wasn't in Toronto, preferring to be the big fish in a small pond.

Practicing was fun, but nothing beat getting on stage under the hot lights to feed off the energy of the audience, in René's books.

Moxy and Ian had jammed with quite a few students from their school. They said the singers and drummers weren't what they were looking for. So a trio they'd be.

Ian had cited many famous threesomes, starting with Nirvana, Green Day, Blink 182, and Primus. Then there was heavy metal icons Motorhead. As for Canadian groups, Ian had listed The Tea Party, Rush, and Triumph. René had never given the last two a listen. He'd be willing to if those bands had something to help him hone his chops.

Still, having two singers, one drumming especially, was pretty unorthodox. Maybe there was a chance they might find one who fit.

With his gear already waiting at the door, he plopped in the armchair to get a quick check in on the 'net. He still experienced fuzzies from Billy responding to his email. The bad news, though—Billy wasn't happy about his mom or being left behind.

The first email in the list was from Chunk. René quickly opened the message. Perhaps his main man had some good news about coming up earlier, instead of waiting until the end of February. Probably not. Chunk was training a new line cook to take over his duties.

Renny. Wassssup? Missing you, man. It ain't the same without you here.

Warmth filled René. He kept reading about the latest happenings in Thunder Bay. When Chunk mentioned Billy's name, for a moment René's lungs seemed to stop operating.

Yeah, your pal sure is turning into quite the lady killer. But he learned from the best, didn't he? Me. Wink. Wink. Chicks are always in your wheels now. He's been out with Carla Morrisseau lots. Ten bucks they'll be hitting the junior prom together. Haha. That's my boy, huh? He knows how to work the girls. He makes me damn proud.

René pushed away the laptop. The most horrendous knife seemed to pierce his gut. He clutched his stomach. Billy had already moved on? No, this couldn't be true. They loved each other. But hadn't he kept telling Billy to make his high school years the best? Wasn't this why he'd insisted Billy keep his bisexuality a secret from everyone?

He clicked on Billy's last message.

I miss you. I know I'm not supposed to say that kind of stuff, but I do. It's not the same without you here. All I'm doing is going through the motions. I know you don't wanna hear that. I know you keep insisting I have a blast. A blast can't exist unless you're a part of it, though.

The pain shifted from René's stomach to his chest. Was this how Billy had felt last year over the Olivia fiasco? Hurt, betrayed, and piss-mad all balled into one? Of course it was.

René put his hands to his face. He couldn't and wouldn't cry. Still, the darn lump kept expanding in his throat.

He set his finger on the delete button. Billy's email vanished into the cyber wasteland.

He'd let him go. Let him live his life. But the machete buried in René's heart was a hurting, motherfucking son of a bitch.

Billy sat in the computer lab at the school. Each time he logged in to his email account, he was flattened by a steamroller. It'd been over three weeks since he'd last heard from René. What a way to start the first week of February. Maybe their exchange of messages was a simple goodbye deal. Checking up on *the kid* before signing off for good.

The bell rang. Billy snatched his books, since this was the last class of the day. He was meeting Chunk at Gold's Coffee to catch up because work had kept them busy. René's main man was getting more excited about his upcoming move.

Within ten minutes Billy was seated at a booth in the restaurant of rich wood, deep greens, and lush browns. Chunk sat across from him. As always, the big guy had plastered on his mile-wide grin.

"I heard from Renny the other night. They started a new band." Chunk lit a cigarette.

Billy peeked at where Stuart, Andrew, Carla, Meghan, and Bonnie sat. He glanced back at Chunk. "New band?"

"Yep. Madame Moxy. They're a trio."

"Madame Moxy?"

"Y'know they always wanted her in the group before Sheldon and Vince started their whining. With the amount of bitching they did, Moxy had no choice but to back off and let Eddie sit in on bass."

"Yeah, that was pretty shitty. I'm glad she split on Sheldon."

"This time around, Renny wanted a nod to her," Chunk continued on. He always had an air of excitement whenever he spoke. "He mentioned madame, besides being a formal address for a married French woman, is also used for chicks in exotic occupations, such as musicians."

Billy had to hide his smirk. Chunk sounded like he was quoting René word for word.

"Your girl's not joining us?" Chunk winked. He motioned at Carla.

"Girl? We're friends. Why would you think she's my girl?"

"Oh man." Chunk smacked himself upside the head. "Dude, I'm sorry. I thought you two were an item. That's what's making its way through the grapevine. Movies. Coffee. Dinner. Even giving her rides to school."

"She's my friend. Nothing more."

"The next time someone asks, I'll set 'em straight." Chunk drew a horizontal line across the air to emphasize his point.

"Thanks. I appreciate it." People and their fucking gossip. Billy shook his head. "Tell me more about this band."

"Hasn't Renny?" A tiny V appeared between Chunk's

brown brows.

Billy couldn't admit the Oshawees had banned them from speaking. And he had to honor their secret, because poor Chunk remained clueless about their crashed-and-burned romance. "No. He must've forgot."

"Really?" Chunk tilted his head slightly. Then he shrugged. "Yeah, I guess they couldn't find a decent singer, so Moxy and Renny are taking charge of the microphone. Moxy and Ian are all for it. Renny's on the fence. He said the setup is too unorthodox. People want a front man or front woman—if you get my drift. I told him Trent's right."

"Who's Trent? Is he a roadie?" Billy lifted his coffee and sipped.

"Trent? You never heard about Trent? He's Renny's new buddy. I guess they're both taking OAC. Hey, guess what's even better?"

"What's that?"

"Trent's the same as Renny." Chunk lowered his voice and leaned in. "Guess this dude's been a big help."

The air drained from Billy's lungs. He punched his chest to get the oxygen flowing.

"So yeah . . . Trent agreed with Ian and Moxy. He said unorthodox is the way to go. He said Nirvana were very unorthodox. Left-handed guitar player. A trio. Kirk could sing but he sure didn't have the range of Eddie Vedder, Layne Staley, or Chris Cornell. But they still made it big." Chunk puffed on the smoke. "You okay?"

"Uh . . ."

"Dude, I swear you saw a ghost. Man, your face is whiter than a rabbit in the winter."

Was this why René wasn't emailing back? Was he already moving on with some guy named Trent? Billy's gut told him his assumption was wrong. After the bullshit René had pulled last year with Olivia, the guy he loved wouldn't be so fast to move on. Still, he was going to call René right away, even if he had to stand at a payphone and keep inserting quarters.

They had their coffees. Billy didn't bolt for work the way Chunk did. He beelined for the counter, changed a ten-dollar bill for quarters, and darted for the payphone in the lobby.

René should be back to his basement apartment by now. Unless he'd gone somewhere after school. But relaxing and then studying was his routine.

Billy dialed the long-distance number. The operator came on and informed him how much he'd need to deposit. The pile of change was spread out on the steel shelf the phone was suspended to. The directory hung underneath. He inserted the money into the slot.

The lobby door opened.

"What's up?" Stuart asked.

Billy held up his hand. He remained facing the phone. "Super busy and super important call."

"Gotcha." Stuart patted Billy's back.

At least his friends had respected Billy's request for privacy. After three rings, the familiar voice that was satin brushing his skin came through the receiver.

"Hello."

The words Billy wanted to say were stuck to the back of his throat. A decade may as well have flown by since he'd last heard René talk. Dots appeared in front of Billy's eyes, and his breathing became a race car tearing down the highway.

"Hello?"

"It's . . . it's m-m-me." Billy's teeth clattered.

"Billy?" Astonishment emerged in René's question.

Attempting to stifle his rapid breathing, Billy curled his fingers into a fist. He gripped the receiver tighter. "Y-yeah."

"Whoa. What's going on? What's wrong?"

"N-nothing. I . . . I needed to hear . . . hear . . . you . . ." *I needed to hear you speak. It's been forever since I last heard you.* "I . . . I'm . . . I'm not dating anyone."

"What?" Confusion replaced the previous urgency in René's voice.

"The rumor Chunk told you about. We got done doing coffee about five minutes ago. I'm not dating anyone. How could you think I was?" Billy's breathing had returned to normal. Desperation thumped at the back of his neck.

"Oh . . ." There was a long pause from René.

Billy rubbed his finger along the stiff telephone cord. Classmates shuffled by him, on their way to the parking lot. Each time the door opened, a blast of cold swept into the lobby. Some of his buddies slapped him on the back, but he kept facing the phone. "W-well?"

"You're right." René's pitch dropped a smidgen. "I guess I shouldn't have jumped to conclusions."

"Is that why you never emailed me back?" Billy shuffled closer to the phone until his nose almost kissed the buttons.

"I . . . y'know I want you to have a blast. I . . . I don't want to hold you back."

"Don't start. Please," Billy begged. "Tell me how you're really feeling? Is it Trent?"

"Trent? Huh? No. We're just friends." A smidgen of confusion distorted René's normally smooth speech. "How could I have the hots for someone else when —"

"Oh . . . okay." Billy's rattling teeth stopped clacking. "I get it." He ducked his head. "I miss you."

"Me, too."

"Sir, I'll need one dollar more," the operator said.

Billy grabbed the quarters and inserted them.

"Where're you calling from?"

"Gold's. I couldn't call from your crib. Your mom and dad would've saw the long-distance charges."

"Peek-a-boo."

Soft palms covered Billy's eyes. Carla. Dammit.

"What're you doing? I'm on the phone." He didn't mean to

snap, but this was René.

"Is that Carla?" René asked.

Great, he'd also recognized her voice. "Yeah."

"Look, I'll email you. Okay?" René's voice was very distant, and not because he was over fourteen hundred kilometers away, but a different kind of distant, one that told Billy something was up. "I gotta go. My ride's here. Have a great time."

The line went dead, and so did Billy's heart.

Chapter Thirteen: Congratula- tions, I'm Sorry

René stared at his laptop. A week had passed after Billy had called. He kept reminding himself why Mom and Dad had separated them. Yet they were stuck in the same mud pit, fearful of putting the truck into four-wheel drive to get out of the hole that had captured them. If René was going to try make the best of a terrible situation, he had to be the one to give them a shove.

The Valentine's Day dance at the school was coming up. Billy was popular now. He had every right to take a date and enjoy himself. Before that, he'd roadied, because they'd had to hide their love.

Like it or not, Toronto was René's home until he graduated law school. Even then, he'd probably stay, because this neighborhood he lived in accepted gay people. Although Trent had urged René to go to one of the gay restaurants, he'd made an excuse.

Dragging Billy through the dark with him wasn't fair until René found the courage to live his life as a gay man.

"Knock. Knock." Keith poked his head inside the apartment from the entryway in the back that led into the kitchen. "I hope I'm not disturbing you."

"No. C'mon in." René motioned at the sofa since he sat in the armchair.

"How're you doing?" Keith strolled to the living room.

"I'm trying to figure out what to write Billy." René set the laptop on the end table.

"You're corresponding? I assumed your parents forbid—"

"They did," René sheepishly admitted. He reached for his cigarettes. "Billy called last week. He was upset 'cause Chunk told him I'd been given the four-eleven on him dating Carla. He insists he isn't."

"They're friends?" Seated with one leg crossed over the other and a straight posture, Keith was as dapper as James Bond.

René nodded. He bounced the filter along his knee.

"This false information upset you?"

René lit his cigarette. He used his thumb to shut the cap of his platinum lighter. "I thought . . ." Dammit, if only there was a way he could speak about what rolled around inside of his head better. "I was feeling . . . conflicted, I guess."

"That's called love." Keith's reply was gentle. "Wanting to be together isn't selfish or wrong. It's simply how you feel. It's how you proceed that counts. We've been over this before. I'm guessing you've reviewed your thoughts a million times already. It's what's bothered you from the beginning, ever since you informed me you were dating a boy two years younger than you."

"What do you mean?"

"You feel selfish for wanting the relationship. Your conscience is asking you to let him have a chance to live out his high school years with people who can be with him. You're well over fourteen hundred kilometers apart. You don't want him holed up in his bedroom, pining. You want him to date and have fun—because you love him. But the other side of love doesn't want him to forget you and move on."

"You always know what I'm thinking." René took a drag.

"It's not a matter of perception. It's a matter of experience. You're not the first person to consider your options during a new romance, and you won't be the last. Graduating has a big impact on high school relationships. While he's working at the video store, you'll be employed at a law firm."

"True."

"You know your answer. You've known the answer from the first time we spoke," Keith added quietly. "What I came down here to ask is if you're interested in accompanying me and Brooks for dinner tomorrow night."

"Dinner? Where?"

"You know where." Keith's pitch remained quiet. "I think you're more than ready. The restaurant welcomes everyone."

René took another shaky drag. Keith was right. Trent was right. "O-okay."

"Invite your new friend along."

"I will. Sounds cool."

Keith stood. He slowly walked to the kitchen. His hand rested on the dining chair. He glanced over his shoulder. "Use this time to become who you always wanted to be but were too afraid to. If you do, I guarantee you'll discover much about yourself. Have a good evening."

Just as Keith headed up the stairs, the roar of Ian's van carried inside.

René knew what he had to do.

The next day, Billy reread the email, because his heart wouldn't believe what his head was deciphering. René was surrounded by *out* gay men. They were probably ganging up on him, telling him to forget about *the kid* who still had to finish grade eleven.

He glanced around the computer lab. The teacher was busy writing on the chalkboard. The other students stared at their screens and typed on their keyboards, now and then glancing at their open textbooks.

First, I'm not doing this to hurt you. You know I never ever want to hurt you. I love you. And this is why I came to the decision I made. Because I love you so much, I want you to move on. Take a date to the Valentine's Day dance. Ask a girl to junior prom. Go out and have fun. Please. I'm begging you. Two and a half years is a long time, Billy. You got a half more year to finish grade eleven. Another year for grade twelve. And then another year for your OAC.

As corny as it sounds, love is about setting someone free to live their dreams.

"You're my dream," Billy murmured.

I'm not even out, but I'm working on it. You have no problem with being out. Why being bisexual doesn't bother you is beyond me.

That was an easy one. When a guy had nothing to lose, what did it matter if he was laughed at again? From birth, everyone had thought of Billy as a loser Redsky, a joke to chuckle about. Plus, love was bigger than fear. Falling for René had erased any doubts—if there'd been any to start with—from Billy's brain about digging dudes. All that mattered was having René to call his own. If that meant telling the world and having planet Earth laugh at him, big fucking deal.

If I could change our situation, you know I'd do so in a heartbeat, but I can't. We have two and a half years to live separate lives. Thinking of you sitting in your room, merely existing until the time is up . . . dude, it's tearing me apart.

Billy squeezed his eyes shut. Dammit, he didn't want to be responsible for René's guilt and agony.

"Mr. Redsky, is there a problem?" Mrs. Peel had stopped writing on the chalkboard. She bore down the aisle.

Quickly, Billy closed the email. "It's cool. I got stuck on something but I figured it out."

"Good." Mrs. Peel beamed.

Stuart had his own computer at his house. Billy would finish re-reading the rest of his kiss-off at his best bud's crib. When the bell rang, he bolted for his locker. Since he didn't have to work tonight, he drove straight to Castle Oshawee, reviewed his lessons at the breakfast nook, forced down dinner with a tight stomach, and then motored over to Stuart's.

Andrew was already there, playing a video game.

Billy plopped in front of the computer.

I'm going to use this time to try live like a gay man. I'm scared shitless, Billy. But I gotta try. See? That's also unfair to you. I know you want us to live freely, and because of me, you're hiding in the closet, too. I wish I had your courage. Too bad I don't.

"You are courageous," Billy whispered while battleships blasted one another from the TV.

I'm sorry. So sorry. I love you. I'm always here for you if you need me. I mean that. If you need me, call. I know life is shit right now with your mom being in the picture again. I don't want you to feel alone.

"But I do."

For me, please, make the best of our time apart. Love, René.

Stuart whacked Billy's arm. "What about the V-Day dance then? You stagging it? You gonna get a date and come out for dinner with us?"

Billy closed the email. At the same time, his heart also seemed to close. He bowed his head. "Sure. Dinner and the dance sounds cool."

René could barely casually stroll down Church Street because he was stiffer than a board accompanying Keith, Brooks, and Trent to the restaurant. He was the tin man, locked knees needing oiling.

Before leaving his basement apartment, he'd checked his email, but there'd been no message from Billy. This wasn't surprising. Who'd send back a message after being told good-bye?

Life was moving too fast, sort of like the never-ending rush of cars flying by them. Being packed around buildings kept the wind at bay. One thing about the city, nobody ever went home. People waited at bus stops. Some raced in and out of stores. Others joined them on the sidewalk.

Friday night. Billy would be at work by now.

"They got the best onion rings. Be sure and order a plate." Trent gave René's shoulder a slap. "And don't be nervous. It's just a bunch of people in there."

Don't be nervous? Yeah, right. René was about to enter his first gay establishment. A smidgen of guilt goose-pimpled his skin because he should be doing this with Billy.

René offered a smile weaker than the cup of coffee he'd made this morning after forgetting to add the extra spoonful to the filter basket.

Keith opened the door and gestured at everyone to enter.

Brooks went in first, followed by Trent.

René whipped his stare on Keith, who calmly gazed back and again motioned to the lobby, where Trent and Brooks waited.

"You'll be fine. Nobody's going to bite you." Keith's rich voice was reassuring arms wrapping René by the waist. "Remember, your parents trust me."

Oh great, had René looked that panicked? He was

eighteen. An adult. Not some kid needing a hand holding. "It's cool."

"Are you sure?" Tender care gathered in Keith's dark-brown eyes.

"More than sure." René squared his shoulders and stepped through the doorway. The walls closed in a little when he joined Brooks and Trent. *It's just a restaurant. Nothing more.*

He glanced around at men everywhere, some in hip clothing that matched the modern art deco of the interior.

"Brooks. Keith. Great to see you again." The host's hair color was every shade of the rainbow. "And you brought some new meat." His gaze latched onto Trent.

Trent offered the maître d' a smile delicious enough to eat.

The multi-colored-haired host then winked at René.

René glanced away.

Trent snickered under his breath. "Easy. All in good fun," he quietly added.

René shot his new buddy a warning glance.

The patrons were an eclectic bunch. Besides the hipsters, they ranged from businessmen in suits to blue-collared guys. As they followed the host to their table, René's rhythm was more awkward than his ten-year-old self learning how to shuffle a beat on the drums.

Finally, after an agonizing five-year walk and being checked out by everyone in the restaurant, they were seated at the back on a tier.

"Tonight's special is pork tenderloin schnitzel." The maître d' motioned at the bar. "What would you like to start?"

"A beer on tap." Trent kept eyeballing the host.

René stiffened. His bud wasn't old enough to drink.

Trent kicked René ever so lightly under the table.

"Scotch. Neat." This came from Brooks.

"Scotch and soda. Easy on the soda," Keith said.

"A cream soda," René murmured.

The maître d' sauntered off. Trent craned his neck, clearly ogling the guy.

René folded his arms, since smoking wasn't permitted and he needed something to do. No, this wasn't how he'd wanted to come to his first gay establishment. The moment should be memorable, with Billy beside him. He didn't dare look around, either, because his rigid muscles told him the patrons hadn't stopped staring at him and Trent yet.

"Your first time here, Trent?" Keith asked.

"Nope. Came with some buds before." Trent's head kept moving this way and that way. "We had a blast. It's a bummer that Giorgio doesn't remember me."

René wasn't about to ask who Giorgio was.

As if reading his mind, Trent offered up a, "Our host." He reached for the beer a tall, dark, and handsome server set down. "You gotta check out Ice. It's something else."

"René isn't old enough to patronize Ice." Keith's tone was an arching eyebrow of sternness. He motioned at the beer. "Only one."

"Easy." Trent flashed his glimmering straight teeth. "My birthday's in March."

"René's isn't until December twenty-eighth. No Ice until then." Keith picked up his glass of scotch.

Irritation should prickle the back of René's neck, but for once he didn't mind one of the family coming to his rescue. He wasn't curious about a gay dance club or whatever this Ice was, anyway. All he wanted to do was try fit into the neighborhood as his real self without being accosted by other guys. Just because he had to end things with Billy didn't mean his heart had moved on. Yes, he wasn't going to mope in his apartment, but he sure wasn't ready to date.

He opened his menu.

"Well, what do you say? Are we gonna join them? Everyone's going before the dance." Carla stood at the horror section, peeking through the videos.

At almost ten o'clock, she'd gotten into Billy's old habit—when René had worked there and he'd stuck around to help close up.

"Sure." Why not take her out for dinner before the Valentine's Day dance? René wanted him to move on, so Billy would fucking move on.

"I thought for sure you'd go with Heath." Billy snickered. The right wing for the hockey team also had the hots for her, from what he'd overheard in the boys' locker room.

"Oh . . . he asked me. I told him I was flattered and all, but . . ." Carla shrugged.

"I don't get you at times." Billy turned the key to z. "You got all these dudes wanting to date you."

"I'm going on dates." Carla meandered up to the counter. "It's fun and all."

"I know. I know. I heard it a million times. You don't wanna get serious." Billy tapped the keyboard to run the z reading.

"What's wrong with only having fun?" Carla draped her lithe arms across the counter. She had the body of a ballerina, thanks to the dance classes she took twice a week. Honed, yet super-slim.

He should get her to pose for a sketch. She had great bone structure, even though her face was a cute round shape with apple cheeks. Maybe the forever sparkle in her dark eyes was what made her so entrancing. There was always a light seeming to glow from within her. "I get it. You wanna be a dancer. I get it."

Carla did a pirouette. She'd been taking ballet and modern dance ever since she was a kid. Her sisters were also enrolled. Her parents deserved major props for getting their children involved in lots of activities outside of the school and reserve.

"Y'know, I could also get my major in dance in Toronto, besides Winnipeg. I wonder if Renny would let me stay at his crib?" Carla said more to herself. "He could show me around. Introduce me to people."

There wasn't a need for jealousy, because Billy understood she was referring to René in a friendship way. "He's two grades ahead of us. By the time you get to Toronto, he'll be well into uni."

"True." She clasped her hands behind her back. "Okay. Pass me the quarters."

Billy shoved the pile her way.

She started counting. "Do you have drum group this weekend?"

"Yeah. Saturday morning. Over at Ned's." Which reminded Billy he'd better start smudging again. Ned was right. Communing with Creator was important. Maybe this imaginary being might help somehow.

"Are you gonna join him?" Carla rolled up a bundle of quarters.

"Join who?"

"Renny. In Toronto."

For a moment, Billy's blood froze. He'd gotten a kiss-off. A goodbye letter. René was probably planning on dating that Trent guy. His gut twisted. "I dunno."

After dropping off Carla at her pad, Billy held a glass of milk and his plate of dinner he'd retrieved from the microwave. He used his foot to shut the door to his bedroom. All was quiet. The Oshawees retired at ten.

He set his food on the coffee table and turned on his TV. The dog tag on the silver chain continued to sit against his chest, a reminder of the past and what would never be.

He dug inside his sweater and unearthed the locket he kept

beneath his socks in the drawer whenever he wasn't wearing the gift.

Hidden love.

Stolen kisses.

Forbidden.

Always, he was the one fighting for them while René continued to find excuses to stop what they had going. If he truly desired for them to be a couple, the ball was in René's court. Billy's days of fighting were over.

He undid the clasp. The locket lay in his open palm.

No matter how much his heart begged him not to give up hope, his sanity said he must move on.

He stood and marched to the walk-in closet. All was dark. He flipped on the light. The sock drawer waited for him. He clutched the handle and slid it open. Heart tight and breathing quick, he placed the dog tag underneath his socks.

Without looking back, he turned off the light and shut the door.

"Congratulations, René. I'm sorry you got your way." Billy beelined for his plate of dinner. He'd eat. He'd eat every damn morsel, because his stomach wasn't aching. Nope, like hell his belly twisted and turned.

Chapter Fourteen: Up and Crumbling

The bottom of the chair adjacent from René scraped along the floor. He never looked up. Since he was in the cafeteria, the person was most likely one of his buddies.

"Ice. We're going to Ice for my birthday. This time I'm legal." There was a *yahoo* vibe to Trent's announcement. "What you say, my man? We can find you a fake ID to get in."

Although René continued to eat once a week at the gay restaurant, he wasn't ready for an all-male dance club. He wasn't old enough to get in, either. Plus, rehearsals with Moxy and Ian were taking up the minimal spare time he had. Not only were they rehearsing, but they were also working on three new songs.

Finding a booking agent to play the clubs and bars in the greater Toronto area wasn't going to be easy. Their group had to build a rep, which meant more high school dances, weddings, and socials—if they could convince someone to hire them. Honing their chops before sending in an audition tape was a must, along with gaining a solid following.

Already, Matt Gerhard was working on a bulletin board for the newly formed Madame Moxy. He'd mentioned building a website for them, too, using *GeoCities*, a new and extremely popular free hosting company.

Matt had originally wanted to follow René to the city to finish his OAC, but his parents had vetoed the suggestion. Come the fall, he was moving in with Moxy, Ian, and Jennifer.

Whether his twin was following along, René wasn't sure.

"You know I rehearse on weekends." René tapped the end of the pen against his mouth.

"Dude, that's all you do." Trent plopped in the seat. "Are you using this as an excuse?"

"Excuse?" René frowned. "Excuse for what?"

"To not go clubbing." Trent's gaze intensified.

"First, I'm not old enough to go clubbing. Second, if Keith finds out, he'll rat me to my parents like that." René snapped his thumb and finger. "Third, music is my air. I need it to breathe. I haven't had a chance to truly jam ever since Moxy and Ian left in the fall. I'm grateful to have two friends who feel the same way about music."

Trent snickered. "I noticed you get a bit of a lecturing tone when you're all serious."

Funny, Billy had said the same thing. René couldn't help his smile. "Do I really sound that bad?"

"A true teacher. Hell, the principal." Trent poked one of René's biceps. "Damn, you are one responsible cat."

"Cat?" René guffawed. "The nineteen seventies called. They want their groovy slang back."

"Hah. Hah. You're damn funny. What's wrong with cat? I love cats."

"You should. You're gonna be a vet."

"With all the volunteering I do at the animal shelter, I find time to hang, chill, and party. You gotta do the same." Trent sat back. "That's what I mean by excuse."

"I'm going out for dinner once a week."

"Yeah, with a dude old enough to be your father and his boytoy. C'mon, they're geezers."

"Geezers? Keith isn't even closing in on thirty."

"Anyone over twenty-five is collecting pension. What you gotta do is make the scene with us young guys." Trent aimed his finger at his sculpted chest hugged by a t-shirt.

"Keith also isn't a boytoy. He's a really smart guy. Smart enough to have a job part-time with the university, and full-time in the summer."

"Fine. He's hot. Ridiculously hot." Trent made the ogling eyes. "But I prefer my boys under twenty-five. Plus, those two are looking for someone to tag team. Not my thing."

"Tag team?" What was that?

"You're not on to them, are you?" Trent cocked his brow. His grin was sly.

"I don't delve into what's going on upstairs. It's their business, not mine." René shut his textbook and binder. He'd grab a bite to eat before the lunch crowd arrived. "Chunk's still—"

"Chunk's fine. You said he's enjoying himself. Digs his new co-workers."

True. Chunk was loving city life. He'd easily scored a job at a local restaurant as a junior line cook. He worked evenings and weekends, so they didn't see much of each other, even though they lived under the same roof. Right now, he was probably rising. He worked the four-to-eleven shifts on weekdays and four to midnight on weekends, with Mondays and Tuesdays off. Usually, he didn't get home until after one or two, depending on how busy the restaurant was.

"The guy's simply living it up until he starts school in the fall," Trent added.

Another truth, because Chunk would be attending chef school at George Brown. His parents were paying his share of the rent on the apartment, and he was banking the rest for school. His boss had even assured Chunk if he worked hard and performed great, they'd keep him on part-time once his classes started. There was a good chance for Chunk to apprentice as a chef after graduation.

"You gotta do some living, too. Isn't that one of the reasons why you're here?" Trent's deep baritone grew serious, something that rarely happened.

The guy was right, though. Reaching nineteen, the legal drinking age in Ontario, was a milestone. Bar-hopping was a rite of passage. "Okay . . ." René nodded. "For you, I'll go to Ice. But if I get caught—"

"You won't get caught. They'll take one look at your more than fine face and yank you inside. Fuck, you probably won't have to wait in line." Trent waggled his brows. "They'll see you as great for business and roll out the red carpet."

René shivered. "What does that mean?"

"You're a babe. They want hot studs patronizing their club." Trent shrugged.

"I think they're a lot better-looking guys than me in the city." Accepting compliments was always difficult, probably because from the moment René realized he was different from his buddies, he believed himself to be a misfit who had no right hanging with the popular crowd, or even the right to be popular.

"You're getting in. Watch and see." Trent stood. "I need some food. I'm fungry."

René also stood. Ice. They'd go next weekend. Moxy and Ian might not be impressed when he bailed on them for Friday night rehearsal.

"So Mrs. Ash said the University of York?" Billy sat with his feet up on the other seat in front of him. They were in the balcony. *Urban Legend* was about ready to flash on the silver screen.

"Yeah." Carla sipped on her cola. "She said once I nab my BA, I can also go for my master's. Even my doctorate. But I just want my bachelor's. It'll get my foot in the door. She said the best teachers are there. What about you? Have you thought about where you're going?"

"I'd have to talk to Mrs. Ash first." The silver-haired lady with the bluish tint to her bouffant was the guidance counselor. "Constable Oshawee told me to go for my bachelor's in criminology. He said if I ever want to make sergeant or detective, that's the route to take."

"Did he get his?"

"Nah. There wasn't anything like it back then. He told me all he had to do was take the training in Aylmer at the police college. He said it's different now. With my degree, I'd stand a better chance than the other guys applying. There's a law and security course offered by the college, but Constable Oshawee said having a degree is better. I think he's right. I might not want to always work for the *Anishinaabe* Policing Foundation. I might end up in the OPP or maybe the RCMP."

"The Foundation covers a big area." Carla set her pop on the floor. "You could end up working up north first before you get the head office like Constable Oshawee."

"I'll take whatever they offer me. There's a program they host every summer here. Constable Oshawee told me to apply and he'd put in a good word for me."

Carla's wide smile plumped her chipmunk cheeks.

"What?" Billy squinted.

"You." She slowly shook her head, still grinning. "Who woulda thought bad Billy and a cop could become this tight." She crossed her middle finger over her index.

Billy snickered. "Yeah. Guess so, huh? All those times he rode my ass, he ends up being the dude supporting me."

"I'm so proud of you." She leaned in and pecked his nose. "Where's the popcorn?"

The curtain rolled back. The blare of the music for the upcoming previews engulfed the theater.

"Right here." Earlier, Billy had set the tub on the other chair. He reached for their treat and placed the popcorn on the armrest between them.

"Maybe there'll be cannibalism. That would be super cool." She leaned her head on his shoulder.

Eh, why not? He wrapped his arm around her. "You would wanna see someone eat another person. But this is about urban legends. Maybe a *windigo* will show up?" He gave a *hehe*.

"I doubt it. Didn't Mr. Atatise say *windigos* are related to *Algonquian* nations?"

"Yeah." Billy had to speak a bit louder because of the previews blasting through the surround sound.

"This takes place around California . . . I think." Carla pointed at the screen.

The previews ended.

"Oooh. The *windigo*'s gonna eat'cha," Billy whispered into her ear.

"You're so funny." She poked his stomach.

"Get in your mouthful before the cannibalism you want so bad to happen starts. Don't think you'll want to eat then." Billy fed her some popcorn.

Carla munched away. "You know gore doesn't gross me out."

"That's why you're tops in my books. You could eat a ham sandwich through an autopsy."

"C'mon, even I'd get grossed out over that."

The smell of her shampoo was a delicious scent beneath Billy's nose. Sure, his heart still pinched, and he'd probably mourn losing René for a long time, but moving ahead had been the best decision he'd made. Carla was his best girl friend. If not for her, he would've sunk to the bottom of Lake Superior like a cannonball, never able to rise and claw his way to the surface.

Carla kept him buoyant. He had to take the plunge and tell her the truth. She could be trusted.

They stood outside the nightclub in the long line. The music from inside carried to the streets. Never had René been so stiff. Guys kept grinning his way. Some cast him lingering looks. Part of him wished he would've worn a thigh-length jacket.

Trent rapped with two guys ahead of them.

Standing out in the cold to get into a place that played canned music was on the moronic side. Yeah, René could understand if a great live band were on stage, but listening to a DJ spin records? C'mon.

One thing he was learning about Toronto, people loved queuing up to see if they could worm into a local hot spot. This was *so* not him. Maybe he should go home. They could be out here for a good two hours.

Just as René was about to tap Trent on the back of his shoulder, a burly bouncer ambled down the line. He'd snap his fingers at whomever piqued his interest, motion at the guy to enter the exclusive place, and then assess other potential dudes.

When the bouncer set his big hands on his strong hips, assessing René up and down like a chunk of meat, heat torched with annoyance claimed the back of his neck. The bouncer then nodded at Trent and a buddy he'd brought along.

"You three. Go on in." With that, the bouncer kept striding down the line.

"Whoa, we're in. I knew you'd do it for us." Trent yanked René's arm and hauled him along the line of hooting guys straight for the entrance.

The stiffness of René's muscles wouldn't cease. The red velvet rope was unlocked. He was pushed inside of the club to a small lobby where they could check their coats and pay the cover charge.

Two gorgeous guys around his age, who stood behind the counter, sent René mischievous grins. He stared at his boots, stomach churning. Shrugging off his jacket took all of his energy. He handed the leather coat over to the dark-haired clerk.

"Just what we need. A total hottie who isn't a twink." The dude winked.

Huh? What was a twink? René offered a weak smile.

"Let's go." Trent again yanked on René's arm and hauled him into the club, with Brenden already inside.

The smell of sweat shoved its way up René's nostrils. He fought the urge to cover his nose. Above him, disco balls reflected the blue and purple lights bouncing off the silver orbs. In raised cages, six dudes wearing jock straps shook their butts for the cheering crowd. On the upper tier, men lounged on the railings, holding drinks and watching the shirtless dancers mobbing the floor.

The DJ was at the front of the club, spinning tunes.

Trent and Brenden dove straight into the melee. After witnessing someone pinch his new buddy's ass, René hung back. The periphery was the safest spot to be. If someone dared to grab his junk, there'd be a fight, and René wasn't about to get booted out of the club, let alone hauled off in handcuffs.

Staying on the sideline, he worked his way to the bar where attendants in black wifebeaters and tight jeans hurriedly fixed drinks. He set his hand on the sleek chrome counter. A guy glanced up. He was cute. Dark hair. Dark eyes.

"I'll be with you in a second, sweetheart. Don't go anywhere," the server told him. He handed a drink to another customer.

René kept his hand on the bar and glanced back to the mob. There was an awful lot of grinding happening on the dance floor. No doubt Trent and Brenden had thrown themselves into the fray. René made sure not to let his attention linger on anyone in particular. He wasn't about to lock eyes with another guy and send out the wrong signal.

"Okay, hot stuff, what's your poison?" the guy asked while

he used a rag to mop up the counter.

"A Labate Crystal." The same brand of beer René had drunk back in Thunder Bay, a welcoming neighborhood friend to make him feel at home in a place far from his former world.

"Gotcha." The server's smile was a suggestive invitation to hop between the sheets. He reached inside the cooler.

René shifted. The never-ending sea of bodies was generating major heat. Or maybe he was the one on fire. Sure, getting laid would be a welcome respite from jacking off, but not when his heart belonged to Billy. If he was going to indulge in sex, his crotch demanded he save his dick for someone he cared about, so he'd better up the friendship he had happening with his porn mags to lovers.

"Here you go. One Labate Crystal. I don't get that request too often. Are you from around here?" The server flashed his straight teeth. There was the tiniest gap between the front two that were a nice long rectangular shape.

"No." René pushed a five-dollar bill across the counter. "I'm here for school." Oh shit, he was supposed to be nineteen. "University."

"Uni, huh?" The server leaned in. "What'cha taking? I'm going to York. Right now I'm in my second year for my undergrad in Civil Engineering."

"Music. Majoring in music for my under grad."

"Really? Gonna be a musician?"

"Already am." René tipped back the beer and sipped. The cold liquid rolled down his throat and unraveled the knots in his shoulders.

"Really? You in a rock band?" If the server leaned in any closer, he'd jump the bar.

"Yeah. I was in one back home. But you know how it goes. You graduate and move on. It's a trio. We started up about a month ago."

"A month?" The server squinted.

"It's when I reconnected with them. I . . . err . . . transferred from Lakeside to the T of O after the Christmas break."

"You are very new." The server had a cute smile to match his toothy grin. "The name's Juan." He extended his hand.

"René." René shook. The palm he gripped was warm but rough.

"René what?"

"Oshawee."

"Juan Sanchez." The server swiped at his waves of dark hair.

From the corner of his eye, René spied Brooks Avery sauntering to the bar. A young guy clung to his arm. If he saw René, for sure Brooks would tell Keith.

With spooky-like fingers digging into his backside, René whipped on his heel and buried himself in the mob.

"Wait, I never got your digits. C'mon back," Juan called out.

René never stopped skittering through the crowd until he came to the back of the club where round booths and matching round tables were situated.

His eyes almost flew from their sockets. Keith was in one of the booths, necking with a blond-haired guy.

René again spun on his heel. He had to get out of here. What Trent said was true. Keith and Brooks were in an open relationship, and probably manhunting for a threesome, or even a foursome.

A sour taste filled René's mouth. How could Keith allow himself to become involved in something that . . . was *weird* the right word? He set his bottle of beer on the first available table and bolted for the entrance. As he dashed for the doors of safety, he kept his head low, since he was taller than most of the crowd.

Once he snatched his coat from the hat check dude who

asked for his phone number, René rushed outside to the cold air that swept away the heat of anxiety pounding through his chest. He expelled the breath he held.

Back home, he'd never fit in because he was gay. In Toronto, he didn't fit in with gay people. His shoulders almost slumped to the sidewalk. At this rate, he'd never find where he belonged.

The only place he'd ever found complete contentment was with Billy. But he wasn't here.

CHAPTER FIFTEEN: PERFECTLY STILL

For a day Billy had fasted. His hunger pangs were beyond painful. Attempting a vision quest on an empty gut seemed impossible. After they'd gotten off the four-wheeler, Ned had directed them straight into the bush. Walking with Ned through the skeleton underbrush was like trudging through quick-drying cement. Dots were in front of Billy's eyes. His limbs threatened to crumble beneath him.

Not even late April's spring sun could cheer up the darkness sitting in his chest.

"We're almost there," Ned said over his shoulder. "How ya doing?"

"If there was a dirty ol' cheeseburger on the ground, I'd eat it," Billy managed to say through his heavy breaths.

Ned was forcing Billy to *bush walk*—making sure he didn't trample the leaves from last fall, or the branches and twigs *Biboon's* heavy breaths had scattered during his reign of winter terror. This sucked and took too much concentration.

"In time this'll be natural for ya," Ned assured him. "As easy as pie."

Pie. Blueberry pie. Apple pie. Any pie. Billy's mouth watered.

Carla had agreed to fill in for him at the video store. She was excited about his vision quest. She'd even begged to hear all about his experience once he was done. Of course, he'd told her he couldn't share what was revealed to him during his stay from Friday evening to Sunday night in the middle of nowhere.

Ned stopped in a peppering of naked poplar trees. "This is it."

Huh? There wasn't anything to look at other than an old log on the ground and a bunch of leaves from last fall, and more boring poplar trees. "Seriously?"

"Yep. Seriously." Ned glanced over at the stand of spruce a good hike away. "Normally, I'd get you some boughs to lay out your sleeping bag on, but since you're not a rough-it kind of guy, this'll suffice."

He unwrapped the tarp and placed it over a bed of leaves. "This is so your sleeping bag doesn't get wet."

He set down the jug of water. Then he tossed the sleeping bag on the tarp. "This is all ya get to drink."

Billy removed his backpack that contained tobacco bags to tie off, his sketchpad, his charcoal pencils, and an orange for emergency hunger he wasn't supposed to touch unless necessary. Something told him, though, Ned would be lurking about in case Billy needed him.

"Remember. The spirits like to play tricks. Don't accept the first animal unless it feels right. One time, a guy accepted a fly as his spirit guide."

"A fly?" Billy sputtered.

"Yeah. Wrong guide." Ned chuckled. He patted Billy's shoulder. "I'll see you Sunday night."

"Wait," Billy called out.

Ned turned his head. "What is it?"

Aw shit, he'd ask. "I don't know what I'm supposed to do."

"It'll come to ya. Trust me. The first time I came out here, I felt the same way you did. I thought Harvey, the guy who was helping me, was batshit crazy. But the longer I sat out here, I found out why I was here." With that, Ned was off, leaving as quietly as he'd made them approach the spot.

Billy fisted his temples. There weren't any sounds but the odd rustle of something in the leaves. Hopefully, a bunch of hungry wolves or coyotes wouldn't get curious.

To find something to do since he couldn't leave the spot, he spread out his sleeping bag. Each time this supposed *something* went off like a lightbulb in his head, he'd been instructed to tie off his tobacco, and keep tying them off until he formed a circle.

He shoved his hands inside his jeans pockets and gazed upward at the naked poplar trees. They reminded him of that crystalline entity from *Star Trek*.

Well, first he could summarize how he was doing after René had left. Then he could think about his pathetic mother. Their visits were stuck in a rut of Mom mumbling about recovery meetings and her illness. But she'd also smile, something she'd rarely done in the past unless drunk or high. Her dull black eyes shining like polished onyx whenever she gazed at him from across the visitation room had tugged at his heart. Just as quickly, he'd stomped down the feeling.

Out here, under the setting sun, he should assess the *why*. Maybe he couldn't take another rejection after René had upped and split. Maybe after all Mom had done, he feared she'd walk out the door as she'd done when he'd been a small child.

He sank to the sleeping bag. Was hardening his heart to her helping any? Leaves were scattered about him, so he picked up a few. They easily crumbled in his hand. He released them, and the brown pieces twirled to the ground.

Rustling came from one of the naked poplar trees. He glanced up. A red squirrel frowned down at him. The furry critter chucked and stomped its feet.

"Look, we're gonna be here together for the weekend. We'd better get used to each other. I wish I had some peanuts to give you, but I don't have anything but an orange."

The squirrel let loose a loud shrill.

Billy scratched his head.

More chucking noises came from the squirrel. The red critter continued to stomp its feet and even gave a tail flick Billy's way.

"Is that how I look when I get pissed? Hey, I'm doing my best to rein in my temper. I don't throw tantrums like I used to."

The squirrel shrilled again.

"Maybe you're my spirit animal. We're the same way. We get mad if shit doesn't go our way. We push and push until we get what we want. And we're territorial about what's ours." *Like René.*

He scooped up more leaves.

The squirrel chucked some more.

"You're not gonna stop until I split. I can't. I'm stuck here."

All he could do was watch the sun slowly sink behind the trees. This was going to be an awfully long weekend.

The darn squirrel rustling about and chucking poked Billy from his sleep. He yawned and stretched. The late April morning was cold on his face. If he got out of his cozy sleeping bag, he'd better engage in some jumping jacks. That would get his blood flowing. Ned had also said to drink water right away, whether Billy was thirsty or not.

He unzipped the bag and greeted the chill, which wasn't as bad as he'd assumed rolling out of bed might be in the outdoors. There was shelter here. The trees kept any kind of breeze at bay. He uncapped the jug of water and sipped. His mouth thanked him for the refreshing liquid.

Dawn was breaking. He had a squirrel to thank for being up this early.

Once he took care of his morning bathroom call, he did one hundred jumping jacks. Getting the blood pumping was important, but sweating was off the list. If he perspired, he'd freeze once he cooled down.

He drank some more water.

There. Done. He was up and ready to go nowhere.

Well, he could always sketch. He reached inside his backpack and withdrew his pad and charcoal pencil.

For maybe a good two hours he drew noses of different shapes. Long and thin. Wide with a thick bulb. Upturned. Downturned. Beak-shaped. This was getting boring, because the urge to draw René's long, straight but not too thin and not too thick nose kept attempting to control Billy's fingers.

Saturday morning. René was probably fast asleep. In the past, he'd always stayed under the covers if he didn't have to fill in for the opening shift if someone called in sick at the video store. His rising time used to be around ten or ten-thirty, if Anarchic Aggregation hadn't been rehearsing, before he went in for work at two.

Billy bowed his head. How could his life change so quickly in a matter of a mere three months? It was hard to believe René had left in January.

Sure, he was digging his closer friendship with Carla. Before they'd put their budding romance on hold, they'd played too many peek-a-boo games that everyone who was digging on each other played. Now, everything was in the open. They shared their feelings. Talked about what they'd do upon graduation.

The squirrel chucked. The furry critter stood tall in the tree, stomping its feet.

Billy set aside his sketchpad and pencil. What an easy life the tiny bugger had. All Napoleon—yeah, that's what he'd name the red furball—had to do was gather food, get mad, defend his territory, and find a mate.

Ned had said people made life hard. He'd talked about wants and needs. In the old days, needs were met. The people had focused on survival, working as a group to flourish. He'd also mentioned people's desires for their wants was what disturbed their inner peace.

Creator and the Great Mother met the needs of the people, while the people made a mess from ambitiously seeking their wants. Some girls wanted to be cheerleaders and became upset if they didn't make the squad, but their needs were met. Other girls yearned for popularity, but they were outcasts, but still, their needs were met. Some guys desired to play hockey but epically failed the tryouts, but their needs were met. Other dudes were horny to bang chicks but couldn't even get a girlfriend, but their needs were met.

Billy could go on and on about wants. Wanting to nab a top score on a test but only passing. Wanting to earn a scholarship but having to settle for community college. Wanting to be a babe but the genes said a big fat no.

Creator had given him a second chance. Before finding his way to Oshawee Castle, his needs had been met with a roof over his head, food to eat, and clothes to wear. Of course the food had sucked, but in the old days, Ned had mentioned surviving deep in the Boreal forest, where animals played hide and seek in the harsh winter and starvation was too common. This predicament had given birth to the *windigo*, a cannibalistic creature who possessed people and enticed them to eat their own.

Biboon, with his fierce breath of ice, was only doing his job during the long, cold winter, Ned had mentioned. Balance. Life must die for other life to survive or rise from its place of birth. But people feared death now, Ned had added. They opposed the natural circle of life, desperately searching to buy more time all because of their wants.

Ned had called the *windigo* the speckle of greed hiding inside of a person, the jealousy, anger, and grief waiting for the right opportunity to consume someone.

Billy stiffened. Had Mom fallen prey to the *windigo*? Had the terrible creature taken a hold of her? But she was free now.

Free from the ugly clutches of the vilest being to walk the hunting grounds of the *Anishinaabeg*.

Was the *windigo* sitting in him, feeding his pity?

He stiffened and grabbed at the leaves, his heart heaving.

That was why Ned had told Billy he must seek his vision. He'd been sinking deep into dark waters, ready to be swallowed, after he'd come so far to find his way to the red road.

Napoleon had come to Billy purposely. The furry critter — as instructed by Creator from the beginning of Turtle Island to teach the people — was showing Billy how to survive. If a mere wisp of a squirrel could live through a winter of minimal food, freezing weather, and cold silence, surviving was more than a possibility for him, too.

He just had to concentrate on his needs, not his wants. But dammit, his wants were too great. Ned had told him to be careful with wants. They weren't bad, he'd said. Wanting too much was what corrupted people.

As an example, Ned had used the new items the Europeans had brought over. Instead of wearing what the animals provided, the People began donning the pretty cloth material. The fur trade era had aided but at the same time had hindered the Ojibway.

Then the lives of the People had become unbalanced when the Canadian government forced the *Anishinaabeg* into treaties and stripped them of their culture once the residential schools had been implemented.

After they'd stuck them on reserves, the government took tons more land, shrinking their reserves of swamp and bedrock to the bare minimum, while possessing the goods of the Great Mother, such as minerals and farmland. Not need but want.

More reserves were flooded and destroyed to build hydro dams to power the cities for the white people, leaving the natives in the dark, moved to their new spots far from their flooded hunting grounds. Their animal counterparts, the true teachers of the *Anishinaabe,* had also suffered, forced to leave the manmade wetlands and find a new place to live.

Ned had called Mom a victim of colonization. Okay, Billy could try. Mom was making the effort. He was holding them back. To restore balance between them, he must put aside his anger and meet her halfway.

Billy finished his evening jumping jacks. So far, he'd tied off eight tobacco bags. Not too shabby for sitting out in the bush by himself. But his hunger couldn't be denied. His stomach had stopped cramping. He made sure to follow Ned's advice and forced himself to sip the water instead of guzzling back the refreshing liquid, anything to feed his empty gut.

He flopped back on the sleeping bag.

The days were growing longer. The sun was still up. From its position, maybe they were closing in on the dinner hour.

Now that he'd decided to give Mom a chance, he had to think hard on his education. Was he becoming a cop for the right reason? Did he sincerely want to help others? After many discussions with Constable Oshawee, the police officer had told Billy he'd be arresting or warning the same people, weekend after weekend. The same domestic violence. The same loud parties. The same punks who refused to listen and stay out of trouble.

Constable Oshawee had called the routine monotonous. But he'd been on the beat for twelve years. He'd also warned Billy about arresting friends, even family, if he worked in the same community where he grew up.

Well, by the time he was done with his schooling, he'd be twenty-three, more than ready to handle the people on the rez after finishing the last of his training in Aylmer.

As for the Oshawees, he'd learned to accept their decision. He didn't like the verdict, but he could accept the predicament his horny dick had put them in. They were his foster parents and responsible for him. If David Oshawee had gotten wind of what had been going down, he would've moved Billy somewhere else.

That meant no longer acting out in anger after René's kiss-off email. He hadn't done so to be cruel. Telling Billy to move on had probably hurt René terribly. Plus, he'd gotten the shittier end of the deal by having to move to a strange new city and meet new people. Not that making new friends was hard for René.

Billy curled up. For the first time he truly called out to Creator. *Help me. I'm scared. I'm scared of moving on. I'm scared of what this red road will bring.*

He was still holding tight to what he'd shared with René in his fist.

Help me. Help me release him and let him go.

The air was deathly still.

He opened his palm, and the morning's chill grazed his exposed skin.

Carla was hinting about junior prom. Guys had asked her, but she was keeping them on hold. He'd ask her to be his date. Not out of an *I'll show you* as he'd previously done after getting René's email, but because Carla deserved a wonderful night out.

Billy would bet this spot was where Ned came to spend time alone, even a night, or a weekend — the area was clear of underbrush. Even in his forties, Ned still sought his vision. He'd mentioned seeking his truth was a lifetime deal.

As for his spirit animal, maybe Billy was stuck with Napoleon, but his gut told him no. The red squirrel was simply here to guide Billy. He'd learned much already from the furry dude.

When he thought hard, his brain kept connecting the dots to Pumpkin, the stunning cinnamon bear of Thunder Mountain. He'd painted a mural in his bedroom to honor *makwa*.

He'd spent sheets of paper sketching the proud bear's formidable form. While other bears around here were black, Pumpkin stood out. He was different with his coat of fall colors bursting with the hues of red, orange, and brown.

Just as Billy was . . . different.

A partridge lurked in a brush of leaves nearby. It picked away, seeking food.

Billy tied off another tobacco pouch. His circle was almost formed. By the time Ned arrived tomorrow, it'd be complete.

Chapter Sixteen: Face the Dark

Throughout the weekend, Billy had dreamed the same dream. Hoyt was always present. The same for Olivia, who'd taken off for parts unknown after reneging on her promise to testify in court that she'd witnessed Hoyt beating on Billy.

In science class, Mr. McGee proclaimed dreams were the brain simply sorting out the emotions, events, and memories of the day. According to Ned, dreams were one of the ways the spirit world contacted the *Anishinaabeg* on Turtle Island — just as he'd told Billy eagles were messengers, also bringing news from a place he couldn't see or touch.

He rolled over on his sleeping bag. Boot heels crushed leaves. Ned's approach was purposeful, as if his former foster father wanted to be heard.

Billy sat up to darkness and Napoleon having disappeared, probably tucked somewhere safe for the night.

Every tobacco bag was tied off and circled Billy.

His hunger pains were at their worst, sharp cramps fisting his stomach.

"Heya, stranger." Ned pushed aside a few stray twigs that were arms and hands reaching out from the skeletal brush.

"Hey."

"Here." Ned dropped a peeled orange into Billy's palm. "Eat slowly. Very slowly."

"Thanks." Billy tore off a chunk and shoved the tasty fruit into his mouth.

"Ya gotta pause. Don't eat too fast. We're gonna build back

up your energy." Ned sat cross-legged on the sleeping bag. "I take it everything went fine out here."

Billy swallowed the chunk of orange and nodded. "Yeah. I . . . I'm still figuring out stuff, though."

"I told ya. Learning is a lifelong journey. The quest doesn't stop until your physical death."

"I see." Billy held up the orange. "Can I . . ."

"Go ahead. Chew slowly."

In between chomps, Billy said, "It was pretty cool out here. Partridges. A squirrel. The squirrel stayed the whole time."

Ned cocked his brow. "I see Creator sent you a teacher."

Delight filled Billy's chest. He had been right about Napoleon. "Yeah. He did. I'm glad. It was just me and a bunch of boring trees."

"Boring?" Ned cocked his brow. "I don't think the Standing People would take kindly to being called boring."

"Standing People?"

"Yep. The Standing People." Ned made a motion with his hand. "They breathe like we do. We call them people because the two of us are interdependent."

"I know that word. It means we need each other to live."

"That we do. What we breathe out, the Standing People breathe in. And what they breathe out, we breathe in."

"I never thought about it that way."

"They communicate, too. Ask your science teacher how they speak to one another. He won't be able to disagree with you."

Billy pointed at the stand of spruce a hike away. "What about them? How come they get to keep their needles but the poplar can't keep its leaves?"

"Now that is a good question, because the story is a true lesson. Y'see, there was once a chickadee who feared he'd succumb to *Biboon*'s wrath. The chickadee understood Winter Maker was simply doing his job as instructed by Creator. But the chickadee had a job, too. He had to survive and continue the circle of life by mating with his mate come the spring. So he asked a tamarack tree to help by allowing the little bird to sleep in its boughs of soft needles. The tamarack tree, being too proud and arrogant, refused the chickadee's request. A spruce tree overheard their conversation, and he told the chickadee he was more than welcome to hide in his boughs of needles to stay warm. Creator smiled on the spruce tree's generosity but frowned at the tamarack for not helping another of His creatures who needed to stay alive for the sake of his offspring, not for the sake of greed. So every winter, tamarack loses his needles while spruce gets to keep his."

"What about the poplar?"

"They must sleep. Leaves and needles are different. Whereas the spruce stays awake during the winter, the poplar has to hibernate like the bears do. Balance. Some still feed from the Great Mother, while others take their rest to make sure there's enough food during *Biboon*'s reign."

"I used to love when you'd share your stories during Ojibway Culture class."

"There's a reason those stories are passed down. To teach."

Billy glanced up at the resting poplars. "I'm learning lots out here. Now I learned more. I also made a decision."

"Yeah?"

"I'm asking Carla to the junior prom." Billy bit into another piece of orange. The sweetness of the nectar was heaven on his tongue. Once he was able to eat freely, he was going to wolf down twelve pieces of Chunky Chicken.

Ned's mouth moved into a straight line.

"What?" Billy gulped down another piece of orange.

"Ya sure about this? She's a nice gal. Not the kind to be a rebound girlfriend."

"No, you got it wrong." Billy shook his head. "We're friends. She understands and I understand."

"She knows about René then?"

"I want to tell her. I plan on telling her. But would that be wrong? I'll be outing René."

"Ya can tell her about yourself. Being two-spirit."

Yeah, Billy could. Levelling with her about his own sexual orientation was the right start to his new path.

"Pride, man. Pride." Trent set down his tray in the cafeteria. He spoke under his breath. "There's nothing like it. I'm talking a parade. Marches. Parties. DJs. You name it."

"Keith and Brooks already told me about it." Tension surfaced along René's temples.

"So are we going or not?"

The word sat on the tip of René's tongue, and he forced out the *yes*.

"I knew it. I knew you'd do it." Trent reached over and patted René's arm. "We're gonna have you fully out in no time."

"I don't know about that," René murmured. "I'm still trying to digest everything."

"What d'you mean? You're doing dinner every week at the restaurant. You went to a club—"

"But I'm not going there again." René buttered his roll. The memory of almost getting caught by Keith was enough to turn his blood to ice. "Not until my birthday."

"No problemo. Now what about prom?" Trent shoveled a helping of goulash into his mouth.

Thank fuck for the cafeteria specials, along with Keith and Brooks inviting René upstairs for supper a good three times a week. Because he had no clue how to cook, he would've been stuck with a diet of frozen food, which was okay to dine on now and then, but not the least bit appealing for every meal after growing up on homecooked breakfasts, lunches, and dinners.

"Prom?" René squinted. He'd always played at prom. Maybe he could talk them into hiring Madame Moxy. Their first true gig as a trio. "Hey, did the committee hire anyone yet?"

"Yeah, you know DJ Don is spinning the latest tunes."

René snorted. What did people have against live music? "Pass. I'm not into canned tunes."

"That's 'cause you're a musician. C'mon, it'll be fun." Trent snapped his fingers. "Hey, did you ask about Rockfest then?"

"Yeah. I talked to Brooks. He's down with it. But I can't afford to take any more time off this summer. It's my first real job."

"Real job?" Trent flicked his hand that held the fork. A smidgen of sauce hit the table. "You told me you've been working since you were ten."

"A paper route," René dryly replied. "Then at the video store. Those are hardly real jobs."

"Not true. My dad said those jobs prepare you for the real world, and all that jazz."

"All that jazz." A flicker of amusement warmed René's skin. Trent had such a cool way of talking. If anyone else pulled out the disco slang, he'd be laughed at, but on Trent, those seventyisms fit him like the t-shirt molded to his nice set of muscles.

"What's wrong with all that jazz?" Trent snickered.

"Nothing. It's cool on you."

"Maybe I should bust out a powder-blue tux? Ruffled shirt? Bow tie for prom?" Trent waggled his luscious black brows that formed a perfect arc over his black eyes. "My dad might have one kicking around in his closet."

"How old are your parents?"

"I told you. They married in seventy-seven when they were . . . uh . . . twenty-two and twenty-three. Then I came along two years later. They said there was no better time than the seventies. Lookit the resurgence of it. *Dazed and Confused,54, Velvet Goldmine,* and *Boogie Nights* are top choice movies. And everyone watches *That Seventies Show.*"

"I agree on *Velvet Goldmine.* Me and Billy rented it one night. It was really cool. The soundtrack kicks major ass."

"And it's about a bi and gay guy." Trent flashed his long white teeth. "I betcha you enjoyed that part when they're on the bed and Curt Wild's tossing Arthur Stuart's salad—"

René held up his hand. Heat flickered on his cheeks. "Yeah, yeah. You don't need to haul out the chalk and chalkboard. I get it. The scene was hot."

"Hot? It coulda burned down the theater." Trent let out a low whistle.

"Oh c'mon, they didn't show *everything.* They were merely simulating the act for the camera." René stopped from rolling his eyes.

"The act? Seriously? The act?" Trent leaned in and elbowed René.

"Fine. Screwing. Fucking. Banging. Humping. Is that good enough for you?" René couldn't help the teasing in his voice. The longer he hung out with Trent, the more comfortable he was accepting his gay self. No, he wasn't one hundred percent across the finish line yet, but at least he was in the race now.

"So prom?" Trent dug into more goulash. "Are we going or not? Never mind the canned music. I'm serious."

"Oh man..." René stifled his groan. "I'm not sure I'm ready for that."

Yes, taking Trent to the dance would be cool. They were good friends. Before Olivia had dropped out at sixteen, and before René had begun playing at the dances, they'd made a pact in grade eight to go to their senior prom together. Instead, Anarchic Aggregation had played at the big blast last year.

That day, a twinge of hurt had stabbed René because he'd

been unable to take Billy out for dinner, then to prom, and the big party. Instead, René had given a date-less Chunk a hand with setting up the gear so the rest of the band could take their girlfriends out for some chow. Afterward, he'd gone stag to the party, along with his main man.

"Okay, it's cool. I know Pride is gonna be a big enough deal for you. Remember what I told you?" Trent reminded him.

"Yep. Naked people dancing in the streets . . ."

Trent guffawed. "You say it like flaunting your sexuality is a bad thing."

"I'm not one to flaunt anything, least of all my sexuality. It's private. I'm private." René finally dug into his goulash, having finished his salad.

"I know." Bemusement flickered in Trent's gaze. He cupped his chin in his palm. "It's what I dig about you. As studly as you are, as hot as you dress, and even though you made quite the impression on my school, you're a really shy guy underneath it all."

"Maybe I am. Maybe I had no choice." René ran his fork along the soft macaroni.

"I get it. I do." Trent's voice deepened to his serious tone. "I was the same way until I came out. Once I could be myself, there was no holding back. But you, you're a naturally private kind of guy. It's not a matter of sexual orientation."

"You think so?" René finally shoved the helping of goulash into his mouth. His tongue savored the delicious meal of pasta, meat, vegetables, and sauce.

"I know so." Trent's straight lips deepened into a grin. "You know how I know so?"

"Nope. You're gonna have to draw me a picture." René chuckled. "S'okay, reach for the chalkboard and chalk."

"There's chemistry between us, but you haven't made a move yet . . ." Trent's cheeks were drawn in impishly to match his flirty smile. "Any other dude would've. You shoulda seen them at the club before you snuck home. I coulda easily had some fun in the john."

Shock surged through René like a bolt of electricity. "Uh . . . what?"

"You heard me." Trent's smile was more than a hint of wanting to get busy. He had a look of *I wanna suck your dick.*

Fuck, had René given that kind of impression? He'd better set Trent straight. "No. I wasn't trying to give off any vibes. You're my friend. Y'know? A really good friend. If not for you . . ." *I wouldn't even be trying to come out.*

Trent's smile vanished as if a bucket of water had soaked his Cheshire grin. "Come again?"

"You know how I feel." A smidgen of sweat rose on the nape of René's neck. Great, whereas he'd assumed they were only friends who admired one another's physical attributes, for Trent, the attraction ran deeper. How was René going to tactfully worm out of a mess his oversized foot had stuffed into his oversized mouth? "I . . . I told you about Billy."

"I see." Trent rubbed his finger along the outline of his lower lip. "I get it. You need time."

"Time?" René blinked.

"Yeah, time." Trent set down his fork. He clasped his hands. "Time to get over him. And I respect it. I wouldn't expect no less from you. It's what I find makes you major hot. You're a loyal guy. Any homie who snags you, they get this . . ." He aimed his index finger at René's heart. " . . . for keeps."

For keeps . . . The scent of the goulash no longer had a delicious appeal. What was Billy doing right now? Had he listened and moved on?

"Look at me, René." The command was soft.

The words were reassuring fingers kneading René's shoulders, working the tension and knots free. He glanced up.

"I'm serious about giving you time. You're worth the wait.

I don't wanna make you uncomfortable, either. 'Kay? You're a good friend, and I'm glad I met you."

"Thanks. Me, too." René held Trent's gaze.

Maybe there was hope he could move on. He'd asked Billy not to wallow in pity, yet René was swimming in the stuff. His friendship with Trent was the answer to finally getting on with his life.

He'd been granted a chance to start over. A new world, new city, and new friends.

Billy pulled up at the family services building for his weekly Thursday visit. Once he stopped at the reception desk to announce himself, he made his way to the visitation room. His heart didn't growl in anger or resentment. He was going to truly try meet Mom halfway.

He opened the door.

Mom sat in her usual chair, coffee cup shaking in her hands, cigarette dangling from between her thin lips.

First order of business — giving her a half-decent greeting. "Hey, Mom."

Her eyes bulged. She set down the coffee cup on the small round table. "H-h-hello." She cleared her throat. "You're in a good mood." Her normally gruff voice melted to a hint of velvet, what he'd heard in the past before her constant smoking had taken its toll on her lungs.

"Yeah, not too shabby." He plopped on the sofa where he always sat.

"How's school?" She always asked about school now.

"S'okay. Still kicking ass."

She blinked. For the second time, her eyes bulged. "That's great. That's great to hear. You seem . . . happy." She raised her shaky hand and puffed on the cigarette.

"I guess I am." He angled his leg and set his foot on his

knee. "How about you?" He unsnapped the tab on his root beer.

"You brought a drink." She pointed.

"Yeah." He sipped. Before, he'd come empty-handed, intent on putting in his obligatory visit and then splitting right away. "I thought it'd be cool to have something to drink while hanging."

She ran her tongue along her lower lip, still staring.

"I asked how you're doing."

Her eyes did another bulging thing, but a light smile softened the strong wrinkles. Her face even glowed and lost the yellow tinge. "I'm doing good. I . . . I . . . I'm going to meetings every night."

"Every night?" His eyes took their turn to do the bulging thing.

"I have been ever since I got out of rehab." She took another drag off the cigarette. "My sponsor gives me rides. When she can't, I take the bus."

"Take the bus?" Naturally, Hoyt wouldn't let Mom use her own wheels for her very own recovery.

"There's only one meeting a week here at the center. The others are in the city. They have some during the day, too. When I first got out, I went to day meetings, besides the evening meetings."

That was a lot of meetings. "Why do you gotta go to so many?"

"The more meetings I attend, the better my recovery. That's what my sponsor says."

What was this sponsor thing? "How come she has to pay for you?"

"Pay for me?" Mom's eyes darted back and forth in confusion.

"Yeah. She's sponsoring you."

"Oh . . ." When Mom's gentle chuckle rolled from her

mouth, the light laugh was something Billy hadn't heard in years. The giggle stroked his skin in a way he hadn't experienced in well over a decade. "No. She doesn't pay for anything. She helps me with the program. She advises me. We talk."

"I see ..."

"We talk lots about what's going on in my life." Mom picked up her coffee cup. This time her hand didn't shake. Neither did the other one holding the cigarette.

"You mean about your drinking?"

"Staying sober ..." Mom coughed. "It's more than not drinking. We talk about why I drank."

"Then why did you?" Billy remained deep in the sofa, leg still angled and foot on his knee.

"It'll take a long time to explain ..." A hint of regret lingered in Mom's reply. "I'm not sure forty-five minutes is enough."

"Okay. What about dinner one night? I can take you to wherever you wanna go." The words left Billy's mouth before he could think on them.

Mom almost spilled her coffee she was about to sip. "R-really?"

"Yeah. I'll talk to Mr. Oshawee before I leave. I think he's still in his office."

"Yes. I'd like that." Mom glanced down at her sweatpants. The strings of unwashed hair veiled her face. "I'd like that very much."

"Then it's a date. I have Tuesdays and Thursdays off at the video store. Take your pick."

"Why don't we go ... uh ... go tonight?" Hope filled Mom's gaze.

Tonight? Was Billy ready? Well, Ned would say there was no better moment than the present. And Napoleon had shown Billy all that mattered was the day. "Okay. Let's talk to Mr.

Oshawee."

Ned had been right about the vision quest. Finally, Billy was truly walking the red road. If he was walking the correct path, this meant everything had to go right for him now. Nothing bad could happen.

CHAPTER SEVENTEEN: HERE AGAIN

Chunk accompanied René to the airport. To avoid staying overnight anywhere when they picked up the truck, they'd take turns at the wheel.

"You fucking Ontario Scholar . . ." Chunk reached over and gave René a noogie.

"Chill, man. I won't find out until next week if I aced all my exams." Chuckling, René sent one back to his main man.

He'd written his last exam at two this afternoon. Officially, he was finished with high school . . . finally.

Come Monday, he was starting his new job. Brooks had suggested Tuesday, but René wanted to dive straight in and check out what would eventually become his career. Plus, if he gave himself a day off to recoup from the trip, he might sink into melancholy. That was a big fat no, not after how hard he'd worked to move on. He could only hope Billy was taking the same approach.

"And why're you razzing me, whipped boy." René snickered. He teasingly jabbed Chunk in the side of his gut. "I'm surprised you're here. For sure I thought you woulda copped out."

"Hey, buds first. Buds always come first." There was a glow to Chunk—not that he wasn't glowing before—ever since he'd started dating a waitress where he worked.

Shantelle was a pretty girl with ash-blonde hair and deep-blue eyes. Chunk was always raving about her mounds of curves being in the right spots.

"But only for you." Chunk thrust his finger. "Anyone else,

I woulda said no. I am totally digging T-O."

"I guess you are. You got a cool job. A great girlfriend. You're starting trade school in the fall. Life's a bowl of cherries."

"How 'bout you?" Chunk spoke under his breath. "You gonna give Trent a chance?"

René folded his arms and stretched out his legs. He crossed his ankles. A child whined because she had to sit still instead of being allowed to run around. "He wanted to go to prom. I told him I wasn't ready."

"Ready to come out or ready to date?" Chunk's question was quiet. Not often did he push for answers, much less dig inside René's head.

"I dunno. Both. I guess." René shrugged.

Chunk shifted as much as he could in the small chair. "Dude, I know it's none of my biz, and I'm glad you told me about you and Billy, but I hate having a blast when you're . . . I dunno. You're not quite you. Only when you're jamming."

Madame Moxy had lucked out and wound up playing a prom dance. The funny thing was, they'd found a singer at the beginning of May. Kenny, a local Torontonian who happened to wait tables at Ian, Jennifer, and Moxy's fave coffee house. Not only did Kenny have pipes to rival Sheldon's, but he also gelled with the band and even played guitar. He sure wasn't in Ian's league, but Kenny did a nice job holding down the rhythm.

"It's the only thing you're excited about. Are you sure this becoming a lawyer is the real deal you want?" Trepidation was in Chunk's question.

René stiffened. Ever since he'd taken Chunk into his confidence about his real reason for leaving Thunder Bay, his main man was no longer hovering on the periphery but daring to ask hard questions. "I guess I'll find out once I start work."

"Maybe you should do a vision quest."

"Uh . . . what?" René straightened.

"The last email I got from Billy, he told me he went on a vision quest. Your uncle took him."

"Oh that." René waved his hand in a dismissing manner. Sure, he'd previously supported Billy's search into their culture, but for the life of him, René couldn't get into hocus pocus bullshit. Science disproved everything related to spirituality. Science had an answer for everything. Well, almost everything.

Now Chunk was poking his nose into René's culture. Why did people assume just because a person's skin was red, they were supposed to be shaking rattles and praying to trees?

The question left René's mouth, and he didn't mean to bark, either. "Why?"

"Err . . . why what?"

"Why do you assume just 'cause I'm a 'skin, I gotta go native?"

Chunk's mouth dropped open. His face reddened. "Renny, I'm sorry. I didn't mean to—"

René held up his hand. "No, it's cool. It is. I shouldn't have . . ." He'd never gotten annoyed with Chunk before, much less angry. "I'm the one who should be apologizing." He faced his best friend. "Look, I know you mean well. I do."

"I just don't like seeing you . . ." Chunk twiddled his fingers. "I don't like seeing you this way. You're not really happy. I can tell."

"Dude, I've never been truly happy." René glanced to where another mother disciplined her child.

"Why? I thought you accepted the . . . the gay thing."

The gay thing? Seriously? If anyone else would've phrased his sexual orientation in such a way, they'd have received a stare cold enough to freeze their tongues. But not Chunk. The poor guy wasn't sure how to address the topic. Maybe if René was more comfortable in his own skin, Chunk would feel comfortable discussing what he probably thought of as a taboo subject.

"Yes, I accepted it." René kept glancing at the people plopping into the available chairs at their boarding gate. "I opened the door, didn't I?"

"Huh? What door?"

The face Chunk made resembled the emoticon René used for his instant messenger program. The colon for the eyes and an s for the mouth shape. "Figuratively speaking. The closet is what they call guys who aren't out."

"Ah, I get it. Opened the door, huh. Taking a look around?"

"Yeah. A good look around. Trent asked me to go to Pride. I said yes, but I'm not sure I wanna go with him, or Keith and Brooks."

"Who're you going with then?"

"Me."

"Only you?"

"Yeah." The board in front of them changed. Aww, crap. Their flight was delayed. They were supposed to leave at six.

"This is an announcement for passengers of flight number four-o-five departing for Thunder Bay. The flight has been delayed due to mechanical issues. Please note your new flight time of eight-twenty PM."

"Are they for real?" Chunk gasped.

Everyone at their gate groaned, bitched, and moaned.

Perfect. Just perfect. By the time they left Toronto, they wouldn't arrive until eleven-thirty.

René stood. "I'd better call my mom."

"Yeah, I'd better call my mom, too."

They grabbed their carry-on luggage and headed for the line of payphones they'd seen earlier while walking to their boarding gate.

Even though Billy hadn't asked for time off from work, Vernon Oshawee had told him to stay away from the store, making sure to add, "I know how tight you and Renny are. I'm sure you wanna see him." While Billy had been eating dinner with the Oshawees, René had called, informing them of the flight delay. Mr. O had hurried them to the airport anyway, a whole hour early before René's plane was supposed to land.

They waited in the cafeteria area that gave them views of the outside since windows surrounded them. Daniel and his girlfriend and Chunk's parents were present.

Billy kept squeezing his can of root beer. He had no clue how to feel about René's arrival. Five months had passed since they'd last looked each other in the eye, yet ten years might have well gone by, because their time apart was like forever.

"We should get going." Mrs. O hadn't stopped beaming the whole day. "I don't want to miss René coming in."

Everyone stood.

Billy was the last in line as they filed out of the eating area. They headed to René's disembarking gate. Billy lagged behind. For ten minutes he shifted his hips side to side. Then the announcement came over the intercom the plane had landed.

During the ten minutes' wait for the passengers to disembark, the pounding of Billy's heart grew into his throat.

People filed out. They greeted those who came to retrieve them.

Chunk appeared. A flash of black hair was behind him.

Billy held his breath.

When Chunk moved off to the side, René came into view. He must have passed on the barber shop, because his hair had grown to almost one length. Previously, his bangs had been long enough to tuck behind his ears, but the black strands rested a tad below chin-length now, with sharp spiky ends that hugged the oval shape of his jawline and elongated his already prominent chin. Since the temperature was warm, slouched cargo shorts wrapped his slim waist and hips. His rolled-down white socks over slides accentuated his already long legs. The collar to his short-sleeved shirt was flipped up. The hem untucked. A few open buttons allowed a peek at his silver choker.

Billy had taken Carla to prom. They'd had a great time dancing the night away to canned music. For dinner, they'd joined their friends at The Bistro. Afterward, they'd attended the party at some jock's house until two in the morning. The drum group had kept him busy. His job ate up his time. Studying occurred whenever he could grab a moment. Every Thursday he took Mom out for dinner. He was even debating on joining her for an open recovery meeting to learn more about the program that had changed her life.

Everything he'd worked so hard to accomplish after his vision quest fell to the floor and scattered like glass shards flying in every direction.

The intensity in René's dark-brown eyes never drifted to his parents or his brother but zeroed in on Billy.

The breath in his lungs faded. His heart, banging in his throat, collapsed to his feet. A familiar feeling surfaced—the urge to run to René and throw his arms around his wide shoulders.

The Oshawees might have put fourteen hundred kilometers between them, but what they felt for each other stretched across the vast distance and melted them together as one again.

René's elegant yet strong fingers whitened on the strap to his carry-on bag. His usual sauntering gait was a forceful stride, barreling straight for Billy.

The white noise died. A gentle thud filled Billy's ears. He parted his lips, his mouth aching to kiss René's once again, but he couldn't.

"Renny? Renny?" The booming voice of The General pierced the spell.

Billy blinked. He glanced at Mr. O, whose hard stare focused on his son.

René stopped. His gaze shifted from Billy to his father. A strained smile that never lit his eyes emerged. "Dad. Hey. It's good to see you."

Which was a lie, in Billy's case. The Oshawees had flown out on six business trips to Toronto already, and an additional two weekend trips.

"Little brother. Good to see you." Daniel stepped up and patted René's back. Another lie. Business had taken the elder Oshawee son to Toronto twice, so there was nothing to miss.

A flicker of anger curled around Billy's heart. He did his best to fling away the red-hot bitterness ready to consume him.

He'd been on a vision quest. He'd found his path. Nothing was going to goad him into behaving like a child throwing a tantrum from having true love ripped from his grasp.

Billy sat in the back of the crew cab of Mr. O's truck. The last time he'd done this, they'd driven René to the airport. Again, he was across the way, sitting in the same spot. All they'd managed was a *Hi, how you doing?* at the airport. The radio played. Mr. and Mrs. O chatted up front.

He snuck another peek at René, who was gazing out his window at the houses lit by the streetlamps. "Your mom and dad said you have to go back right away."

René's head turned slightly. His perfect profile vanished. "Uh . . . yeah. I start work on Monday." There was a stiffness to his words, the same tension creeping along Billy's muscles.

"Cool. My exams are done. I start full-time at the police building the first week of July. Your uncle's gonna hire a couple of students to fill in for me. My job'll be waiting once I go back in September."

"Yeah?" The darkness couldn't hide the pride in René's gaze. "Mom mentioned you were going on a trip with Uncle Ned and Aunt Ellen to her home reserve for the Sun Dance ceremony."

"I wanted to go. I really did. But the job at the police building only lasts until the end of August. I talked about it with Ned, and he said to wait until next year. He said working with Constable Oshawee will give me a good idea of policing and if it's really what I wanna do."

"Funny, Brooks said the same thing to me. It's why he's letting me work at the firm."

"Congrats."

"Congrats?"

"For finishing your OAC. You're done now. Starting uni."

"Yeah . . . I guess I am," René replied quietly. He shifted his gaze to the window.

Something was wrong. Very wrong.

They pulled up at the house.

"She's in her stall. I took good care of her for you." Billy pointed at the door, since Mr. O's stall was separate from Mrs. O's and René's vehicles.

"I knew you would. I wasn't worried." The overnight case was between them. René reached for the carrying strap.

"I bet you're tired. You probably wanna sleep right away." Billy wiped his palms on his pants.

"S'okay. I'm gonna have a cig first." René opened the door.

The Oshawees also got out. Mr. O blabbed, so Billy slunk from the truck and meandered from the garage.

There was no moon tonight. The sky was midnight black. Crickets sang. Frogs croaked. The scent of summer lingered under Billy's nose. He dragged his feet along the path leading up to the deck but stopped once he reached the top. The pool water was partially black instead of chlorine blue.

The General and Colonel probably wouldn't leave them alone so they could speak. Then again, maybe René might not want to talk. Billy slipped his hands inside his pockets. The air was on the stuffy side. Before leaving for the airport, he'd donned his favorite pair of shorts.

Mr. O unlocked the back door. "I imagine you're tired and want to sleep right away."

"What I need is a dart. I'll see you inside." A hint of finality was in René's statement, as if saying *don't argue with me*. He set down the overnight case, reached inside his shirt pocket, and withdrew his packet of smokes and platinum lighter. "I haven't had one since we arrived at the airport in T-O eight years ago."

Mr. O and Mrs. O glanced at each other. With stiff shoulders, they marched inside like a couple of low-ranking privates chastised by their drill sergeant.

"Billy?" Mrs. O called out.

"I'll be right there." Billy leaned his butt on the railing of the deck.

The back door quietly shut. Ten bucks they'd wait somewhere in the house. Probably the breakfast nook. Those two weren't going anywhere near the royal chamber.

"Well? You seeing anyone?" Why Billy started their conversation with that question was beyond him.

René was in the middle of taking a drag and coughed. He'd never blown a toke whenever they'd smoked a joint, much less choked on a cigarette before. "Uh . . . seriously?"

"Chunk told me you and Trent are pretty tight." Jealousy didn't simmer in Billy's chest. Why? He wasn't sure. Maybe after tucking the locket away and placing the ball officially in René's court, Billy had finally found some peace, instead of clinging to something tight he shouldn't have to. Or he could be outright lying to himself.

"No. We're friends. Nothing more. I heard you took Carla to junior prom." Jealousy didn't slither into René's voice, either.

"We've been chilling." Billy shrugged.

"How about your mom? How's that going?" A light breeze ruffled René's hair. Ever since he'd gotten off the plane, his familiar scent of crisp and clean had been teasing Billy.

"Pretty good. We're talking. Getting to know each other. Been out for dinner once a week."

"That's great. I'm glad to hear that."

Their conversation might as well be a scripted play, both nailing their roles of two guys who'd moved on, or maybe they were trying to convince themselves they had.

The itch of an ache in Billy's throat reaffirmed he never had — that he was trying his darned best to live his life, but the tiny hole in his heart could only be filled by René, whose cigarette was burning lower. Too soon, they'd be due inside.

"Have any parties yet?" René motioned at the pool.

René had thrown a few when he'd lived at home. Naturally, no alcohol had been involved, but the revelers had snuck off to the pool house to smoke the odd joint to liven up the bash.

"I'm having the usual gang over on Canada Day." Billy kept his hands in his pockets or they'd shake, because he was beginning to tremble.

There was a hint of shakiness to René's hands. He flicked the last of the burned-down cigarette into the tin can where he used to toss his butts when he'd lived at home.

Light came from the French doors in front of the breakfast nook.

"I guess we should get inside." Billy stared at the glowing ember in the cigarette can.

"Yeah . . . we should."

Chapter Eighteen: Major Lodge Victory

René sat quietly observing the meeting that had dragged on for over two hours. The legal jargon volleying back and forth went over his head, even after studying up on the terms.

His mind was wandering again. Rolling back a week and a half ago to his visit home. Of course Mom and Dad hadn't given him a moment alone with Billy after they'd stood on the deck. Sheldon, Vince, Eddie, and other guys from René's graduating class had stopped over to see him. By the time he got on the road at nine o'clock on Saturday night, Billy had long vanished to work, insisting he couldn't let someone else fill in for him again.

He'd expected laying eyes on Billy to hurt like a bitch. René still hurt. When did a person's heart stop aching after losing someone they loved? Yet, Billy's reconciliation with his mother had given René courage he didn't believe he possessed.

This weekend was Pride, and he was determined to go by himself, since all he had to do was walk out the door of his crib and he'd be swallowed in the craziness. Taking in such a big event alone was something he must do, so he could assess everything and then reflect.

Chunk was stuck working during Pride. He'd mentioned the restaurant made major coin then. The big event brought in tourists from all over Canada, even the States, and some flew in from Europe.

Now that René had his truck, Ian didn't have to retrieve him for rehearsal anymore. When he told his bandmates why he couldn't jam this weekend, they'd hear the truth from his lips—he was going to Pride.

If Billy could bite the bullet and embrace his new life full throttle, so could René.

Funny, everyone had assumed he'd saved Billy. People didn't have a clue. By saving a guy who'd once been heading down the wrong path, Billy had turned around and had saved René, too.

René kept thumping the bass drum. He held the sticks in his hands. Moxy and Ian set aside their instruments. They were in the basement of the rental house. As for Kenny, he'd bolted right away to clock in for the graveyard shift, but the other two could tell him afterward what René had to say. Jennifer should be home soon. She always brought back foot-long subs from a local fast-food joint where she worked from two till ten.

Courage.

He needed more than courage. Try a drink. A whiskey and cola was on the agenda. Rising from behind his kit, he headed upstairs to mix himself one. Ian followed him.

"You got the right idea. I need something, too." Ian slapped René on the back.

"Get me some of my wine," Moxy called out.

René opened the fridge to labelled containers and jars of food. Some said Ian and Jennifer. Others read Moxy. He grabbed the wine and cola.

Ian opened a lower drawer and retrieved a beer.

Once René fixed the drinks, he followed Ian back down the stairs. Hopefully, the liquid courage could get him to open his constantly sealed lips. Trent was right. Maybe René was shy.

Or maybe he'd spent his life holding so tight to his secret that living a double life had forced him to hide his feelings and thoughts.

He parked his butt back behind the kit. His smokes were on the small table he kept nearby. He reached for one. After he lit the cigarette and took a big gulp of booze, he blurted out, "I won't be able to make rehearsal this weekend." There was no other way to confess the truth, other than cold turkey.

Ian frowned. A normally easygoing guy, downturned lips didn't happen often on his face, unless music was the subject. "Why?"

"I'm going to Pride." The evenness of his voice and smoothness of his tone surprised René.

"The fag parade?" Ian squinted.

The viciously cruel word was the tip of a knife sinking into René's chest.

"Why you going to that?" Ian held his beer and swallowed back some.

"Because I'm one of those . . . *fags*." René gritted his teeth.

"What the fuck?" Ian whipped his gaze to an open-mouthed Moxy. Just as fast he fixed his rounded eyes on René. "You're kidding. Right?"

Sweat sprang up on René's back and the nape of his neck. A buzzing sounded in his ears. His bladder threatened to empty. "No. I'm dead serious. I'm going to Pride because I'm one of those *fags* you thought to call them."

"Whoa. Easy. Ren-Man." Ian held up both hands while still clutching the beer. "I wasn't razzing you. Okay? You're not a fag."

"No, I'm not a fag. I prefer the word . . ." René heaved in a big breath. "I prefer the word *gay*. I think they do, too. When I was at Ice, I didn't see any *fags*. I saw a bunch of men who prefer men there."

"Ice?" Ian rapidly blinked. "That's the fa — gay club."

René nodded. "I went there with Trent."

"Trent?" Ian's face whitened. "He's gay, too?"

"Yeah, he's gay. He's out. He's been a good friend." Where René was finding the courage to keep speaking, even though his teeth rattled inside his mouth, was beyond him.

"You two aren't . . ." Ian moved his index and middle fingers back and forth.

"Just 'cause two guys are gay doesn't mean they hook up. Do you hook up with every straight girl who crosses your path?" The fear was ebbing off René like the sweat running down his back and vanishing into his underwear. In its place was courage.

"Uh . . . no. *No.*" Ian reached for his own smokes. He fumbled with them. "I don't. And I . . . Renny, I just never expected this. Okay? Can you cut me a break? Please? This came out of nowhere."

Moxy was still staring, openmouthed.

"It's cool. It is." The courage that had been the size of a golf ball was expanding into a baseball.

"Does . . . does the Chunkster know?" Ian still fumbled to get a cigarette from the packet.

"He was one of the first people I told last March."

"L-last March?" Ian shoved the smoke between his lips.

"Yeah. It's when I told my fam the truth. Mom, Dad, Danny."

"D-does B-Billy know? You two were pretty tight."

Hearing his name was a pinch to René's heart. He nodded. "Yeah. He's cool with it, too."

"Oh . . ." Ian turned toward Moxy.

She finally peeled her gaze off René and fixed her attention on Ian.

The silence in the basement was sharp enough to pierce René's ears. With shaky hands, he picked up his sticks. "If you want me to leave—"

"No." Ian's reply came out so fast, the word was almost on top of René's question. "No. We're . . . you're my friend, man. We both dig . . . before I met you, d'you know how much I wanted to meet someone who loved music as much as I do?"

Grade nine. Music class. René had played the snare drum, while Ian had been on the tuba. Being back-beat instruments, Ian had sat just below René. They'd both hated their instruments. Learning to read music had been cool, but playing only a snare, when he'd been four years into drumming, had sucked. He'd pointed the band out to Ian—Sheldon on trumpet and Vince stuck on clarinet. Anarchic Aggregation had been born when they'd added Eddie, who'd been glaring at his French horn, three weeks later—all wanting to rock out, not join an orchestra.

"I did, too." René's reply was almost a croak. Their passion for their instruments and jamming was an electrical current of sizzling chemistry they'd experienced the first morning of music class.

"Renny, what he's trying to say is he doesn't give a fuck. And neither do I." Moxy wiggled her hips as she strutted over to the kit. She stood behind him and wrapped her willowy arms around his shoulders. Her lips brushed the top of his head. "And I'd still fuck you. Gay or not."

"Hah hah, you're so funny. Not." René tilted his head and accepted the sweet kiss on his lips Moxy offered.

He'd passed a major hurdle. His bandmates were still down with him. Maybe Kenny would also feel the same way. He was a Torontonian and had probably seen everything by the time he was ten.

Billy clutched his can of cola. He sat beside Mom in the back row of the stuffy room reminiscent of the seventies, having picked her up for the recovery meeting. His first one.

The jargon had messed with his head, and the same for the slogans. He wasn't sure what they talked about, but when they'd first arrived, he'd expected to meet crying people bawling in their coffee cups, not happy older men and women teasing one another, joking, laughing.

Sure, there'd been two people who'd huddled in their chairs, shaking, but the rest might as well have been kicked back in their living rooms, ready to enjoy some family time and a night of TV.

Everyone had greeted Mom, too. They'd given her hugs, while she'd proudly introduced Billy to the former pack of drunks. She'd called this a speaker meeting. Which simply meant someone from the group had gone to the podium at the front of the room and shared their drinking days story. Not concentrating on how much they'd drank, but how they'd changed because of the program.

Billy's eyes stung from the amount of cigarette smoke in the room that had turned the air blue.

"Remember. One day at a time. The program only works if you work it. And don't drink. Call your sponsor." The speaker, who'd announced himself as John R., winked at everyone.

The chairperson stood. She glanced over the crowd. "Can you help me close the meeting with the Lord's Prayer."

People formed a circle and joined hands. Billy grasped Mom's. A shiver of gooseflesh popped up on his skin, because he hadn't touched her in eons. Her palm was warm, a bit on the rough side, but comforting. The same palm that had kneaded the back of his neck as a child was again fingers softly digging into his shoulders, magically weaving him into a spell. Soothing. Relaxing. Beckoning him to acquiesce to the enchanting feelings and relinquish control.

The person to Billy's right grabbed his other hand.

Since he had no clue what the Lord's Prayer was or the

words, he simply listened to the former drunks say their chant to Creator aka Higher Power, as they called Him.

After the meeting, he met the sober people helping Mom keeping the bottle corked. They weren't weirdos, either. Nice older people. Friendly.

They left the church basement where the meeting had gone down and headed for Mrs. O's boss town car. That was another change in Mom. In the past, she wouldn't have accepted a ride. She would've screamed she wasn't going anywhere near what an Oshawee owned.

Mom even buckled up her seat belt after Billy told her if he wanted to earn his full license next January, everyone he chauffeured had to follow the rules. She didn't even complain. He couldn't remember when he'd last heard Mom complain after she'd finished rehab. She was famous for finding fault with everything, even blaming a broom she'd tripped over for her messed-up life.

"That was pretty cool." Billy started the engine.

"I'm glad you enjoyed it." Mom hadn't even complained when he'd told her she couldn't smoke in the car. "They have different meeting formats."

"Yeah? What kind?" Billy backed out of the parking spot.

"Oh . . . round table. It's when we all get to talk. Women only. Men only. Topics. Steps. That kind of stuff." She fiddled with her purse strap. "We . . . the program teaches us honesty. Honesty with ourselves. Honesty with others without hurting them."

"Hurting them?" He guided them down the street.

"Yes. We-we can't be honest if it means . . ." She glanced around. "If it means we'll hurt the other person."

"I don't get it."

"Say a guy is cheating on his ol' lady. He can't tell her . . . if he does, it'll hurt her. He has to . . . uh . . . live with his guilt and betrayal. Telling her he cheated when he was out on a bender . . . it's his problem. Not hers. Telling her to relieve his guilt is at her expense then, and not his. Am I making sense?"

"Yeah, you sure are." Billy gripped the steering wheel.

Shit, now he had a dilemma. If he told Carla the truth about him, he had to figure out if his confession was for honesty because of their friendship, or if he was trying to relieve his own guilt. But there wasn't any guilt in play, at least he assumed so.

From the beginning, he'd never wanted to hide the truth from her. He wanted her to know the *real* him. Not the fake him René had forced Billy to become.

"Mom. Five. Gimme five." Thanks to her, he'd made his decision. Damn, never in his wildest dreams had he imagined Mom could offer wise advice.

"Five? What for?" She laid five.

"'Cause you and your program helped me solve something."

"Oh? I did? It did?" Surprise was in her rough voice, and delight. She sounded on the verge of giggling.

"Yeah, you sure did." He couldn't help the warm glow expanding in his chest. He faced her, grinning.

She returned his grin with a big, beautiful smile of her own that produced a striking radiance to her face. Lately, the radiance was erasing the rough years of drinking. She was beginning to look like her former self, when his young buddies would razz Billy with *Your mom's pretty hot, totally MILF,* which had left him gagging.

Now, he wasn't gagging. He was proud to have a stunning mom, because he . . . loved her. Yes, he loved her. He'd always loved her. And no matter what she did, he'd keep on loving her.

He braked at the stop sign.

She reached over and touched his arm. "I love you, Billy." In the dark confines of the car, her voice had reverted to the shaky, unsure-of-herself, smokey gravel.

He laid his hand over hers. "I love you, too, Mom."

They sat by the pool. The Oshawees had gone into the city for dinner and a movie. With the sun still up at eight-thirty, Carla remained in her bikini, stretched out on one of the chaise lounges. Billy was in a chair, also in his trunks. They'd finished swimming fifteen minutes ago. The warm June weather was easily drying them off.

"I bet you're loving your new work hours, hey?" she said, more to herself.

He had René's previous summer hours of Monday to Friday from nine to five. But he had to go in for ten to ten on the weekdays to do the till reading. On the weekends, he went to do the x reading at two, and for close up.

"Yeah, loving them way better. I'll miss that place once I start at the police building." He sipped his root beer. For the past two hours he'd been trying to figure out the best way to start the conversation.

Wait, there was a way. "What'd you think of Rob Halford coming out this year?"

Carla shrugged. "Some weren't cool with it. Others were."

"I mean, how did you feel?"

"I dunno. It's his life. Y'know? His biz. Why should I care?"

"You mean it doesn't bother you the singer of one of the biggest heavy metal bands is gay?"

She shifted and lifted her sunglasses. "Billy, is there something you're trying to tell me?"

"Uh . . . huh?"

She propped on her elbow. "Why should you care if The Metal God came out or not? You're not even into metal anymore. Remember?"

"Just 'cause I found my music style doesn't mean I still don't dig metal."

"Then where are you trying to steer this?" She squinted.

Dammit, she knew him too well. "I figured if Halford came out . . ."

Her eyes narrowed, and her lips formed into an O. "Are you trying to tell me . . ." She slapped her hand over her mouth.

"Yeah . . . I'm bi." He held his breath. Everything in his body stood still—heart, pulse, and blood.

The color drained from Carla's copper skin. She no longer lounged but set her bare feet on the concrete and gripped the chaise. Her gaping stare ripped right into him. "Are you serious?"

Billy nodded. The heat from the sun was intense, but the fire seemed to come from within him.

"Does . . . does Renny know? Do the Oshawees know?" She kept sputtering.

"Y-yeah . . . th-they . . . th-they do."

"They don't care?"

"No . . ." Billy slowly shook his head. "They're totally cool. Same for Ned."

"And me now." She set her long, slim fingers on her chest.

"And . . . you. You're my friend. I . . . I didn't like keeping the truth from you."

"Is this why you wouldn't go out with me when we were crushing on each other?" She tilted her head. An *I get it now* flashed in her dark eyes.

"I . . . I didn't feel it was fair to date you unless you knew the truth." With shaky hands, Billy reached for his root beer.

"You're . . ." Her O-shaped mouth formed into a big smile, plumping her cute chipmunk cheeks. "You're the best guy I've ever known." She jumped up.

Before he knew what was happening, she threw her arms around him. Her soft skin melted along his. He was drawn against her breasts and into a warm embrace.

"Billy . . ." she whispered into his ear, her voice a loving caress. "Billy, did you expect me to hate you? Hate you for something you can't control? You're my best guy friend. I'd never hate you. Ever." She clutched him tighter.

He wrapped his arms around her tiny waist. For some reason tears brimmed in his eyes. Never had he met someone before who could except everything about him — faults and all.

Keith and Brooks had already left the house. The revelry coming from Church and Wellesley was so loud, the noise carried into the basement apartment.

Ten in the morning.

René stood at the full-length mirror in his bedroom. Cargo shorts. Wifebeater. Casual collared, short-sleeved shirt. Sandals. He slipped on his aviator sunglasses.

There was nothing keeping him here anymore. Earlier, he'd eaten breakfast, sipped a cup of coffee, glanced through some more books on law to help him at work, and smoked half a joint to calm his nerves.

He opened the door and stepped into the kitchen. Snores came from Chunk's room. His best buddy had gotten home around two in the morning, eaten, and gone to bed. He'd probably sleep until one or two o'clock, shower, and then head to work.

With purposeful strides, René closed the distance from where he stood to the back door. He stepped out into cheers, music, clapping, and chants. The parade must have already started. He strolled down the narrow walkway between the two houses and popped out on the sidewalk.

Gloucester was crowded. People headed for Church Street. There wasn't a parking spot to be seen.

Brooks had told René the parade didn't happen in the village, because that was where the main events were held. So

René started west to Yonge Street against the mob who were making their way east for the other festivities.

He gaped at the dress of people. Some half-naked. Chain mail, leather, rainbow-colored clothing, superhero outfits, speedos, drag, chaps, and G-strings . . . the list was endless. He was a complete dud in his getup.

The laughter of the crowd was contagious. He couldn't help the tugging of his lips demanding to grin. Pride. Yeah, now he understood. A light bulb snapped on. This was their week to shine. Their week for *normal*. Their week to tell the city they were taking over and making gay the new straight.

Couples held hands. Heck, three guys held hands. Whatever floated their boat, perhaps. Who was René to judge if consenting adults wanted to be paired into threes?

The trio of dudes flashed René big smiles. One winked. He gave them a teasing salute and kept walking as he passed them.

"Sexy," a deep voice called out.

Two girls were locked at the lips, leaning on a streetlamp.

"Sexy! Shades! Sandals! Cargo shorts!"

René stopped. Why was the trio speaking to him? He pivoted to the three dudes who'd also stopped and eyeballed him. They were outfitted in leather.

"First time?" the one asked.

René nodded.

"Enjoy yourself. We'll be over at the beer gardens if you're interested." The guy slyly smiled.

René wasn't offended. The freedom in the air swamped his lungs, pumped through his blood, and beat in his heart. "Sounds, cool. Checking out the parade. Later." He turned and strode down the sidewalk.

The wolf whistle from behind him sent a chuckle from his stomach up through his throat. Those guys were crazy, in a damned good way. Yes, he never should've judged Keith and

Brooks for engaging in an open relationship. They were honest with each other, and nobody was getting hurt.

He kept passing the strangest costumes until he arrived at Yonge Street. The sidewalks were crowded. Floats crawled by. The rainbow colors were out in full force. Some shaped into rainbows. Others made up by balloons. A flatbed trailer full of guys in jockstraps wiggled and waved at the crowd they passed. All René saw were white asses. Another float spelled out the letters l-o-v-e.

Although Brooks was on vacation during Pride week, like Chunk, René had to go into the office on Monday, but he had the weekend to enjoy himself. He found a place to stand in the throng of people and kept watching the floats crawling by.

If only Billy was here to experience this amazing event. Imagine holding hands like everyone else without fear of harassment or assault. Being respected. Being treated as normal. An equal in a world where heterosexual was the default orientation.

This was probably the reason why so many gay people flocked to live in Toronto's gayborhood. He was lucky to be one of them.

CHAPTER NINETEEN: IDIOT SUMMER

"Can I ask you something?" Carla leaned on the counter and folded her arms. She'd landed one of the positions to work at the video store for the summer.

"Sure." Billy hit the required keys on the keyboard to start the z reading. Coming here at ten to ten every night was a pain in the ass, but working from eight to four at the police building made up for the bogus shifts at the video store. Plus, Vernon Oshawee paid Billy to close up each night and do the x reading of the till on Saturday and Sunday afternoons.

"I know you haven't forgotten those gay rumors that were going around about Renny last year . . ." Carla began. " . . . so I don't have to start with the *do you remember?*"

Although Billy's breathing hitched, he kept rifling through the printout. He nodded.

"Renny sure upped and split for Toronto pretty quick. One minute he was back at school after Christmas break, and then — poof." She snapped her thumb and finger. "He's gone. Everyone thought it was cool he wanted to get a jumpstart on his schooling, but . . ." She gathered up the quarters.

"Billy, look at me." Her voice was a gentle command.

He kept staring at the paper.

"I'm not gonna judge you. I told you already, I'm glad you were honest. We're friends."

The reassurance in her words coaxed his head up and focused his gaze on her understanding dark eyes.

She touched his cheek. "Something happened between you two, didn't it? That's why he left. The Oshawees made him leave, didn't they?"

For a moment Billy's pulse points ceased.

"I always thought it was cute how you were stuck to him like glue. Y'know, big brother hero worship and all. But it wasn't hero worship, was it? Maybe it was at first, but it became something more, didn't it?" She kept her fingers on his cheek.

Billy wet his lips. Sweat broke out on his palms. He fisted his hands. "I can't . . . I can't level with you. I can't 'cause there're some things — "

"That's why you were upset when he left," she added. Her fingers now stroked his cheek in reassurance. "You were in love with him, weren't you?"

I'm still in love with him. "Carla . . . I can't — "

" . . . say anything to me because he's not out. Right? I get it. Don't worry. Your secret's safe. You know I'd never do anything to betray you." Her fingers left his cheek. She locked her arms around his waist. "I'm sorry. So sorry this happened to you." She gently moved his head to her shoulder.

Gladly, he nestled his head on the delicate but comforting spot. Even after he'd deceived her, albeit he hadn't wanted to keep everything on the down low, she was here for him.

"That's what you were trying to tell me at the Waffle Wigwam. Remember?" Her breath was moist on his earlobe. "The day I got mad and accused you of playing me. You weren't. You were trying to tell me the *why* but couldn't."

"I'm sorry," he murmured. He gripped her tiny waist tighter. "I'm so sorry, Carla. If not for René . . . gosh, if not for him, I'd . . ." *I'd easily fall for you, but he has my heart.*

"I know. And it's cool. We make better friends. Y'know?" She kept holding him close. "I love hanging. It's different than chilling with Bonnie and Meghan."

"I get it. I do." There were things he could tell Carla he wasn't comfortable speaking to Stuart and Andrew about, but with her, the words easily tumbled from his mouth.

He lifted his head off her shoulder and pressed his nose against her cute upturned one. "What would I do without you?"

"You'd be bummed. Admit it." Her chipmunk cheeks plumped. "And don't feel like you betrayed Renny by telling me. We can only hold things in for so long before secrets drive us crazy. I'm sure Renny has someone to talk to."

"Him?" Billy almost grunted. "He's got a zipper sealing his mouth shut."

"He's bunking with Chunk now. Maybe Chunk knows, but Renny told him not to say anything."

Billy squinted. Hmm, Chunk had thrown him a curious sort of glance at the airport in June. If René had told Chunk about them, this meant he was starting to chink away at the walls he'd built around himself.

"Are you taking your mom out for dinner again this week?" Carla untangled herself from their bear hug.

"Yeah. Tomorrow night. Hey, you're not scheduled then. Wanna come?"

"Sure." Delight filled her big eyes. "It's a date. I'm glad you two are getting along now. I really am." She leaned in and pecked his lips.

His mouth thanked her for the soft kiss that filled him with the fluffiest of cotton balls. Heck, he kissed her again.

Lights flashed in the window. Stuart was here. They were going to Gold's for coffee.

"Dude . . ." Chunk slapped René on the shoulder. "This is your time. Your chance. A guy doesn't take a girl out for dinner with his mom unless it's serious."

The noise of the cheering crowd had forced Chunk to shout. Not that René was paying attention to the band on stage at Rockfest. They were one of the unsigned groups that had won a contest to perform, and not a very good band, either, at least to his ears.

Ian and Kenny had sought out the mosh pit. Trent had gone to get more beer. Jennifer and Moxy had found a spot by the sound board and grooved to the music. As for Jagmeet, Abbas, and Fernando, they were lost somewhere in the crowd. Kyle had missed out due to work.

The music festival of one full weekend was packed. They'd managed to peg down their tents together, at least. Moxy, Jennifer, and Ian in one. Kenny, René, and Chunk in another. And Trent, Jagmeet, Abbas, and Fernando were squashed into the last one.

René should've deleted Stuart's email upon receipt, because his hunch had told him the message was about Billy. Of course his second cousin hadn't known the pain René would experience from reading the damned thing. Stuart was simply keeping René updated about the happenings back home. Kissing at the video store and taking Carla out for dinner to officially meet Mrs. Redsky was what any guy did with a girl he totally respected.

Trent wove his way through the crowd. He carried three beers. "Here you go, man. Drink up."

René took the cup. The line-ups at the bar were longer than usual because the servers were checking age of majority cards. The one thing René could thank the band up on stage for was taking a hose to the audience. Not that he'd gotten splashed, but he could use a soak down. The wifebeater, shorts, and flip-flops weren't doing their job of keeping him cool.

"Are these guys still playing?" Trent frowned. "Damn, they suck."

"We could do a better job." René slipped his cigarettes and lighter from his cargo shorts pocket.

"Why didn't you guys enter the contest?" Trent, like Chunk, had to holler.

"Still too new." Maybe they could enter next year. René lit the smoke. He had a nice buzz going on. People were passing joints along the line, and he'd taken a few tokes. He was on his third beer. This would be his last and he'd then switch to water. He didn't want to get wasted and miss out on seeing Our Lady Peace.

"Let's split." Trent made a face. "We'll be back in time for OLP."

"Sure." As much as René loved live music, standing in the baking sun for a lame band wasn't worth the sweat.

"You guys go on ahead," Chunk called out. "I'm gonna make my way to the front."

"Belly splash them in the mosh pit," René couldn't resist taunting.

"You got it." Chunk gave a thumbs-up.

"We'll be at the tents," Trent shouted.

Our Lady Peace went on at nine to close the first day of the festival, so they had enough time, since it was only eight in the evening. Two stages were set up, the headliners on stage A, while smaller bands played stage B.

René had never seen so many boobs in his life. Every girl in twenty was flaunting their tits. Too bad he wasn't straight or he could've appreciated the nice show.

"Having a good time?" Trent took a swig of his beer.

"Who wouldn't be?" The top bands on the main stage so far had been Finger Eleven and The Age of Electric.

After a good hike, they finally reached their camping spot. The area was quiet, only a handful of people in tent city the place had become for the festival. About four spots over, a guy was tossing his cookies. No doubt he'd miss the last show and be laid out stone cold in a few minutes. Why did people get too wasted at concerts? They missed the point of a show —

to breathe in the magic of music.

Trent plopped in one of the lawn chairs that were allowed at the site but not on the concert grounds.

René crawled into his tent to grab the insect repellent he'd need once the sun started setting. He'd slather some on before they made their way back to the festival.

"Whassup?"

Trent's laughter carried into the tent.

René glanced over his shoulder, since he was on his hands and knees, in the middle of unzipping the luggage he used for carrying onto an airplane. "What're you doing? I'm only gonna be a sec. I'm a wuss and hate getting bitten."

"Nothing." Trent stretched out across Chunk's sleeping bag. "Just wanted to get a good look."

"A good look at what?" Bug spray in hand, René sat back with his calves under his thighs on his own sleeping bag.

"Your ass, what else?" Trent quirked a brow and snickered.

The teasing answer produced a sheen of heat on René's skin. He'd never had anyone outright comment on his butt before. Sure, girls had hit on him in the past, even Moxy, but they hadn't been bold enough to follow René into his sleeping place.

With the way Trent was stretched out, elbow on the pillow, palm cupping the side of his face, and legs crossed at the ankles, the open invitation was louder than the music coming from the concert.

"Is that the beer talking?" René did his best to offer a joking rebuttal, even though every muscle tensed. He shook a cigarette from the packet.

"You know it isn't." Trent held his beer with his free hand. He raised the cup in a *cheers* kind of manner. "I told you how I feel."

"Yeah . . . uh . . ." René stuck the smoke between his lips.

Trent set his beer aside. He fastened his fingers around the butt end and drew the cigarette from René's mouth. "You don't need to light that." He set the smoke on the packet.

René tilted his cup and took a big gulp of beer. There was a swollen feeling to his throat. Trying to gulp down the drink took a couple of tries.

"I know you're still hung up on Billy. And I respect it." Trent shifted and moved in closer, close enough for René to pick up the scent of sweat after rocking out under the hot sun all day. "The thing is, he's not here. You get?"

What Trent said was true. René's ears understood the message, but his heart remained the same shriveled pea as when he'd left Thunder Bay in January. He continued to sit with his calves tucked under his thighs.

Trent reached out. He drew his finger along René's exposed knee. Skin on bare flesh after being denied another's touch for the last six months awakened a need buried deep in René. The circles Trent kept drawing while inching upward, slowly moving to René's thigh, sent the pattering of his heart into overdrive. The hairs on the back of René's neck stood at attention.

His crotch was coming to life for once outside of the bathroom where he took care of business a good three times a week. He wouldn't have to jerk himself off. There was someone here wanting to do the job. It'd be so easy to give in to the ache in his balls.

"Why not Kyle?" he murmured.

"I told you already. Just 'cause a guy is gay doesn't mean he finds every gay dude hot. Kyle's too young. Only going into OAC. We're both going into university."

Trent's words were hot on René's ear. His thick lips trailed René's neck, steaming his skin. The prickles of light stubble grazed his flesh. He shivered. This was a nineteen-year-old experienced guy, not an inexperienced, seventeen-year-old virgin. He gulped for air. This was no mistake. Trent had brought them back here for a reason.

A thick fog seemed to penetrate René's thoughts. No matter how he tried to reach for them to clear his head, he couldn't. Trent's big hand was on René's thigh, just below his knee. The silky sensation from the light massage left him shaking.

Trent kept offering light pecks. He was slowly creeping his way to René's chin, and shifting higher.

René held his breath. Trent's thick lips claimed his mouth. René stiffened. The thought finally pushed through the fog. A loud thought of *move back*. He did. Trent shifted to his knees. He was slightly above René now, his mouth still determined to claim his lips.

Billy . . .

But Billy had moved on. He was dating Carla, taking her for dinner with his mom. Building a new life as René had asked.

His mouth was being smothered with hot kisses. Trent's hand had returned to massaging René's thigh. Goosepimples popped from somewhere deep in him and pushed through his flesh. His heart was pounding in his throat. He couldn't catch his breath. He'd lost the last bit of oxygen when Trent's fingertips had begun trailing up his thigh. Never was he so aware of the hairs on his leg. The light brushing Trent lavished on him was a melodic song, coaxing René to lie back in plush velvet and let the heady sensations consume him.

He belonged in Toronto—a place where he could live a normal life in a neighborhood that welcomed gay people.

When Trent's tongue eased between René's lips, his whole body screamed with excitement. His mouth was being explored, feasted on. He licked back. The hint of beer and saliva was ambrosia to his taste buds. Trent groaned. His exploration became that of hunger, his tongue playing with René's in the most teasing manner.

René was guided up on his knees. He was drawn against

Trent's hard pecs. Their crotches melted together. Meeting Trent's hard dick almost bursting from his shorts gripped René with fear and exhilaration. Their kisses were no longer lavishing licks but deep probes of each other's mouths.

Trent's hand was on the small of René's back and inched lower. A roar filled René's ears. He was in deep water, treading for his life, and ready to cease the fight and let the refreshing liquid claim him in its deathly grip. If he sank, there was no turning back. He could never face Billy again.

No matter if they were kaput, he wasn't ready to sink. His heart hollered at him to fight the lust pumping through his veins. All he had to do was grab the life preserver.

He broke the kiss, panting, chest heaving up and down.

Trent's eyes flew open, and so did his mouth. "What is it?"

"I-I'm sorry. I-I can't." René wiggled back. He untangled himself from Trent's grasp.

"You're nervous?" Trent drew his finger along René's cheekbone.

Sure, René could lie, but a guy as wonderful as Trent deserved honesty. "No. Not nervous. I . . ." He clasped his fingers together. "I . . . before I do anything, I need time to get over, well, what I left in T. Bay."

A spark of pain reflected in Trent's dark eyes, but he nodded. "I get it. I do."

"You're . . ." René picked at the cuticle on his pinky finger. "You're too good of a guy to have his chain yanked—"

"I wish you'd yank something else on me." Trent's voice was low. He moved his hand up and down. Wistfulness was light on his words, and a smidgen of teasing.

René forced a chuckle. "Yeah, it'd be cool. It would. Don't think my nuts aren't hurting." They were. His balls were full and his schlong hard.

"I understand." Trent pushed back his dreads that had fallen forward. "I can even respect it. It's why . . . why I really dig you."

"I don't know what you mean." René tilted his head.

"Your loyalty. I told you before — when a guy wins this . . ." Trent tapped where René's heart lay. " . . . he gets it all from you. Every little drop. I picked up that vibe from the first time we met. Even when you leveled with me, I'm not gonna lie, I wanted us to be more than friends."

Trent sat back on his haunches. "The dudes around the clubs and restaurants, they only wanna get their rocks off. Y'know? I was jazzed at first, but now . . . it's old hat." He let out a low whistle. "Okay, you're worth the wait."

Heat spread across René's cheeks. "I can't give you a date when the timer runs out."

"It's cool. I know it's not gonna be until the fall, maybe. Like I said, you're that kind of guy. Go on now . . ." Trent's laughter never reached his eyes tipped downward. "The show's probably gonna start soon."

"You're not coming?"

"No. You go on ahead. I'll be there soon."

Rejection wasn't fun. Of course Trent needed a moment to reflect. This was René's signal to duck out. "Sure. I'll see you in a bit. I'm going to try make my way to the stage, if it's do-able."

"Gotcha." Trent winked. He raised his thumb and extended his index finger in his usual gun position.

René turned and crawled from the tent. Putting on the brakes should fill him with relief, not guilt. But guilt was present. Guilt for blue-balling a great friend.

CHAPTER TWENTY: I CAN'T FIGURE YOU OUT

"I can't believe we did it. Can't fucking believe it." Stuart flopped on the bed, chuckling.

Billy sat on the loveseat. For over fifteen minutes he'd listened to his buddy give the lowdown on getting to jump on top of Meghan. Personally, Billy wouldn't be offering up details if he'd done the deed. Sure, dudes in the locker room bragged about their hookups, but not him. Maybe he was a geek for wanting to keep intimate details private.

"I thought for sure I'd be ringing in the New Year as the only guy in the senior class who hasn't gotten laid. What an awesome early Christmas present." Stuart sat up. His grin matched a floppy-eared dog with its tongue hanging out. "Wait." His voice grew serious. "You and Carla are banging, aren't you?"

What the fuck? They were friends. Billy had enjoyed taking her to the latest horror flick, scarfing down some Chunky Chicken, or hitting the school dances, but that didn't mean they were slipping under the sheets. "Don't go there. Don't even go there."

Stuart cocked his brow. "When a guy says that, it means he's not seeing any action."

Thank fuck Billy could close down this conversation soon. He was taking Mom out for dinner that had turned into a two-nights-a-week event after she'd told him she loved him and he'd said he loved her. Mom's sponsor had even joined them a few times. Naturally, he continued to accompany her to the open recovery meetings. The people were tops in his book for saving his mother. He couldn't thank them enough for all they'd done for her, and for him, for them.

The phone rang. Although he didn't have his own line like René previously had, the Oshawees installed a cordless in Billy's bedroom so he didn't have to keep running down the stairs to answer or dart into their royal chamber done up in a massive four-poster bed, two walk-in closets, a sitting area with a couch, chaise lounge, TV, and two armchairs. The bathroom was fit for a king and queen with not only a separate jacuzzi tub but also a tricked-out shower, two separate sinks, and some kind of makeup place where Mrs. O painted on her face every morning.

Billy picked up the receiver that was out of its charger. "Hello."

"H-hey . . . umm . . . uh . . . I'm not feeling very well." Something was off in Mom's voice. She must be massively sick.

Billy clutched the phone. "What's wrong? Is it the cirrhosis? Did you need me to take you to the hospital?" Because Hoyt sure wouldn't, which was the reason why Billy had regretfully declined Mom's offer to come over for Christmas dinner, and also why David Oshawee had vetoed the suggestion.

But Mom and Billy had made plans to spend Boxing Day together. He'd already checked with the Oshawees to have Mom over for the evening in the basement where they could watch a movie, rap for a bit, and scarf down munchies he'd planned on whipping up. Then he'd give her the special present he'd bought.

"N-no . . . N-no. I-I-I n-need to rest. That's all. W-we c-can g-go another n-night."

Something was wrong. Very wrong. She was slurring, not

stuttering. Cold dread spread across Billy's chest and seeped down his spine. His head became a hollowed-out shell. He sank to the love seat. The bitter accusation flew from his mouth. "You're drinking again. Aren't you?"

"No. N-no. N-no. I'm drinking not."

"It's *I'm not drinking*. You can't even speak straight," he spat out. "Fuck you. Fuck you, bitch." He switched off the cordless as the stuffed-down hate he'd believed was finished reared up like the Devil rising from the bowels of Hell.

Stuart gaped.

"I need . . . I need to be alone." Trembling, Billy scrubbed his face and bowed his head.

She'd gone and done the unthinkable—and he'd been gullible enough to believe she'd really wanted to change. Everything had been a show for him and the doctor like she used to do with her false made-up face and stupid little outfit to con a man or men into buying her booze.

"Dude . . . oh hell. I'm really sorry." Stuart sank down beside him.

"Go. Go. Please, go." Billy kept his face buried in his hands.

In two days, René was flying in from Toronto, but Billy wasn't sure if he wanted him to know the truth, not after having spoken to him since June.

"When are you going to provide Trent with an answer?" Keith held one of the onboard complimentary drinks. Scotch and water. His leg was crossed over the other. Even while traveling he was primed—knit sweater, collared, pressed shirt, and dress pants.

René had an aisle seat. He didn't have a window to glance out. Not that there was anything to see but darkness at nine at night.

"I told him I'd call him. I'm only gonna be here for a week, anyway." Debating on whether to attend the New Year's Eve party at Ice as Trent's date had weighed on René's mind ever since he'd been asked.

Keith's light laughter was as rich and luxurious as his voice. No hee-hawing or guffawing for him. "May I assume you held off on accepting his offer because of Billy?"

Heat spread across the nape of René's neck. He glanced out the window of the airplane to a sea of black. "Trent understands. He knows I don't wanna jack him around. If we're gonna date, it has to move slow. I'm talking a turtle's crawl. It's why I told him I'd call him over the holidays. Plus, I got all this other shit going on."

"The first year's always difficult. I'm glad you gave yourself time to adjust. Many leave because they feel overwhelmed. University is much different from high school."

"I'm talking about the band. Auditions are in March." The mere thought of acing the audition and getting to play Rockfest in front of thousands of people gave René the shivers.

The band was going full steam. They were not only playing high school dances, weddings, and other social events, but writing songs and demoing them in hopes of landing a booking agent.

"Ah, Madame Moxy." Keith swirled the liquid in the plastic glass. "You seem to be at a crossroads between law and music."

René set his foot on his knee and attempted to angle his leg, but being stuffed inside a tube with seats bumping seats, he chose to simply keep his thighs slightly splayed. "Not really. I'm juggling both."

"True. But you're left without a social life." Keith stared straight ahead.

"It doesn't matter." René drained the last of the cola he'd ordered, since the plane didn't carry cream soda. "I like how—"

"Pardon my intrusion. As wonderful as it is to discover pastimes that allow you to expand your creativity, you can't forget about people."

"Who says I'm forgetting?" René stiffened.

"Aren't you?" Keith turned his head. His dark-brown eyes were quizzical.

René's knee involuntarily bobbed. "Fine." An attendant was passing by. He held up his empty cola glass. "Maybe I'm getting caught up in school and the band . . . a little too much, but he knows what music means to me."

"It's been almost a year," Keith kindly pointed out.

"I know. I know." René offered the attendant his empty cup. "Another, please." After thanking her, he glanced back at Keith. "I . . ." *I feel like Billy needs me.*

"He turns eighteen on the eighth. You have to trust Billy to make proper decisions for himself." Keith tapped his chin. "Or is it because he is turning eighteen?"

René gripped the arm of the chair. Of course Billy's upcoming birthday had intruded into his thoughts.

"Remember, he may be in his senior year, but he still has his OAC to complete."

"I get it. I get it." René didn't need a reminding on how they were at different stages in their lives. For almost two years the lecture had been shoved down his throat.

Because of his schedule, they'd left Toronto later than expected. Today was the twenty-third. Tomorrow was Christmas Eve. He'd be splitting on the thirtieth to attend the New Year's Eve party at Ice on the thirty-first with—if he said yes to the date—Trent.

He'd miss Billy's birthday.

Half an hour later, the pilot announced they were landing in ten minutes. While waiting, René couldn't stop squirming and fiddling in the chair.

He tried thinking about Chunk, who couldn't come home

because the restaurant had asked him to work over the holidays. His main man sure hadn't said no. Once Chunk completed his schooling, the restaurant was taking him on as an apprentice chef. Mr. and Mrs. Bradley were flying out after Boxing Day to meet Shantelle. Not that Chunk minded. He was feasting at his girlfriend's house on Christmas Day, having already joined her family for Thanksgiving and other special meals.

The plane landed. During the moment of disembarking, René's stomach gurgled. He retrieved his carry-on bag and followed Keith out to where Mom, Dad, and Danny, along with Mrs. Harlow and Keith's sister, stood.

René's gaze searched the crowd, but there was no Billy. Maybe he was working. Annoyance pounded at the base of René's neck. Billy could've asked Uncle Vernon for time off if he truly wanted to be present.

After receiving a hug from Mom and taking in her familiar floral scent, René motioned straight ahead. "We'd better get the rest of my stuff." He'd brought his presents along. They were wrapped and waiting in an additional suitcase.

Mom studied him.

Everyone else was too busy listening to Keith regaling them about the flight.

"He's . . . at work . . ." Mom held René's hands as people passed by them.

"Who's at work?" René attempted to feign ignorance while the intercom came on, asking a Mr. So-and-So to pick up the red courtesy phone.

"You know who I'm referring to." Mom seemed close to clucking her tongue. "He hasn't been . . . it's been going on for two days now."

"He's been holed up in his room?" René's concern ramped up to eleven.

Mom nodded. "We tried talking to him. He insists he's

shaking off the flu . . . But I know something's wrong. I don't know what it could be. He was doing so well. Good grades. Going to every school event. Involved in his cultural activities. Painting. Sketching."

Taking Carla out on dates René kept from adding. At least Billy's lack of presence didn't have anything to do with him. "I'll talk to him when we get home."

"Come . . . tell me how you're doing." She slipped her arm through René's.

The last time he'd seen his parents had been at the beginning of December when they'd flown down on one of Dad's business trips. There wasn't anything new to tell. "I already have . . . a million times."

Even if the parents didn't fly down, Mom always called, and he touched base with her on Sunday nights to inform her about his week.

The room seemed strange. Keith had likened being home to visiting an old friend. After having his own pad for almost a year, the bedroom René had grown up in did feel as if he was stopping in to check in on an old buddy. Even unpacking his clothes in his former walk-in closet was a little off. The same for setting his toiletries in his bathroom.

He'd already placed the wrapped presents under the massive tree set up in the living room.

All he had left to do was walk across the hall to check in on Billy, who'd gotten home from work and had gone straight to his bedroom.

René had changed into his sweatpants, t-shirt, and thick white socks. He opened the door, strode across the hall, and banged on Billy's door.

"I'm already in bed," Billy muttered. "I said I'm not feeling well."

René opened the door anyway because the missive was

probably for Mom. He stepped inside to the mural of Cinnamon Bear flooding the one wall. The lighting at the sitting area was off. Only the table lamp by the bed burned low.

Too many emotions choked René—pain, regret, joy, relief. He swallowed and forced his feet to walk across the room to the sleeping area where Billy lay huddled beneath the covers. His jeans and t-shirt were slung over a chair. His socks were balled up beneath.

"Hey." René spoke quietly. He sank on the edge of the mattress.

Billy merely blinked.

"Mom said you haven't been feeling well." René's tongue grew too big for his mouth. Maybe Billy and Carla had fought.

The silence pushed hard into René's ears. Okay, he was donning the boxing gloves and spinning backward in time when he used to give Billy a good push. "What's going on? Spill." And a big *whatever* to his lecturing tone.

A scowl spread across Billy's flat mouth. His eyes shifted to the side, zeroing in on René. "The hell do you care?"

Well, well. Misery hadn't completely consumed Billy. The one who'd captured René's heart had surfaced. "What's going on?"

"What else?" Billy sat up. He flung aside the covers. In the six months that had passed, his chest had completely filled out to hard, sculpted pecs—not that he'd been a skinny punk beforehand, but this wasn't a boy anymore.

René's eyes almost rolled out of their sockets. He had to tell himself to stay in the conversation and not let his dick interfere. "Care to elaborate?"

"What's there to elaborate on?" Billy snorted. He set his hands on the comforter.

His shoulders were the size of baseballs. His smooth brown skin was soft to the eye, but underneath were muscles meant to caress. René slapped aside the thought. He forced his gaze back to Billy's face. "Try me."

"Try you?" Billy again snarled. He gripped the sheets and then let go of them. "She's boozing."

René's stomach sank. "Your mom?"

"Who else?" The snap in Billy's reply almost bit René's hand.

"When? Where?" The building disgust kicked away the lingering lustful thoughts that had tried to creep into René's brain.

"A couple of nights ago. We were s'posed to go out for chow. Bitch called me half shot. Tried to say she was sick, but I wasn't buying."

"Is she still drinking?"

"Fucked if I know," Billy muttered.

Oh boy, she probably was. "Remember, the holidays can be hard on people. It's a tough time, especially if a person is trying to cork the bottle."

"Are you taking her side?" Billy's tone was incredulous.

"I'm not taking her side. What she did is downright shitty, but booze is tough to beat. Almost sixty percent of the rez is hooked on drugs or booze."

"I don't give a flying fuck about sixty percent of the rez. We're talking about that bitch. I can't believe . . ." Billy swatted the air. "No. Delete that. I can believe she'd turn around and knife me in the back."

Whenever Billy got this angry, he was attempting to hide his pain. René reached for Billy's hand and tangled their fingers.

Defiance blinked in Billy's eyes. He almost shoved his thrusting chin down René's throat.

"I'm sorry. I really am." Pain seeped across René's chest.

"Don't be sorry. And don't feel bad." Billy's chin remained raised. "I was a stupid idiot to believe she—"

"Hey . . . hey . . . hey." René set his finger over Billy's lips that were silky to the touch. "Don't be beating yourself up. You gave an honest effort. It's not your fault she fucked up."

"But it's my fault for giving her a chance." A sheen of moisture glazed over the disgust simmering in Billy's eyes. "For . . . letting myself . . . letting myself . . . letting myself love her again." His voice broke.

"C'mere." René released their hands. He drew Billy into his arms and clasped him around his slim waist.

At first Billy's muscles tensed, but then they relaxed. He rested his head on René's shoulder.

Time had stopped for them. Elation shimmied along René's skin. They could slip into the secret place when they'd been the best of friends. Mom and Dad hadn't stolen the connection they shared. He clutched Billy tighter.

Billy's own grip on René intensified. "I swore I wasn't gonna cry. I swore I wasn't."

"Sometimes we have to. She's your mom. She let you down. If my mom did that to me, she might as well cut off my balls." René spoke quietly into Billy's ear where a nest of warmth resided.

Billy sniffled. "I hate her, man. I fucking hate her."

René rocked Billy back and forth. Muffled sobs filled the room. He held Billy while he cried. But he belonged to someone else now — Carla. All René could be was a friend, and he'd be the best friend possible. Anything for Billy.

Chapter Twenty-One—As Long as It Matters

Today was Christmas Eve. A day Billy had once spent alone but didn't have to anymore after meeting René. Whenever he truly needed the guy, he magically appeared to ease the pain. Last night hadn't been any different. No words had been spoken afterward. René had simply held Billy until their tired bodies demanded rest. He'd been laid out on the bed, the covers tucked over him. Sleep had easily claimed him with René across the hall.

Funny, he'd undergone a vision quest and had spent the last year attempting to find his path. No matter which direction he took, the road led back to René. This was why he'd been honest with Carla. If not for her, Billy wasn't sure how he would've gotten through the year.

The door opened. René entered, still in his bathrobe and cotton pants. He held two mugs of coffee.

The bright sun outside the window matched the radiance inside Billy. He sat up. "Morning."

"Good morning." René handed over the mug. He claimed his spot from last night on the edge of the bed. "How you feeling?"

Billy sipped the welcome caffeine of whole milk and plenty of sugar—just how he preferred his cup of joe. "Better. Now that you're here." Maybe he should've refrained from adding the last four words, but he was done with hiding his feelings and tiptoeing around everyone. In two weeks, he was turning eighteen.

A smile erased the pucker of René's lips that had once been full of concern. He set his palm on the comforter. "I'm glad to hear that. Mom said you wouldn't speak to anyone. It really —"

"It's cool. It is." And it was. "How about you? How're you doing? Stu told me Madame Moxy's kicking some major ass."

The intensity of René's smile was brighter and had the same curve as a rainbow. "You nailed it. We're kicking major ass. Serious ass. Guess what's up for us?"

"What's that?" Billy sipped more coffee. Time hadn't moved on for them. The bullshit awkwardness back in June wasn't present.

"Auditions for Rockfest ninety-nine happens in March. We're gearing up for it. We want the gig." René's grin was big enough to produce those fine lines coming close to dimples. "When we went there in the summer, they had an amateur band opening. Fuck, we shit all over those guys. Easily. If bands like that can get the gig, it means we stand a good chance."

"Cool." The enthusiasm pounding through Billy's blood screeched to a halt. This was nothing but a pity trip. The pure bred pampered dog once again offering his filet mignon to the kicked-around rez mongrel who'd never stood a chance. "Well, I bet you got tons of friends to visit. Gotta brag about how well the band's doing, huh? I should get dressed." He set his mug on the nightstand.

"Uh . . ." René blinked. His face was a mask of shock.

Billy flipped aside the covers and reached for his robe. The corner of his eye didn't miss the stroking gaze René lavished on Billy's bare flesh. He stopped, stiffening. Had he assumed wrong? The flames in René's eyes were enough to melt metal.

"Maybe I should finish my coffee first." Billy scrambled for the mug.

"Oh . . ." René again blinked. He was a puzzle missing a few pieces.

"I . . ." Billy ran his palm along his thigh buried under the blanket. "I . . . I . . ." *Fucking say it. You got bigger balls than René, whose mouth is kept shut by a broken, rusty zipper.* "I . . . I'm glad you're back. It blows you're not staying for the full visit."

"I changed my mind. I'm not going back until the fourth. Classes start on the fifth. I just need to make a phone call." René's reply was cotton stroking Billy.

He shivered. "You-you are?"

"Yeah." René folded one lip over the other. He glanced to the window and peeked back. "That's if . . . y'know, you don't mind me sticking around."

"Huh? Why would I? It's your house," Billy sputtered.

"Cool." The sexy lines beneath René's cheekbones reappeared. "Did you have any major plans? Parties? Stuff like that?"

"There is a party. I promised Carla I'd take her—"

"Yeah, well, I understand." René stood faster than soldiers under the command of the meanest drill sergeant. "I should finish unpacking."

Now what was going through his head? Enough of this dance of two steps forward and one step back. "Cut it. Level, man. Something's ping-ponging around in your brain that you're not sharing."

"I . . . I understand. I do." Red seeped across René's face. "Carla's a great girl—"

"What the fuck? Not you, too." Billy slammed his palm against the side of his head. "Geez, what's with everyone? Why can't everyone believe a guy and a girl can hang and not a dime more? I told you over eight months ago we're only friends."

René slowly sank to the mattress, mouth open, eyes almost popping from his sockets. "Uh, what? Stu said—"

"That guy runs his mouth so much, he should go for his bachelor of journalism instead of occupational therapist." Billy scowled. "Do you seriously think I can get over you . . . us . . . what we had going, all because your mom and dad made us break up?"

"I . . . err . . . I . . ." Relief and disbelief at the same time consumed René's gaze. "I thought you —"

"I tried. I really did." Pain filled Billy's words. "I gave it my best shot."

"I did, too." René bit down on his lower lip. "You wouldn't believe how hard I tried. But . . . I kept telling everyone I needed time."

"What about your friend, Trent?"

A hint of pink coated René's cheeks. "He's been . . . he's been wanting to . . . well, be more than friends —"

"What?" Billy almost scrambled from the sheets, ready to toss on his clothes, drive to the airport, get on a plane, disembark in Toronto, and tell Trent to stay the hell away from *his* guy.

René held up his hand. "It isn't what you think. He's a great friend. He was there for me from the get-go. Maybe . . ." He gazed down at the coffee he held and looked back up. "Maybe the time apart did do us some good. I . . . it helped me figure out what I want. Fuck, I'm still trying to figure out what I wanna do. But there's one thing I do know — I couldn't get over you. Over us."

"Y'know your mom and dad are against us . . ."

"But that was only because they're your foster parents and you're underage. You're gonna be eighteen in two weeks." Hope was in René's declaration.

"Yeah, I am." Billy started trembling again. "I . . . I changed up my music. Your CD player was pretty pissed at me. Didn't you notice?"

René cocked his head. "What're you listening to?"

"Gin Blossoms. Goo Goo Dolls. The Cranberries. Hootie and the Blowfish. The Wallflowers."

Snickering, René nodded. "Hey, if you found your groove . . ."

"Eat it." Billy extended his middle finger. "If you call them chick bands . . ."

"You'll what?" René leaned in, smirking.

"I can't stand Rage Against the Machine, Fear Factory, Tool . . . I tried. I tried to dig them, but they're—"

"Freaking awesome," René finished, his lips still in a smirk. "What about you? What'd you find?"

"Lots." René stood. "C'mon, I need my morning cig. Mom and Dad said I can smoke in my room, but I have to stand at the window."

"You're gonna be nineteen. You'd think they'd—"

"Easy. They just hate the smell of smoke. They're respectful of the fact I'm turning the big one-nine."

They shimmied across the hall, both chuckling. Billy swore they were two kids racing for where the Oshawees had stashed the presents. He shut the door to the room and hurried over to the window where René already stood, lighting his cigarette.

Something happier than the sun outside flooded Billy's chest. Seeing René's room as it once was—laptop on the desk, jeans slung over the chair, textbooks spread out on the coffee table—came close to melting Billy into a puddle of mush. But this was only temporary. Come the new year, René would leave him again. At least this time they'd be together.

"So, about T-O . . ." Billy sat on the edge of the bed.

René blew the smoke out the window. "It sucked but also rocked. At Pride . . ." His eyes brightened. "I went by myself—"

"You did? Not with Keith and his roommate? Or Trent and the guys?"

René shook his head. "I wanted time alone. It was a big deal for me. And I found it really cool. Everything about Church and Wellesley. Locals call it the gayborhood."

"Gayborhood?" Billy snickered. "That's pretty neat."

"Yeah . . . it's aptly named. Everyone's out. And they behave like they're out. You see guys and girls holding hands everywhere. They're restaurants specifically for gay people. I ate at one once a week with Keith and Brooks. There's even a dance club called Ice where I—"

"You're not old enough to go." A flicker of jealousy appeared.

"Yeah, but it wasn't my scene. I dunno. It wasn't for me." René shrugged. "I left right away. Y'know how I operate. If I'm going to a bar, I wanna hear live music. Not that canned bullshit." Then his eyes shone. "Finally, I could be myself. My real self. I even told the band."

The floor almost opened up on Billy. "Seriously? Ian and Moxy know?"

René nodded. "I even . . . don't get mad. Please."

"Mad? Why?"

"I told Chunk about us. I—"

"I told Carla about us."

They stared at each other.

"Why'd you tell Chunk about us?" Billy squinted.

René flushed. He peeked out the window while sucking on the cigarette filter. "I needed . . . I needed someone to talk to. At the time . . . Keith, well . . ."

"What about Keith?"

"It doesn't matter. I wasn't comfortable talking to Keith. Chunk was there. Y'know? He's been my main man since grade three. I had to stop shutting him out. He was crazy about this girl at work and always sharing stuff about her. I realized it was time I started . . . reciprocating. I didn't want our friendship to always be one-sided. And that's what it was for the longest time. He deserved to know the truth."

Billy almost keeled over from shock. Maybe the Oshawees had been right. Maybe being apart for the year had forced both of them to take a good long look at themselves.

"It-it was the same thing with Carla for me. She's been there. Really has my back. She also wants to go to T-O. Be a dancer. I . . . I wanted her to know why we couldn't hook up when we first got to know each other."

A big smile spread across René's face. "Sounds like me and Trent. He's had my back ever since I moved. I wasn't gonna yank his chain. He's too good of a guy."

"So, you dug Pride? Dug the gayborhood?"

"I sure did." René's smile faded. "But it wasn't the same without you. When I was at Pride watching those couples hold hands, the first person I thought of was you. A person is free there. Everyone accepts them. Another thing, every color of the rainbow lives there. My buddies are all different nationalities. It's really cool."

"Y'mean no red and white like here?"

René nodded. "You'd like it there."

Just then Mrs. O hollered for René.

"They must be checking up on us." Billy turned toward the door.

"Maybe. Oh well . . ." René flicked his butt out the window. "It's our life now. They can't say anything." He left the room.

Billy leaned against the windowsill. René was right.

The festivities taking place in the house had squashed any more talking they wanted to engage in. After they spoke at ten, both had to have breakfast and then shower and dress for the party. Since Keith and René had flown in later than expected, a buffet was being served.

In the fall, Billy had gotten a new suit. He checked himself in the full-length mirror in the bathroom. ZZ Top must have had him in mind when they wrote *Sharp Dressed Man*. Now he wouldn't look like a scraggly teenaged punk as he had last year when up against Mr. Metrosexual. Instead of letting his bangs flop and spike over his forehead, he'd slicked back the top with some gel. Rather dapper, he'd say.

The door across the hall opened.

Billy darted from the bathroom and bolted from his bedroom. He met René and let out a low whistle. "Hot. Major hot."

"When'd you get a suit?" René's admiring gaze traveled up and down.

"Your mom got me one in September. She dug how I looked in my tux for junior prom, so she said it was about time I got one." Billy smoothed the lapels. "Pretty boss, huh?"

"Very." René arched a brow.

"When are we gonna tell your mom and dad?"

They strode down the hall.

René adjusted his jacket. "After Christmas. Maybe Boxing Day?"

That was when they had a nice meal of leftovers, and the turkey bones were boiled for rice soup. "Sounds like a plan."

Christmas music carried upstairs.

Billy followed René down to the foyer. To his right was a packed living room. Ned and Ellen were present, along with their children who'd driven in from Winnipeg for the holidays. Mrs. Harlow and her daughter sat on the sofa. Daniel and his girlfriend stood by the tree. One of René's cousins mentioned Vernon Oshawee and his family were in the dining room, enjoying the buffet. Everyone was taking turns eating.

The massive Christmas tree was lit. Red, green, blue, and purple lights twinkled from the icicles dangling from the branches.

For a moment, Billy's chest clenched. Mom was probably already drunk or halfway to getting loaded.

"C'mon." René set his hand on the small of Billy's back, as if sensing his discomfort.

Billy was steered into the living room.

"Merry Christmas." Keith held up his glass of eggnog. "It's good seeing you again."

"Good seeing you, too. Thanks for taking care of René for me." Billy reached out to shake.

Keith's thick brows furrowed. He shook. "Always a pleasure."

"René told me he enjoyed Pride."

"He sure did." Keith's brows remained knitted. "Did he tell you he attended alone? Such valor."

"Yeah. He said he wished I could've been there." Why Billy had to throw shade, he wasn't sure. Maybe he'd always feel a twinge of inadequacy around Keith.

"In due time you might. Have you determined your area of study for your post-secondary schooling?" Keith motioned at the bowl of punch. He led Billy to the table.

"Yeah. Criminology. My BA."

"There's Trent to consider." Keith filled a glass of punch.

Billy stiffened. "René told me they're only friends."

A light chuckle escaped from between Keith's lips. He handed over the punch. "I mean Trent University. I hear they offer a wonderful program, and the campus is in the GTA."

"What's the GTA?"

"Greater Toronto Area. Durham."

"Oh . . ." Talk about wanting the floor to swallow Billy whole. He took the punch. "Err . . . where's Durham?"

"About forty-five minutes northeast of Toronto." Keith fixed himself another rum and eggnog.

"We'll see." Billy sipped the alcohol-free drink. Shit, last year they'd let René toss back a few, and he was again, since he held a beer while yapping with Daniel and his girlfriend.

"Yes, there's still lots of time for you."

When Billy finished his secondary schooling, René would be done his sophomore year. Maybe there was a way he could talk him into transferring to Lakeside University. But René loved the freedom Toronto offered. He'd come so far with accepting himself as a gay man all because of the gayborhood.

Dammit, this meant leaving Mom in Hoyt's clutches. She wouldn't stand a chance.

"Penny for your thoughts." Keith tipped his glass toward Billy.

"Oh . . ." Billy licked his lips. "Sorry. I was thinking about my mom."

"Yes, I hear you two are having a wonderful time reacquainting yourselves." There was always an *ahh* to Keith's voice.

The back of Billy's neck pinched. He shrugged.

"Did you invite her?" Keith glanced around.

"Nope." Fuck it, everyone was going to find out sooner or later. "She's drunk."

The rich dark brown of Keith's irises seemed to darken and almost blend with his pupils. "I'm very sorry."

"It doesn't matter. She is what she is." Billy took a big gulp of punch.

"Does René know?"

"He was the first and only person I told. Now you know." Bitterness seeped across Billy's tongue. "I got her a present. I ordered it early. But it'll sit under the tree." He flopped his hand at the pile of gifts waiting to be unwrapped.

His heart tugged at the shiny red paper and golden ribbon with the matching bow on top. He'd bought the book because Mom's sponsor had a copy and loved reading the sobriety passages she swore helped her maintain a no-drinking stance for eighteen years. Hope had flooded him after he'd laid out cash for the present, fingers crossed with anticipation the book could produce the same magic for Mom.

If only the stupid, drunken bitch would read the damned thing. Now she wouldn't, unless he tied her in a chair and forced her to listen to him recite what was in the special pages.

"C'mon, I need a cig." René seemed to appear out of nowhere.

The guy had again surfaced when Billy needed him. "Sure. Let's go."

"What were you and Keith rapping about?" René stopped in the mudroom and retrieved a jacket.

Billy reached for his parka. "Mom."

"Oh man . . ." René threw his arm around Billy and guided them outside. "Fuck, I'm so sorry. I really am. If I could make her stop drinking for you, that is the one gift I wish money could buy."

Billy was drawn into a deep hug out on the deck. He laid his head on René's shoulder.

Chapter Twenty-Two: Something Wrong

There was only one gift left under the Christmas tree. The one wrapped in red with the gold ribbon and bow. At ten, Mr. O had settled in the chair, cup of coffee and plum pudding on hand, to begin calling out the names on the presents, a tradition the family had performed once the kids were born. Each time Mr. O said the name, the person would rise and accept the gift, and then return to their position in the living room to unwrap, while Mr. O set his aside for later.

Last night while they'd been chowing down on the buffet, Billy had told the Oshawees about Mom.

Mr. O lifted the last present, glanced at the name, and then set the gift Billy had bought Mom back under the tree. "I'm happy you're here again to celebrate another Christmas with us. Especially now since Daniel's engaged."

Last night Daniel had gotten on bended knee in front of everyone and had proposed to Paula. Of course she'd said yes.

"I'm glad to be here, too." Billy was. He forced his gaze from the lonely present and glanced over his own swag he'd gotten. More oil paints. Watercolors. Canvas boards. Brushes. Sketchpads. Charcoal pencils. Clothes. A gift certificate for Music Music to buy new CDs.

René's gifts were stacked a mile high beside him. He was going to have to borrow his parents' suitcases to get his haul back to Toronto. A new leather jacket. Boots. Pants and jeans.

Shirts. The latest boombox to roll off the assembly line. A new laptop for the Windows 98 operating system that had come out in the spring. There had been mention after he'd opened the present Billy could keep René's old one.

Mr. O cleared his throat. "You know how much people in the community suffer from alcoholism—"

"It's cool. It is." Billy held up his hand. He'd never interrupted The General before, but he refused to hear anyone try excuse what Mom did.

"No, it's not okay." Mr. O shook his head. He set aside his coffee and plum pudding. "You trusted her, and she let you down."

"It's not like it matters." Billy shrugged. "I'm gonna be eighteen. I don't need her now."

Mr. O rubbed his chin. "Renny still needs us, and he's turning nineteen. I think he would've been devastated if we'd told him to move out on his eighteenth birthday. Our home is always welcome to him. The same for Daniel. And the offer extends to you. Is that what you think?" His gaze was assessing. "On your birthday we'll tell you to find your own place?"

"No. I know you won't kick me out." Billy sighed. How to explain himself? For once his running mouth wouldn't get out of the starting gate. "She . . . she made me care about her."

"Of course she did." Mr. O's tone was fingers kneading Billy's shoulders. "She's your mother. I know this is hard to understand, and you probably heard it at the meetings you attend with her, but alcoholism is a disease, the same as cancer, or even mental illness. She can't stop it, but she can arrest it."

"That's it. She won't kick Hoyt to the curb." Billy threw out his hands. "I told you about Grace. Her sponsor. Grace told me for an alcoholic to succeed in the beginning, they have to be in a supportive environment, and Mom's not."

"Did you talk to her about Hoyt?"

"Yeah. I told her to boot his ass straight off the back steps." A scowl formed on Billy's lips. Yeah, he shouldn't have used profanity around the Oshawees, but he couldn't help himself. "She gave some lame excuse about already losing one kid to care, and she wasn't going to lose Hoyt."

"I think losing you bothered her more than she let on." Mr. O's voice remained soothing. "When a parent's deemed unfit to care for their own child, many feel they failed the biggest test of their lives. I know I'd feel like a failure if my nephew would've taken you from us."

Billy blinked. "You would've?"

"Yes." Mr. O nodded. "This is the very reason why we had to separate you two. If David had learned the truth, he would've accused me of negligence and rehomed you faster than I can eat a container of Chunky Chicken."

Billy had to stop his laughter from escaping. The General never joked around, but poking fun at himself said how much the top dog gave a shit and was trying to lighten the tense conversation. Chunky Chicken was something Mrs. O forbade because of Mr. O's diabetes.

"Nephew or not—he has a job to do, and he takes it very seriously. He's in charge of the well-being of minors. Our community's children. As the chief of this reserve, I don't expect any preferential treatment." Mr. O sipped his coffee. He'd turned back into his serious self.

"You never told Mr. Oshawee?"

"I did after the fact. I informed him of what occurred and how we dealt with it. I owed him that much. Honesty."

"He knows the *whole* truth?" Billy gasped.

From René came a sharp intake of breath.

"Yes. Just as he's your caseworker, he's mine, too. As I said, being the chief doesn't mean I am pardoned from following the rules."

"Wh-what did he say?"

"He was thankful how I handled everything before it became a . . . well, as Daniel witnessed, leading to a very big problem." Mr. O raised one brow.

"What about now? I'm turning eighteen." Billy glanced at a white-faced René.

Mr. O's shoulders caved. "I take it you two have . . . well, I guess you wish to resume your relationship?"

The saliva in Billy's mouth vanished. Everything was on the table. He peeked at René, who remained whiter than a ghost, but he did sit forward.

René reached for his coffee. "We're old enough now, Dad. I know you wanted us to have time apart, and we did benefit. We did."

"I know you did." Mr. O glanced at Mrs. O.

She was in her lounging outfit and slippers. A robe draped her slim form. "You both showed extreme maturity with how you handled yourselves by respecting our wishes." She sighed. "Honey, you're going to be nineteen in three days." Her gaze was on René. "You know I can't tell you what to do. But I would like to speak with you during Boxing Day dinner."

More rules, even when they were now of age? Billy would hear out his foster parents. Ever since he'd started living here, one thing he'd learned — they dealt fairly and squarely and were open-minded.

After the Oshawees had given their speech, they'd surprised them by announcing René could have his birthday present early and the gift was downstairs. When they'd entered the rehearsal room, a keyboard was set up. As part of his major in music for his BA, he'd selected to learn the keyboards for his performance study.

He sat on the stool, his fingers not quite as dexterous as his drumming since he was still learning. Earlier, he'd told Billy he'd chosen keyboards to aid in him in songwriting. The only noise made were the keys being struck. The music he was creating was fed through his earphones.

He could now quietly play at the apartment, Mr. O had informed them, beaming. They'd taken into consideration René's complaints about not being able to practice unless he was at the university.

Billy's heart tugged. He was back on the sofa — a place he'd stopped visiting after René had left for Toronto, because there'd been no point in coming down to sketch by himself. His tugging heart had nothing to do with René again receiving a top-notch present, but the fact his parents cared enough to listen, and had given him what he'd yearned for. Not in a million years would Mom do that for Billy.

There had to be a way to make her give sobriety a second chance. Goddammit, she'd given him the same hope when he'd been four years old.

Funny how at such a young age, he'd learned how to make his own milk from the powder and water, and then pour the mixture in the cereal bowl without spilling anything. Mom hadn't shown him, either. Hoyt had, because he'd been doing the same thing as Billy — fending for himself his whole life.

"What's wrong?" René reached for his coffee.

They were still in their bathrobes at one o' clock.

"It's cool," Billy muttered.

"No, it's not cool." René stood. "Let's go up to my room. I need a dart."

"Sure." Billy set aside his sketchpad and charcoal pencil. Strange how he'd been drawing a picture of Mom when the bitch didn't deserve a second of his thoughts. But he'd couldn't resist sketching her as he remembered her — sober while driving her to meetings and perhaps even happy.

Perhaps . . .

Because if she was sincerely happy, she wouldn't have

uncorked the bottle.

"Your mom . . ." René glanced at the sketchpad Billy had set on the coffee table.

Billy shrugged. "It sucks. I forgot to put a bottle in her hand. Let's go." He huffed to the door.

In a few minutes they were upstairs in René's room, having stopped at the buffet in the breakfast nook to refill their mugs of coffee.

René had the window open and blew the smoke outside. "Maybe after the new year and all the parties are done, she'll go back to her meetings."

"As if." Billy sipped. "Ain't gonna happen as long as Hoyt's living there. The doctor told her if she doesn't stop, she'll die."

"Cirrhosis is as serious as it gets."

"No shit. That's why she quit. She was puking up blood." Billy shook his head. "When I first met with her, she was a fucking mess. She kept herself covered up, but she couldn't hide the color of her skin. It was gross. Like an alien. Greenish yellow. And so were the whites of her eyes. She had these spider veins on her nose. When I saw her in a t-shirt, they were all over her arms. Just covered in them. Her hair was thin. Like, really thin."

René wrinkled his nose. "Whoa, that's heavy."

"The thing is, the more she kept going to meetings, she was starting to look like Mom again. She was even wearing makeup. Mom was always into that stuff. Was putting on some jeans. Nice shirts and stuff. Doing her hair."

She'd looked like the woman in the sketch he'd been working on downstairs. Completely beautiful. A true *Anishinaabe-kwe* with her jet-black hair and the blue undertones, satin-brown skin, and razor-cutting cheekbones. Her once skeletal frame had begun filling out. Mom had always been thin, but now she was simply slim. Model slim like Kate Moss.

He couldn't leave her there. He couldn't get her out of his thoughts — as if she was calling for him. "We gotta get her. We can keep her in the guest room until she sobers up." Never had such determination filled his voice before.

René's mouth fell open. The smoke he didn't blow out the window filled where they stood, but he'd managed to flick the butt into the cold. "Wh-what?"

"I'm serious. Fucking serious. We gotta get her. I ain't leaving her there. He'll kill her. All he gives a flying fuck about is himself." His words were hot enough to start a fire. He whipped on his heel and barreled for his bedroom to change his clothes.

"Will you please stop? We're not even dressed. Or showered." René's slippered feet were hot on Billy's trail.

"I don't care." Billy yanked his sweatpants off the chair and donned them. "It's Christmas. I'm not leaving her lying there in her puke. I may have in the past, but not anymore. I know she can do this." He snatched the t-shirt, also slung over the chair.

"We don't even have wheels. How're we gonna get her here?" René was halfway out of the bedroom.

"Use your dad's truck. I'll ride in the box with her in case she pukes." Billy darted into René's room.

"This is nuts." René scrambled into his sweatpants, t-shirt, and socks. "She's gonna claw us to death if we try take her from the house. Remember last time? Outside the video store? She was piss mad. Slapping. Kicking. Biting. Scratching."

"I don't care." Billy dashed from the bedroom. His feet stomped along the hallway rug. If anyone tried to stop him, they were getting a bloody nose. He hurried down the stairs.

The Oshawees were in the living room visiting with a few of Rene's many uncles and aunts, since Mr. O had about a bazillion brothers and sisters.

Billy marched down the hall and through the breakfast

nook. He threw open the door to the mudroom.

René scurried inside. He lifted the set of keys belonging to the top dog off the rack where all the sets hung.

No longer did René's empty spot bother Billy. Soon, those set of keys would be back because the two of them couldn't bunk together in Toronto come the fall, not with Mom needing Billy. René would just have to suck it up and transfer to Lakeside University in September.

They both slipped on their coats. Billy bolted for the garage.

René got behind the wheel, muttering, "This is nuts. They're not gonna go for this. No way in hell are my folks gonna go for this."

"If they don't, then I'm moving out and back to that garbage dump. I'm not leaving her there with him. I'll move my stuff in and kick his ass to the curb." Billy shut the passenger door. "He know she's sick. He knows one more drink can kill her. I won't let him do that to her. He's hurt enough people."

René hit the button on the visor. The garage door opened. Since there were three vehicles in the driveway, he had to maneuver the big truck around them. Billy was thankful he didn't have to try that stunt. But René got them out and going like a pro.

"What if the door's locked?" René glanced at Billy and then back to the road. They drove down the cul-de-sac. "How're we gonna get inside?"

"We'll kick it open." Billy ground his teeth and stared straight ahead at the winter wonderland.

"That's called breaking and entering," René dryly replied. He stopped at the red sign and turned left.

"It's my house. It's hardly breaking and entering."

"Whatever you say. But if my cousin hears about this, you're gonna have to explain yourself. And you wanna be a cop." René shook his head.

"Spare me the lecture." Billy folded his arms. "I know what I'm doing."

"I'm telling you, Mom and Dad aren't gonna go for this." René drummed his fingers on the steering wheel. "The things I do for you."

"That's 'cause you love me." The anxiety coursing through Billy's veins diminished. He gazed at René. "Love means doing anything for the person you love."

"Yes, it does," René began slowly. "But it also means— Never mind. We'll do it." He reached across and entwined their fingers.

Billy gripped René's hand. They veered onto Wolf Street. His house was up ahead, a field over from Castle Oshawee.

René eased the big truck into the driveway. Mom's broken-down pickup wasn't present, but Hoyt could've taken their wheels somewhere, probably for more booze from one of the bootleggers.

Without waiting for René, Billy bailed from the truck. He dashed up the steps and tried the back door. Lady Luck was on his side. Not locked. When he stepped into the utility room, the most horrendous stench of booze, grunge, and puke hit his nostrils. He almost keeled over backward because his nose couldn't take the disgusting odor.

He bolted into the kitchen. There was empty beer, vodka, and whiskey bottles strewn everywhere and on the table. Caked-on food was stuck to the dishes piled in the sink and all over the counter. Dirt covered the floor, along with beer cases full of booze-drained bottles.

A sharp intake of breath came from behind him. Mom's bedroom was off the utility room. He should've looked there first. Her door closed with a click, meaning she'd locked him out. He spun on his heel. René had vanished. For sure he'd followed Billy inside. Seconds ago, he'd heard René's boots quietly moving along the floor.

What the hell was going on? "Hey," he called out. He banged on Mom's door. "What's going on?"

"Billy . . . please . . . just . . . just . . . give me a minute." Begging saturated René's frightful pitch that was an octave higher.

Dread opened up in front of Billy, ready to suck him into its nightmare. Something was wrong. Very wrong. René wouldn't lock himself inside Mom's bedroom for any reason, unless . . .

CHAPTER TWENTY-THREE: STILL SOME ROOM IN HEAVEN

The coldest chill René had ever experienced ghosted his spine. Today's temperature was around minus twenty-five Celsius, and the awful icy wind seemed to have blown its way inside Mrs. Redsky's room.

He crept to the bed where she lay on her side. One arm was flung behind her and the other stretched to the end of the mattress where her fingers curled into the blankets. Her knees were bent. Something resembling sticky tar and coffee grounds stained her brown pants and white t-shirt. The weird substance also rimmed her half-open mouth and coated the bedding, as if she'd wretched the stuff from her gut. A bottle lay by her skinny thigh. There was a blemished circle there. Probably from the contents draining out and onto the sheets.

Billy banged on the door. "What's going on? Let me in. Let me in."

"Please . . ." René called out. He moved onto the double bed and sank beside Mrs. Redsky, who never stirred. When he put his hand on her bony arm, warmth came from her flesh. Thank fuck she was alive.

He wrapped his fingers around her wrist and pressed his thumb down. His hope-filled heart dropped a splash. No pulse. He checked her neck, but nothing beat beneath her skin. Maybe he couldn't find anything because she was in a drunken stupor. He put his hand under her nose. No air greeted his palm.

"Please," he whispered. "Be alive. You gotta be alive."

He checked her temporal pulse point, but nothing beat. He leaned his ear against her chest, but nothing stirred.

Her parted lips and half-open eyes staring at nothing proclaimed she was dead. She'd probably passed an hour or two ago.

Billy's banging became frantic pounding.

René craned his neck. His heart kept plummeting. He had to call the police.

"Open it or I'm gonna kick it in," Billy hollered.

There wasn't a chance René was allowing Billy to fight his way inside. He stumbled from the bed and unlocked the door. Just as Billy attempted to shove his way into the bedroom, René set his hands on Billy's chest and shoved right back with all the force he could muster.

Billy stumbled backward. He was falling. At lightning speed, René reached out and grabbed Billy before he crashed into the empty cases of beer. He drew the man he loved against his chest, clutching him tightly while steering them into the living room.

Squirming, Billy frantically shouted, "What's going on? What's going on? Let go. Let go of me."

"No." René strengthened his hold on Billy by locking his fingers together. "Stay here with me. Please, stay."

Billy stiffened.

They were face to face.

Billy's lips parted. "She's . . . she's . . . she's . . ."

"I'm sorry . . . so sorry." God, how was René supposed to tell Billy his mother was lying dead in the bedroom? Seeing her that way still fucked with his mind. The creepy cold still ghosted him.

"She's dead, isn't she . . ." Billy blinked. He limpened.

René again retightened his grip. "I'm sorry. There's nothing that can be done."

"She's . . . dead." Billy kept blinking, never averting his spooked gaze anywhere else.

"I'm sorry. I'm so sorry." René palmed the back of Billy's neck and urged him to lay his head on a shoulder he could always count on to be there for him, even during his darkest hour.

"I . . . I gotta see her," Billy murmured, voice cracking.

"Please, don't. Please, don't. I'm begging you not to go in there. She wouldn't want it this way. She'd want you to remember her from the last time you saw her." René had never held someone so tight. He swore he'd break Billy in half, but he couldn't stop clutching at him.

Agony wound its way through René's limbs and fisted his heart. He couldn't stand how this had ended. Billy didn't deserve any more pain. René would rather be the one in this position than having to witness someone he loved facing such agony.

Billy didn't fight to release himself. He clutched René, his fingers almost clawing into his skin.

All René could do was hold Billy. He didn't have Uncle Ned's magical words to take away the suffering. Or Dad's logic to calm someone. Or Mom's soothing whispers to ease another.

He kept kissing the top of Billy's head, who'd buried himself in René's chest, his tears from his heartbreaking sobs saturating René's t-shirt and jacket.

They sank to the garbage-covered living room floor. While still holding Billy, René punched in the number to the police building. There was no use dialing nine-one-one because Mrs. Kabatay was dead.

When Warren's deep baritone came through, René breathed in relief.

"We need you at Billy's old house. Mrs. Kabatay's . . . gone . . . she's gone."

"I'll be right there," Warren replied in his deep, calm voice. "Call Mom and Dad right away. Please." René hung up.

Billy's tears had stopped. They stood outside in the freezing cold to let the police and ambulance attendants inside. They were waiting on the coroner who was coming from the city. The body couldn't be moved without Dr. Mitchell's consent, Warren had explained, after taking René's statement earlier.

Mom had her arm around Billy. She rubbed one of his biceps while he shivered and stamped his feet. René also continued to hold Billy. Dad stood by the yellow tape, since the police had secured the house.

Winter's reign never ceased, creeping in every nook and cranny about the reserve, a horrible ghost of ice spooking the back of René's neck.

The flashing red lights from the two police cruisers and ambulance bounced off everywhere. People stood outside their cribs. Some had been walking down the road and also crowded by the Redsky's house.

A beat-up truck weaved down the road.

René stiffened.

The pickup rolled to the snowbank and parked with its front tire and fender deep in the snow. Hoyt stumbled from the truck. His big boots sank in the snow. He swayed back and forth, attempting to vacate the mess he'd left himself in.

Olivia emerged from the vehicle with Hoyt and Billy's cousin, Nigel. When had she come back, and why?

"The hell's going on?" Hoyt slurred. He lifted his big finger. "Get the hell away from my house."

"You fucking prick! You piece of fucking shit! You killed her!" Billy ripped himself from René's clutches and darted straight for Hoyt.

René scrambled after him.

Mom was quick on his boot heels.

Dad bellowed something.

Just as Hoyt staggered up the driveaway, Billy launched his fist at his brother's jaw and sent the bastard reeling. Hoyt fell over. Olivia screamed and dropped to her haunches to attend to him.

Billy pushed her out of the way. He jumped on top of Hoyt and started throwing punches.

"Easy. Easy." René grabbed Billy and hauled him off Hoyt, which wasn't an easy feat. The Redsky brothers were built like bulls.

"Billy. Enough." Dad's booming order carried into the screams, hollering, and shouts.

René finally had his arms around Billy's waist and managed to drag him away. Billy's struggling forced René to use every bit of strength he possessed.

"You shut your fucking trap, you fucking pussy. I didn't kill anyone." With Olivia offering both her arms to stabilize him, Hoyt got to a standing position.

"Up against the cruiser," Warren told Hoyt. "I believe we're looking at driving under the influence."

"What the fuck?" Hoyt clenched his big hands. "I'm not doing anything, you fucking cocksucker." He hawked back a good helping of saliva and blew a mound of spit on the snow.

"If you don't, I'll charge you with resisting arrest." Warren's voice remained calm and deep. "Up against the cruiser. You can barely stand. And that's a nice parking job." He pointed at the truck half in and half out of the snowbank. "C'mon, let's go."

"Suck my dick, you fucking pig cop." Again, Hoyt spit.

"She's dead, you fucking loser." Billy remained in René's grasp. "Fucking dead, and you killed her."

"Who's dead?" When Hoyt swiveled to face Billy and René, he almost toppled over. He held out his arms to steady himself.

"Mom. What d'you think's going on here? Do you actually believe everyone stopped by to wish you a Merry fucking Christmas?" Billy struggled to free himself.

René retightened his grip. "Let's go. There's no reason for us to be here anymore."

"Go?" Billy squirmed and managed to turn himself. "Mom's dead in there." He shoved his chin at the house. "I'm not fucking going anywhere."

"M-mom's d-dead?" Through his drunken bleary eyes, Hoyt gaped at them. "What d'ya fucking mean she's dead?"

"Like I said, you dumbass. She's fucking dead." Billy huffed. "Dead. D-e-a-d. Dead."

"D-dead." Hoyt stumbled backward.

Olivia reached for him. She gasped and looked toward the house.

A fancy European-model car pulled up. René guessed the person was Dr. Mitchell, because nobody on the reserve owned that kind of expensive set of wheels. Not even Mom.

Hoyt's jaw slackened. Then his brows furrowed. He glared at Warren. "You're gonna book me on a DUI when my mother's inside there, fucking dead?" His tone was incredulous.

"And we need to question you," Warren added.

"Question me for what? I didn't kill my own mother, you cocksucking son of a bitch. The hell you think you are?" Hoyt shoved his finger into Warren's chest.

"You so did kill her," Billy shouted. He again tried to worm from René's grasp. "You fucking killed her."

"Touch me again, and you're also going down for assaulting a police officer." Warren didn't bat an eye. "Let's go. Into the cruiser."

"Leave him alone." Nigel shoved his way through the crowd. "His mother's fucking dead. My fucking auntie. You don't treat a man like this when he lost his fucking mom, you fucking toy cops. Always pushing your weight around 'cause you got no power anywhere but only on the rez. Even then, you gotta call in the big guns for shit like this 'cause you're fucking useless."

"You can't take him," Olivia screeched. "He lost his mother. He needs me." Tears brimmed in her blue eyes.

"You fucking son of a bitch. Fucking pussies. Fucking useless pigs." Fire roared in Hoyt's dark eyes.

Warren's partner latched on to Hoyt's other arm. A struggle broke out. Both cops had to drag Hoyt to the cruiser, while he kept cursing and thrashing to free himself.

"Miss, you'd better call a taxi and get yourself home," another officer said to Olivia. "This house is off-limits for tonight."

"C'mon, Olivia." This came from Nigel. "You can crash at our crib. The fucking Oshawees always gotta throw their weight around. They're the biggest fucking warts on everyone's cocks."

"I'm not going anywhere." Tears streamed down Olivia's face. She searched the crowd. Her desperate gaze landed on René. "Renny, you gotta help us. They can't take Hoyt. He has to see his mother. He can't go to jail. Make them stop. Please, Renny."

Help? After the way she'd backstabbed him and Billy, now she had the nerve to show her face after fleeing to parts unknown during the court case? "There's only one person I'm concerned about, and I'm doing my best to hold him off at this moment from kicking the shit out of you all."

René steered Billy to Mom's car that was parked on the road. Dad's truck was blocked in by the ambulance and a police cruiser.

Mom followed.

René set the cup of tea in Billy's trembling hands. All the way to the house he'd kept repeating his mother's death was his fault.

They were in the family room. Billy was huddled on the sectional with a blanket wrapped around him because his teeth wouldn't stop clattering and his knees wouldn't cease shaking, maybe from being out in the cold, or even worse, he could be going into shock.

Mom sat beside him, her arm around Billy. She kept whispering "I'm here" to him in her soothing voice that was a lullaby of pure cotton.

René sat on the other side of Billy. He draped his arm around Billy's shoulder.

"Do you think he'll be okay?" he mouthed to Mom.

Mom glanced at Billy. "Let me fix you something else. It'll help." She gently took the cup from Billy's still-shaking hands and headed out of the family room and crossed over to the kitchen.

Billy continued to shiver. "What am I gonna do?" He turned his big eyes on René. "What am I gonna do?"

"You're with me." René nuzzled Billy's cheek. "You're gonna be okay. We're all here for you. You're not doing this alone."

Minutes later, Mom came back with a fresh cup. "Here. Make sure and drink it all."

"I . . . I . . ." Billy bit down on his lower lip.

"Here. I'll help." René took the cup and pressed the rim against Billy's mouth. "Drink."

Billy sipped. He made a face. "There's booze in it. I don't want any booze. I don't wanna see booze around me again. It killed her."

At least he wasn't blaming himself anymore. "You have to drink it. It'll help warm you up and calm you." René kept his words soothing.

"It's a hot toddy," Mom reassured him. "A harmless drink. Please, take it. I'm making you another right now. The kettle's boiling. I'm making us all one."

Billy nodded. He sipped the drink while Mom returned to the kitchen. His hands had stopped shaking. He finally relaxed and nestled his head in the pit of René's arm.

"Keep drinking, baby."

"You never called me that before." Billy sipped some more.

"It's 'cause you need me. And I'm here for you." He kissed the top of Billy's head.

The back door opened and closed. Dad was home.

Then the front door opened and closed.

"Dad?" Danny called out. "I'm here."

"They're in the family room." Mom stood at the kitchen island, fixing the teas.

Danny appeared, gaze full of concern. "I came as soon as I heard. Damn, Billy, damn I'm sorry."

"I'm . . . I'm managing." Billy drank more tea.

Danny's gaze skimmed the sectional, but he parked his butt in the recliner. He removed his parka.

Dad strode in. His normally wide shoulders were caved. He rubbed Billy's knee and then sat in the other recliner.

Billy handed René the cup. He spread his palms and fingers over his face. His body trembled.

René set aside the cup. He drew Billy into his arms. "I'm gonna take him upstairs. Danny, do me a favor and bring the drink. Get Mom to bring the other one when it's done."

"Gotcha." Danny stood.

They were stretched out on René's bed. He puffed on the cigarette. The can of cream soda he'd brought upstairs — and had drunk — served as his ashtray. Mom and Dad wouldn't give him grief. He needed a smoke badly, and he wasn't about to leave Billy to go stand at the window.

They'd finished the hot toddies. Having two had done the job. Billy no longer trembled. He lay quietly, simply staring.

"You'll sleep in here tonight. I don't care what Mom and Dad say. I'm not letting you sleep by yourself." René petted Billy's hair.

Billy nestled his head back on René's chest.

The vision of Mrs. Redsky's corpse wouldn't stop flashing in front of René's eyes. He'd never seen a dead body before. Thank God she hadn't been in full rigor or he would have hurled. But the woman lying in the bedroom had been Billy's mom, which made digesting the horrendous experience a bit easier. At least Billy hadn't witnessed his mother's tragic death pose.

A knock came on the door across the hall. Great, Mom was checking in on Billy.

Moments later, a knock was at his door.

Billy's breathing deepened.

René carefully slipped his arm out from Billy and gently got off the bed. He was close to tiptoeing over to Mom and met her at the door.

They left the bedroom.

"I wanted to see how he was doing," Mom whispered.

"He's finally sleeping. He stopped shaking." René kept his voice low.

Mom wrung her hands. She glanced at the partially open door and then back to him. "Your father's not going to like this."

"Tell Dad it can't be helped. He needs someone right now. And he's too old to be cuddling with you and Dad." René folded his arms.

"We still want to speak to you both. Now isn't the time. Maybe a week after the funeral." She knitted her brows.

"What is it?"

"I'm counting. I'm trying to determine when you're due

back at school."

René stifled his gasp. "Mom, I can't—"

"We're talking about your education. As I said, we'll speak later." Mom touched his cheek. "Goodnight." She turned and headed for the master chamber.

Chapter Twenty-Four—Angels To-night

In two days the new year would arrive. René's big one-nine had been a bust. They'd spent the evening simply watching movies because neither had been in the mood to celebrate.

The funeral home had informed Billy he could hold the service on the thirtieth or the second. He'd chosen the former.

Since Mom wasn't traditional or religious, her casket was set up at the recreation center. The reserve had paid for the cost because Billy didn't have any money, and neither did Hoyt, or at least so he'd said.

Billy sat in the chair about ten feet from the casket. People he'd seen at the recovery meetings were present. If not for the men and women who'd taken Mom under their wing, she would've had a bare bones crowd. Only the family was present because Mom sure hadn't been the most upstanding citizen who'd contributed to the community.

Hoyt had been sprung to attend the funeral. Then he'd be escorted back to his cell because he was waiting on his hearing for the charges he was up against. No doubt the Sons of Satan would buy the same hotshot lawyer from Winnipeg to clear him of the charges.

Olivia was present. She clutched Hoyt's arm. He stared down in the coffin.

A growl sat in Billy's chest. The fucker had a lot of nerve swiping at his eyes, as if upset over Mom's death. Cousin Nigel ambled over and patted the *mourning* Hoyt on the back.

Get real. His loser brother wasn't upset. He now had the house, whatever contents hadn't been wrecked, and Mom's truck. The fucker was probably quietly rejoicing.

Uncle Henry meandered by, holding a cup of coffee in his shaking hand. Red-eyed and face drawn, he'd most likely come off a bender, since he'd been a regular at the house, always mooching booze if Mom had any. Aunt Betty followed behind. Her torn sweatpants and rumpled oversized parka said she'd also been on a bender.

Billy would've preferred to mourn in private, but people expected a send-off. He wasn't going to speak to any of his family. They could all suck his dick. If Mom had truly meant anything to them, they would've tried to help her instead of using her house as a place to booze and crash.

The only sincere people present were the Oshawees, Ned and Ellen Atatise, and the recovery group.

Even if Billy hadn't been fostered by the Oshawees, they would have come. The top dog attended every funeral in the community. He was even known to cancel important business trips to be present to support the families in mourning. And Mrs. O always accompanied him.

Mr. O stood at the podium to offer some words on Mom, since Billy had asked him to.

"The hell does he think he's doing?" The snarling question came from Hoyt, who remained at the casket, his fiery stare on the chief. "He caused all this. It's their fault. Him. His wife. And their fucking son. They killed her. They made her drink. If they would've left Billy with us, she wouldn't have gone off the deep end."

Billy stiffened. René gripped him by the elbow. The silent gesture was loud and clear—he wanted Billy to maintain his cool and not cause a brawl at Mom's funeral.

Hoyt shrugged off Olivia's arm and stormed over to the podium. "The hell you think you're doing?"

Mr. O had on his reading glasses and held a piece of paper. "I am readying to eulogize your mother."

"Yeah? That so?" Hoyt set his hands on his hips. "I know for a fucking fact she wouldn't want you speaking about her. She couldn't stand you and your fucking family."

Billy pushed off René's arm and stormed over to Mr. O and Hoyt. Boot heels clicking along the floor followed him.

Someone groaned.

"Mom let it go. She told me so." Billy stepped in between them.

Hoyt's face puckered in disgust. "The fuck do you know? You didn't even live with us, ya pussy."

"I talked to her when she was sober. Something you sure as shit didn't do. She told me her days of resentment were done. He has every right to speak."

"Listen here . . ." Hoyt raised his finger.

Constable Oshawee approached. "If you don't sit down, I'm taking you back, funeral or no funeral. Understood?"

Hoyt scowled. "See?" He thrust his finger at nobody in particular. "That fucking family's always gotta get their way. They're killing everyone on the rez. People drink 'cause of the royal family trying to control everybody." He stormed off over to a chair.

Olivia scampered after him.

Billy nodded at Mr. O, then turned to head back to his seat accompanied by René. At least the drama was over . . . for now. But man, when he became a First Nations constable, he was gunning for Hoyt. The fucker was going to pay.

For once Billy was glad he'd listened to Mrs. O and had worn his parka. The air outside was cold enough to freeze the fat off a seal's rump. To stay warm, he shifted back and forth.

They stood at the dug grave, which had taken a big effort from the diggers who'd had to light a fire first to unthaw the ground.

There was nobody to send off Mom. Everyone merely stood and paid their last respects.

Billy clutched the book he'd planned on giving to her. He hadn't been able to put the pages of prayers in her casket at the recreation center thanks to his brother. Some laid roses. At least there wasn't any wind present. He eased forward to where he'd finally received the love he'd wanted from a woman who'd made his life hell, and set the red hardcover on the big wreath.

He stepped back. René's ever-present arm came around Billy. Sure, everyone assumed he was being a best friend by staying at Billy's side, but he knew the truth — René was here out of love. True love.

The casket began lowering into the cold, hard earth.

Billy couldn't believe he had any more tears left in him, and they came, falling from his half-closed lashes.

"Oh God." Hoyt kept his hand on the lowering casket, head bowed, knee flexed. He brought his palm to his face.

Olivia rubbed his back.

"Step off, bitch," Hoyt muttered. His jaw clenched and Adam's apple bobbed. Clearly, he was fighting off his tears.

Mom was fully in the ground.

The funeral director glanced at Hoyt and Billy. "Would one of you care to do the honors?" He motioned at the shovel.

Billy stiffened and shook his head. He wasn't throwing dirt on Mom.

Hoyt nodded and took the shovel.

Billy turned and walked away. René kept his arm on Billy's shoulder. Mrs. Oshawee was at his other side, hugging him. He was led to Mr. O's truck.

Billy tossed off his tie. His stomach growled. He'd passed on the lunch spread at the recreation center after Mom's burial. He opened the walk-in closet. Once he managed to get his suit off and hung, he meandered to the bed and sat on the edge.

Was this how death operated? Find a person, hold a funeral, bury them, and then go home to normal? But there was nothing normal about his life, from the time he'd been born up until today. What teenager buried their mother? Lots, from what he saw on *Forensic Files*.

The door opened. René wandered in, also changed out of his suit and into his sweatpants, t-shirt, and white socks.

Jaw twitching, Billy glanced up. "I'm not sure what I'm supposed to do."

"What would Uncle Ned tell you?" René joined Billy on the bed.

"He'd tell me to feel the pain. He'd tell me death is part of the circle. He'd tell me not to run away from my feelings. He'd say we grow through these kinds of things."

"Then let yourself feel it," René murmured.

"I'm not sure I wanna *feel* anymore. It's all I did since she died." Billy rubbed his palms along his thighs.

"Let me put it this way. What do you think your cousins, aunts, and uncles are doing right now?"

"Drinking." Billy shrugged.

"Yeah. And when they wake up with a hangover, how're they gonna feel?"

"Probably the same before they got drunk." Billy gazed at René.

"There you go. They're not dealing with anything. Instead, they're creating the same vicious cycle. What did we do over the last year?"

"We dealt . . ." Billy set his hand on René's leg and rubbed.

"Yeah, we did. I couldn't keep running, could I? You kept telling me I had to face it, and I did."

"How am I s'posed to face death?" Billy blinked.

"By grieving, Uncle Ned would say. And be a bit thankful, although that's not what you wanna hear right now. Think about it, though. She was sober. You got to know the real her for a short time. Isn't that what you always wanted?"

Billy nodded. "Yeah."

"Did Hoyt?"

"Nope."

"Then who benefited? You. Remember, she had cirrhosis. There's no cure but a transplant. Unfortunately, not drinking was buying her time."

"But the doctor said some people live—"

"Some. Not all. And you don't know if she would've had two years or fifteen years if she'd kept going to her meetings."

"I know. I know." Billy yanked at his hair. "But it still fucking hurts. It hurts really bad."

René wrapped his arms around Billy. "I wish I could say something to take it all away, but I can't. And I hate seeing you this way. You don't . . . dammit, you don't deserve this."

Billy clutched René tightly. "I don't want you feeling bad." He spoke into René's t-shirt. "I'm just glad you're here and we're together."

"Me, too."

"What am I gonna do when you leave?" The thought of having to go on alone until he graduated high school was pure agony for Billy.

"We'll figure something out. Maybe I can take some time off from uni."

"I don't wanna interfere. I know how hard university is." He laid his head on René's shoulder. "I'm gonna be eighteen. Maybe I can go to Toronto with you? Finish my last semester there? Then take my OAC like you did?"

"Let's not talk about this right now. We still got a week to think things through." René's voice was reassuring.

Billy nodded.

René sat in the living room with no TV or stereo to create sound. Just what the doctor ordered. There was peacefulness to this part of the house, even though he didn't sit here and relax too often. Maybe the built-in shelves housing the collection of books were responsible for lulling a person into quietness. Billy loved sitting in here and reading. Or perhaps the fireplace, whenever one was lit, was soothing. Or maybe the shades of hunter green with rich dark browns created the right amount of color for a dab of mellowness.

Whatever was responsible, whenever René had to think, this room was the best place to be, because he had to figure out a way for them to be together sooner than expected. Before shit had hit the fan, he'd intended on finishing his first year in Toronto and then discussing with Billy their next step.

There was Madame Moxy to consider. The audition for Rockfest '99 was in March.

Mom entered. She carried two mugs. "How is he?"

René stretched out his legs and crossed them at the ankles. "Sleeping."

"You look like you have a lot on your mind." She handed over the mug and then sat in the matching chair.

"Thanks."

"I'm betting you're thinking about what you're going to do." Mom used her prodding tone.

René nodded. "Yeah." He tipped the mug to the refreshing taste of eggnog, sans the alcohol, on his tongue.

"Please remember you have your education to consider." She shifted.

"I know."

"You're nineteen now. Your father and I can't tell you what to do. Try making your decision with your head, not your heart." She let out a deep breath. "I know that's not going to be easy."

René almost snorted. He rubbed his face. "No, it won't."

"Also remember you can't fix him." She reached over and patted René's forearm. "No matter how bad we want to, we can only be there for one another."

Again, René nodded. "I wish I could. It's what I tried to do from the very beginning." He wiggled his toes that bumped around beneath his socks.

"Have you thought of when you're going back?"

René stiffened. Guilt created tension at the back of his neck. He glanced at Mom. "How can I leave him when—"

"I know it's hard. But you can return for Reading Week. It's at the end of February."

René rubbed the handle on the mug. "He-he mentioned coming with me to Toronto."

"Oh, René . . ." Mom gasped. "I hate to say this, and as I said, I'm doing my best not to interfere, but that is the last thing he should do. It's too much change for him."

"He . . ." René again curled and uncurled his toes. "He mentioned finishing high school there and then enrolling for his OAC. I . . ." He peeked at Mom through the fringe of his lashes. "At least we can be *us* there. Do y'know how much it killed me not to be able to hold him the way I wanted to at the funeral? I'm sick of playing his main man here."

"Then you're going to have to make a decision on how long you want to hide who you really are." Mom's voice firmed.

René whipped his gaze back to her. "Wh-what do you mean?"

"Do you like leading two lives, honey?" Concern saturated her stare.

No, he didn't.

"Keith does it." René bit down on his lower lip.

"Do you think Keith's happy?"

"It seems to work for him," René honestly answered.

"But . . ."

Keith was hiding Brooks by lying about their housing arrangement. Brooks never visited for Christmas or any other special event. The two also had an open relationship, which René had never questioned Keith about, but something was up with why neither wanted to commit, or maybe René's assumptions were wrong. Perhaps they were happy maintaining the status quo. Still, whenever they dined together, they didn't portray a happy couple in love. More like roommates with benefits. Try as he might, René couldn't bring himself to dig deeper, because — well, their relationship wasn't his business.

"I guess he's going stag to Danny's wedding, huh?" he said more to himself.

"I'm assuming so. He is Daniel's best man. Which reminds me . . ." Mom sighed. "They want to have it outside, here, next to the pool. The following summer."

René sat downstairs in the basement. Billy was sleeping again. He'd probably sleep lots after all he'd been through. The emotional exhaustion had finally weighed him down.

Keith stood at the bar, fixing their drinks.

"Can I ask you something?"

"Of course." Keith picked up the tumblers and meandered over to the sectional. He held out René's glass.

"Thanks." He was having a simple rum and cola.

Keith sat. He crossed a leg over the other.

"What's the, uh, what's the deal with you and Brooks?" He coughed into his fist.

Keith's brows formed a half-moon.

"It's not any of my biz. Never mind." René took a gulp of the drink.

"Oh. It's okay. I don't mind. I never had anyone inquire before, that's all." Keith's smile did seem a bit forced. "Well, as you know, we live together."

"Does your mom and sister know?"

Keith flicked at a piece of lint that wasn't there off his pants. "No." His pitch was low. "No."

"Does anyone know?" René shifted. "I mean, do you go to his office Christmas parties? That sort of stuff."

Keith shook his head. "The less people know, the better off we are. The goal is to keep our professional and personal lives separate."

"I see." René pressed his lips together. Lately, his socks had become very interesting. "You like to compartmentalize everything."

"Yes. I find life is much easier this way. There's my professional persona, my personal persona, and my intimate persona." Keith held up his glass of scotch on the rocks.

"Which persona am I getting?" A knot formed at the base of René's spine. Had he ever truly known Keith? Was he providing René with another persona?

Oh geez. He straightened. He had no right judging Keith when he'd been playing Renny and Ren-Man for his whole life. This was why he'd switched gears with Chunk by presenting the real René to his main man, why he'd fought to be himself in Toronto.

But as for here, Mom was right.

Did he want to spend the rest of his life like Keith—hiding who he was by cutting himself into something resembling a jigsaw puzzle and digging out this piece or that piece to show?

Yes, he understood people had to restrain themselves and behave a certain way depending on the company. That was simply the way of the world. But around people he loved or cared about?

The funeral continued to tap at the back of his head.

"Penny for your thoughts." Even Keith's chuckle sounded

forced. He sipped more scotch.

"I . . . I . . . I'm trying to make up my mind. What to do about Billy." René clenched the glass.

"I gather you two have resumed your relationship." Keith studied him.

René nodded. "Yeah. I . . . uh . . . it was before Mrs. Redsky died. We both . . . we missed each other. I had a chance to date a great guy, but he's not Billy, and Trent doesn't deserve that. He deserves someone who sincerely wants him."

"Well, I will say fate has granted you a wonderful opportunity. At your age, I didn't believe in love."

And do you now? Do you believe in love? René glanced away. Strange, he'd always viewed Keith's life as perfect. A man who had all the answers. But at this moment, he seemed to be struggling.

Keith set aside the drink. "I'll say one thing." He rose and patted René's shoulder. "Whatever you are contemplating, don't doubt yourself. You're smarter than you believe." With those words, he headed for the basement stairs.

CHAPTER TWENTY-FIVE—HEART AWAY

René had to begin packing soon. Five minutes ago, he'd banged on Billy's door, telling him they needed to talk. Maybe they could pack together. No matter the outcome of their conversation, and how much his heart broke, he had to accompany Keith on the plane.

"You're looking wide awake." René stood at the walk-in closet.

"Yeah." Billy meandered over. He wrapped his arms around René's waist and rested his head on his shoulder.

René gathered Billy against him. Dammit, leaving was going to be the hardest thing he ever did. "I love you."

"Why do I feel like I'm not gonna like what you're gonna say?" Billy's spoken breath penetrated René's t-shirt and was hot on the skin of his shoulder.

While rubbing Billy's lower back, René managed to choke out, "I have to pack."

Billy stiffened. His head popped up. Fear blazed behind his eyes. "I'm going with you."

"Baby, you can't . . ." René palmed Billy's cheeks and gently rubbed. "You gotta stay here. There's too much—"

"Stay here? What for?" Black irises flashing, Billy struggled to wrench himself free.

René's heart cracked. He held tight to Billy. The words flew from his mouth. "Please don't do this. I'll be back. I'll be back for Reading Week at the end of February. In April . . . I'll be back for good."

Billy ceased struggling. He blinked. The stiffness in his muscles vanished. "Wh-what?"

"Yes. For good. In April. I'm transferring to Lakeside." René pressed his forehead on Billy's. Their warm skin connected.

"F-for me?" Billy sputtered.

"Yes, for you. For us. I . . . I . . ." *I can't keep hiding me . . . you . . . us. I don't want to end up like Keith. I don't want us to end up like Keith and Brooks.*

"What about Madame Moxy? What about the big audition?" Billy's scleral became even whiter if that were possible.

"I have a band here." The soft words easily left René's lips. He did have an awesome rock group waiting here. Although Anarchic Aggregation was sans Ian, they could still forge on. Sheldon, Vince, and Eddie had stopped over to visit and informed him the band was on hiatus, because they couldn't find a decent drummer.

"You know they're not going anywhere. They're gonna be a cover band playing weddings and socials for the rest of their lives." Concern was in Billy's voice. "I know what music means to you."

"It's okay." René kept massaging Billy's cheeks. "Music is music. We'll find a way."

"I don't wanna take music away from you."

"You're not." René set the tip of his nose on Billy's. "And you're more important than music. I had all the music I could handle in Toronto. But I wasn't happy until we got back together. Doesn't that tell you something?"

"Yeah. I get it. I do." Billy threw his arms back around René. "If you're sure this is what you wanna do, then let's do it."

René clutched Billy. His scent and warmth were pure heaven. "I'm more than sure."

Now that they'd finished dinner and had eaten dessert, talking over coffee was the best time to break the news to the parents. In the past, confronting Mom and Dad had been pure fear strangling René's throat. Not this evening. He was sharing his plans with them because at nineteen, he didn't need their permission, only their blessing.

"I think we have a good hunch what you need to speak to us about." Dad lifted the carafe and poured.

"I know you hoped I'd stay in Toronto. I know you thought it was best for me . . ." René took the carafe from Mom. "But I made up my mind."

Since Dad took his coffee black, he simply sipped. "Go on." He wasn't frowning. Nor were his eyebrows flat in a straight line. This was a good sign.

"I talked with Mom about it." René glanced at his mother. "She . . ." He grabbed the creamer and poured. "She made a lot of sense." He plucked two cubes of sugar from the crystal bowl. "After visiting with Keith last night, I thought about what he said. He has his reasons for being there, but they're not mine."

Billy was silent, staring at his empty mug.

René reached over and filled Billy's cup. "At first, I didn't want to leave." He glanced at Mom. "She's right, though. I have to finish the school year out."

Dad's eyes lit.

"Billy and I also talked about him moving to Toronto—"

"Renny . . ." Dad began.

"We nixed the idea."

The lines of tension along Dad's forehead faded.

"I'm going to transfer to Lakeside." René held his breath.

Dad looked over to Mom, who nodded. "You do understand you're passing up a chance to work at a great firm. It's very rare they employ anyone but law students when they're considering summer employment."

"I know. And I'm grateful. I enjoyed the job and I learned lots. But—"

"And you're also passing up a chance to audition for the music festival," Dad continued on.

"I'm gonna talk to Ian and Moxy. I know they won't be happy. The thing is, I gotta start doing what's best for me . . . .and Billy." René's throat tightened. "I'd say for the first eighteen years of my life, I lived to please others. And when I make decisions, they gotta include Billy."

"I understand." Dad again glanced at Mom.

The slight tip of her head said she agreed.

"I'm sure we can find a place to live—"

"What do you mean?" Dad squinted.

"I know you wouldn't approve of us—"

"Renny . . ." Dad held up his hand. "Billy's going to be completing his OAC in the fall. I'd prefer he stayed here. And you, as well. You're not even out yet to the community."

René stomped down the blanch ready to wrinkle his face. Great. They'd be like two kids sneaking into one another's rooms. "I get it, I do. If we stay, I know you don't want us sharing the same room, but can we . . . at least be given the respect and privacy of adults?"

"Of course." Dad rubbed his chin. "Just don't be obvious about it. Understood?"

"Yeah." Okay, he'd managed to bring up *sex* without heating his cheeks to the temperature of Arizona. "We will."

"This'll allow you to save money. Living on your own isn't cheap." Dad picked up his mug. "Keep in mind you have three more years to finish your undergraduate degree. Then there's your Juris Doctor. That's another three more years. Afterward, you have to decide whether to articulate or take the LLP. The LLP is two months shorter, but it isn't always the best route, depending on what you decide to practice. Then you have to study for the bar exam. It's going to be very demanding for you.

"If you can, please live at home as long as possible. We supported Daniel's post-secondary education, and we want to support yours, too."

"Sure." René glanced at Billy.

Billy gave a quick little nod.

"We want to do the same for you." Dad fixed his stare on Billy. "I know how much becoming a police officer means to you."

"Thanks. Your support means lots to me." Billy's voice, for once, was on the shy side.

René sank back with his coffee. They'd climbed one hurdle.

The evening was cold, but not the minus twenty-five cold that had haunted the reserve over Christmas and New Year's. Maybe around minus sixteen. Billy rode on the back of the two-up. They were blazing down the trail where René dug taking his dirt bike for a rat.

The moon was out, casting shadows everywhere from its silvery light. After talking to the Oshawees, René had suggested they spend their last night alone snowmobiling. The brush on the trail came close to sweeping the sides of the machine. There were many humps and bumps, twists and turns. René drove fast, the trail of white ahead of them coming at full force while the blast of snow they left in their wake dusted the air.

They were deep in the spruce stand. Because of the chill, frost clung to the needles. They were silver trees wrapped in the wonder of winter. Maybe this was why Billy loved this season. Both of them, actually. They'd been born during *Biboon*'s reign. Naturally, they'd find peace in his heavy, cold breaths.

Since the seat Billy sat on was higher than the one René was on, he had a great view and could set his hands on the bars beside him. He lifted the visor of his helmet to take in the refreshing air hitting his face.

The snowmobile slowed. They were at the turnaround, having already clocked in a good fifteen clicks on the trail. Billy was next up to drive.

René also removed his helmet. He glanced over his shoulder. "Ready?"

"Yep. It's time someone showed you how to really open up the engine on this baby." Billy snickered and got off the machine.

"Lemme have a dart first." René stood. He stretched and then reached inside his top-of-the-line snowmobile outfit made of black leather with bright-green reflectors on the arms and back of the jacket and sides of the pant legs. The suit could even float if he went through the ice, but they were nowhere near water.

At least Mr. and Mrs. O had bought Billy decent gear to wear on the trail. No, his wasn't leather, but the pants, jacket, and boots kept him toasty.

René removed his leather gloves and donned a light pair while he smoked his cigarette.

"Need some warming up?" Billy motioned at the gloves covering René's long fingers. He trudged around the snowmobile and hugged René's waist.

"I'm not cold, but go on ahead. I'm all for it." Under the moonlight, René's teeth were an even brighter white than usual. "The hand warmers are doing their job. How about you?"

"The hand warmers on my bars are tops." Billy couldn't resist nuzzling René. There wasn't a breeze here. Only dead cold air. "I almost had to take my gloves off 'cause my palms were getting too hot. Man, your parents really go for the best, don't they?"

"From the day I was born, it was drilled into my head to go for gold." There was a hint of teasing to René's cheeky remark, but also a sliver of melancholy, as if he wished his parents had told him to reach for bronze instead.

"Is this why they bought a new one?" Billy glanced at the machine the Oshawees had purchased last winter after trading in the previous one.

"They got it 'cause they knew you'd wanna use it with your friends." René shrugged.

"Really? For me?" Billy blinked.

René nodded. "They're that way. You can't take it with you."

No, all Mom had taken was her soul to the spirit world.

"Hey . . ." René slid his finger under Billy's chin. "I love you."

"I love you, too." The wave of sadness rolled off Billy from the sweet chocolate cocoa René's eyes had become. While thinking about cocoa . . ."How's about some hot chocolate when we get back?"

"Sure." René took a drag. He ran his gloved fingers along Billy's short hair. "I'm glad we came out here tonight."

"Yeah?" Billy tilted his head.

René nodded. "There's nothing I love more than us being out here, spending time together."

"When you come back, we'll have lots more time." Billy couldn't stop staring into René's eyes.

"Yeah . . . we'll come out here when I fly back for Reading Week. That's a promise." René's lips came down on Billy's.

He was enveloped in a kiss cozy enough to unthaw Billy's toes if they'd been frostbitten.

Billy snapped René's last suitcase shut. There wasn't much to take, because the Christmas gifts he'd received were staying put. The same for his keyboard.

"That's it." René set his hands on his hips. His gaze studied every corner of his bedroom. "I'm pretty sure I got it all."

"You do. You didn't forget anything last time." Billy hauled the suitcase off the bed and set it by the door with the other luggage.

"René. Billy. Time to go." Mrs. O's voice carried up the stairs and into the bedroom.

A point of a knife seemed to nick Billy's heart. "You won't be here for my birthday."

"Remember what we talked about last night. I'll be here in February. We'll celebrate then. Okay?" René cupped Billy's chin. "You got my old laptop. We can message each other. Phones exist. We'll call."

"I know, but it's not the same." Ah hell, Billy wasn't going to complain. Come April, René would be back permanently. "In a way, I wish I could see this gayborhood."

"You woulda dug it. Totally dug it." A light smile graced René's soft-to-the-eye mouth. "Maybe someday we can visit. We'll see. Money's gonna be pretty tight."

"Do you think you'll be able to work?"

"Danny only worked during the summer when he was in uni. I gotta admit, the studying's insane. It's nothing compared to high school. If I wanna be on the dean's list every term, and graduate *summa cum laude*, I have to hit the books hard."

"So all you pretty much did was drum, learn how to play the keyboards, and study, hey?"

"Yep. And go out for dinner once a week." René chuckled.

"Of course you couldn't resist hitting the books here, too." Billy motioned at the briefcase that contained René's textbooks and binders.

"I told you already, it's been drilled into me from birth to go for gold." The same melancholy from last night glazed over René's eyes, but he did chuckle. "We gotta get going."

He reached into Billy's shirt and slipped the dog tag free. He fingered the locket. "I'm glad you're wearing this again."

His palm moved to Billy's cheek. When René leaned in, Billy closed his eyes and was smothered with a gentle kiss sweet enough tell him how much he was loved.

"Don't forget what I want for my birthday." Billy spoke with their lips pressed together. He couldn't resist bumping their crotches.

"Oh, you'll get something for your birthday. Guaranteed." René laid another kiss on Billy.

This time on their way to the airport, they held hands in the back seat of Mr. O's truck, even though the carry-on was between them. Billy's heart wasn't cracking. Nor was his chest. There wasn't even a lump in his throat. He kept squeezing René's fingers.

When they arrived at the terminal building, he walked beside René. The sun was out on the cold January morning, spreading its light across the city and offering rays of warmth.

Keith, his mom, and his sister fell in step with them. Everyone chatted all the way into the building, through check-in, and up to the eating lounge to have a coffee before René and Keith would head for security and vanish.

Forty-five minutes later, the time came. Billy stood with René in line. While Keith was checked through, Billy kept his gaze pinned on René.

"Call me as soon as you get there. Okay?"

"I will." There was something in René's eyes Billy couldn't read. "I'll call you before I even unpack."

The attendant motioned at René now that Keith had cleared security.

René set his carry-on in the bin. He unzipped the laptop case and turned on the computer for the guard to inspect. The guard nodded. René passed through without the alarm going off. Once he gathered up his belongings, he stopped and looked over his shoulder. His lips puckered ever so slightly.

Billy could almost feel the kiss on his mouth.

René swiveled on his heel and vanished from sight.

"You ready?" Mr. O asked.

Billy nodded. "As ready as I'll ever be." *Because he's coming back. He's coming back to me for keeps.* He rested his hand on his shirt where the dog tag lay hidden.

You may also enjoy the following from Devine Destinies:

After The Snow Melts
Maggie Blackbird

Excerpt

The video game didn't interest Elliot, whereas he always picked up the joystick to lose himself in *Invaders from Venus*. Neither did the sixty-inch rear-projection TV in the rec room downstairs at the Deschamps' house. Whenever he was here, he dug tossing in a video because Bryan always had the latest newly released movies.

The stupid card kept flooding Elliot's mind, turning his brain to cotton. A big ball of fluff that couldn't concentrate on anything. Part of him was flattered, but the other part had frozen his blood, churned his gut, and left a slick layer of sweat on his palms, fearful of having his secret on everyone's mouths in the hall at school.

Was the card a joke? Maybe from Raquel? Had she disguised her writing?

Or did someone suspect the truth?

Or did someone *like* him?

Bryan was chewing on his thumb again.

Elliot reached into the bowl of suckers and held one out.

"Suck on this, or you won't have any skin left."

"S-suck?" Bryan shifted.

"Err . . ." It was time to book, or something bad might happen in Elliot's pants, very bad, bad enough that Bryan was almost breakdancing on the sofa. "Uh yeah, it'll help . . . err . . . help with the . . . with the eating your thumb thing."

Bryan stopped squirming and scowled. "Whatever." He snatched the sucker and tore open the wrapper.

There was a bathroom downstairs. A safe place for Elliot to still his churning gut and get his wood under control.

He stood. "Gotta use the john."

Mirroring a bleary-eyed space cadet, Bryan said nothing and stared straight ahead at nothing.

Elliot bolted for the washroom. He shut and locked the door. His breaths came fast. He set his hand on the marble vanity counter. The card remained in his back pocket. He grabbed it to reread it for the bazillionth time.

A cool music note was on the cover, but it was the inner contents that had left him breathless after discovering it in his locker. Even during supper at his boarding wardens, he'd had to force down his food. While dressing and waiting for Bryan to get him, he'd paced and racked his brain over who would send him this.

Music is the rhythm of your beating heart.

So true. He couldn't help smiling. That was exactly how he felt when he listened to Megadeth, Iron Maiden, or Judas Priest. An even cooler sound was the *thump-thump* of his hand drum while he sang his morning song to Creator as Rufus had taught Elliot to do. But it was the personal message making his heart bang like the old man's water drum.

I know you dig music as much as I do. We may think different bands are way cool, but it doesn't mean shit. Music is music. Give new wave a listen. Really listen to it. I'm willing to give metal a try if you're willing to do the same.

The weird thing was, Bryan lived and breathed new wave. He was such a total waver, nobody had heard of half the bands he had on cassette in his car. But a lot of other guys dug new wave, too. Fuck, it was the most popular beat at school.

"What're you doing in there?"

Elliot froze and shoved the card back into his pocket. "Nothing, man." He threw open the door.

"You didn't flush." Curiosity and something else filled Bryan's blue eyes. He glanced up and down.

Elliot couldn't tell his best bud the truth, no matter if he trusted Bryan. It was bad enough being a red, but a two-spirit red was ten times worse. As Rufus had said, their own people had long forgotten the gift and believed what Western society had taught them.

"What's eating you?" Bryan's scrutinizing stare was a dagger piercing Elliot's skin. "You've been acting weird ever since you found the invite in your locker from the chess club."

"Nothing." Elliot bolted for the sofa and scooped up the joystick for the video game.

ABOUT THE AUTHOR

An Ojibway from Northwestern Ontario, Maggie resides in the country with her husband and their fur babies, two beautiful Alaskan Malamutes. When she's not writing, she can be found pulling weeds in the flower beds, mowing the huge lawn, walking the Mals deep in the bush, teeing up a ball at the golf course, fishing in the boat for walleye, or sitting on the deck at her sister's house, making more wonderful memories with the people she loves most.

Web Site: https://maggieblackbird.com/

Facebook Page: https://www.facebook.com/maggieblackbirdauthor/

Twitter: https://twitter.com/BlackbirdMaggie/

BookbBub: https://www.bookbub.com/profile/maggieblackbird

Linked In: https://www.linkedin.com/in/maggie-blackbird-032798169/

eXtasy Books Author Page: https://www.extasybooks.com/maggie-blackbird/

Newsletter Sign-Up: eepurl.com/gJu2VL